THE GUARDIAN FOREST

ELANRAIGH BOOK 1

SANDRA A HUNTER

Previously Published by Eternal Press (2012)
As
Elanraigh: The Vow
By S.A. Hunter

DEDICATION

To my husband, Bill and daughter, Leslie who put up with
my absent mindedness while I wrestled with the Muse—
meanwhile the roast burned...

And with gratitude to my writing buddies from W.I.P. for
their enthusiastic
support and encouragement.

THE GUARDIAN FOREST
Elanraigh Book 1

Thera doesn't know why the Elanraigh forest-mind chose
her, of all the Allenholme folk, to hear its voice and to
awaken her gifts of mind and spirit.

The Elanraigh sends a warning dream; black sails swooping
toward Allenholme from across the western sea—the
Memteth, an ancient enemy, armed with blue fire that
hungers to consume life.

As Thera awakens to her gifts of bonding with raptor birds
and reading hearts, the *knowing*; she also awakens to love.
Will she choose Chamakin, the young Ttamarini warrior
who is kindred in spirit to her, or the polished young
nobleman who covets her beauty even more than her
estate?

Forest-mind is aware she is yet too young for such power
and responsibility. It has no choice—the lives of all Thera's
people and the existence of the Elanraigh Forest itself,
depend on Thera fulfilling her destiny.

Can she learn what she must of gift, and heart, to survive
what comes their way?

REVIEWS

From its opening pages when Thera of Allenholme, melded in mind and spirit with a young sea hawk, first explores her extraordinary gifts, this well-wrought coming of age novel is an engrossing read. Thera's world, with its haunting west coast ambience of storm and raging surf and rainforest, is vividly realized.Thera herself, as she grows in self-knowledge, awareness of her inherited duty, and her mystical affinity with the natural world, has a hero's moral strength, and a young girl's touching vulnerability.

I'd recommend Elanraigh to readers of any age who love fantasy fiction in the classic tradition of Ursula LeGuin's Earthsea books or Robin McKinley's The Blue Sword. -- Eileen Kernaghan, author of Wild Talent: a Novel of the Supernatural

Reviewer: Constant Reader

~

...I have to say this is one of the best-written books I've read lately. The writing is so descriptive and poetic it had me in tears at several points...I really enjoyed the mixture of Native cultural concepts with Mythology and Wicca and Druidism and Fantasy. S. A. Hunter obviously did her share of research in order to design such plausible cultures and rituals. I felt every bit of the love Thera felt for the forest and the elementals, the animals and plants. But it wasn't sappy. Thera is a genuine bad-ass teenaged character with a lot of charm and ... character. I wouldn't mind knowing her... or being her mother. She held her own in some pretty nasty battles and the antagonists were truly disgusting.

Overall I flew through this book in a matter of hours because I couldn't stop turning the page to see what would happen next.

Reviewer: Rebecca Russell

≈

Author has superb writing skills. Her imagination in creating this story amazes me. You will enjoy. I don't usually read fantasies but loved this book and looking forward to her next book.

Reviewer: Ida

≈

...the author created an interesting fantasy world differing from any other that I've ever read.

It is a world where some are able to sense/communicate with the sentient mind of the natural elements that live around them. The young heroine of the story, Thera, is one person that has this ability and to a much greater degree than the rest of her people. It is basically a coming-of-age story where she is being is trained to reach her full potential so she can become a leader during a time of crisis and restore her people's ability to commune with Elanraigh, the `forest-mind.

I really liked the main character, Thera and how she handled all her various relationships with the people around her. She is a heroine that sets a fine example to young people in showing respect, courtesy, bravery, and love of home & family.

I really enjoyed this book and would recommend it to young & old. It is definitely an introductory story since the book ends with our heroine prepared for future challenges. So, I hope that there will be more books in this intriquing fantasy world.

Reviewer: Mac

∾

Many times have I bought a book based on the summary or cover only to be vastly disappointed. You can imagine that it came as a big surprise to me how unlike anything I have ever read before this book was. The author's use of descriptions and imagery really capture the attention.

I really loved how she gave Thera strengths and weaknesses in equal measure, balancing her character, yet at the same time endearing her to the reader. Thera could be pushy and stubborn sometimes but she was also loyal and kind. Her flaws made her human and it made me happy to see that this author was imaginative and creative enough to think outside the box in a world obsessed with werewolves, vampires, demons and the like.

I cannot wait to read the next book, so far this one has only served to whet my appetite for more info on Thera,

Chamakin, the forest mind, and even their enemy the Memteth. Hopefully the next one will be as good as the first.

Reviewer: C.Willis

∾

Love this book. The nature/telepathy/ valuing the feminine is appealing, but even more so that love relationships are not the main point, but part of a complex life. Fabulous fabulous fabulous.

The words paint a deep, rich picture of the world Thera (protagonist) lives in.

Reviewer: Jennifer S.

∾

The book started out a little slow for me. By the time I was at 300, I realized that everything I read and lead up to where I was. It was needed. I LOVE this book. The story is beautiful. I really do hope that more books will be written. I don't want to spoil anything so I have to cut my review short. But you'll understand what I mean when you get to the end of this book. We need to know more about the people and Elanraigh. ~:)

Reviewer: Angelina M. Krell

CHAPTER 1

"Take her, child," said Teacher's voice in her mind. "She is here for you. Join with her."

Thera reached with her mind, as Teacher had shown her, slowly and cautiously. The young sea hawk rustled and shifted nervously, and then, in a dizzying kaleidoscope of sight and sound she spread her wings and stroked upward, uttering shrill, joyful cries. Thera marveled at this new lightness of physical form coupled with such great strength. To her hawk's eyes, colors were more vivid and her vision more sharply focused. The sounds of activity in Allenholme Keep below, so well known to Thera, were of little importance to the hawk, but no movement escaped her notice. The sea hawk yearned for the cliffs by the sea and the warm spiraling thermals there, but for a moment, Thera insisted on hovering, delighted with this unusual perspective of her home. Her mother's garden was a mere patch of vibrant green amidst the grey granite of the keep — its stone paths bordered with myriad blooms of spring flowers. She eyed the tall lace fronds, beneath whose leaves her physical self lay concealed. Even the hawk could see nothing of her body there. She heard the clack and clangor of arms drills near the stables at the east wall, and the warhorses neighing an eager response. Then she veered and drifted over the market. She spun herself higher over the clamor and calls of the street vendors, and over the rumble of carts, wagons, and barrows.

They spiraled upward and banked toward the waterfront. Far below, Thera saw a dark-haired dancer twirling joyously by the Southgate, her red skirts fanned like a blooming flower amidst the dust and smoke. Fishermen and off-duty soldiers tossed bright coppers that fell glinting at her feet.

She drifted through a miasma of smoke and closed her inner eyelid. *How convenient to have such a thing,* Thera thought. It was then she smelled the cooking odors and was struck with *hunger.*

Thera reeled in surprise at the impact of this need on her hawk's body. The demands of the sea hawk's needs, this driving imperative to hunt and to kill, consumed her. They winged to the cliffs. The air here blew clean and fresh. She caught a scent of fish, but it was dead and distasteful to her. She lowered her head and scanned for the promising glint of silver or blue beneath the waves. Small clouds of herring flitted through the water, but no succulent bluefish pursued them.

Hunger drove her harder. Becoming sullen and fractious, she dove at a flock of seabirds just to send them squawking aloft, and turned for shore.

Then, in the mix of starmoss and thistle that mortared the rocks and clung to ledges of the cliffs, she saw a fat waddle of grey-brown fur lumbering toward a small crevice.

A sedgemole, a wonderful meal! An excellent meal! Bloodlust throbbed, her neck feathers fanned once as her skin tightened and her body filled with powerful, compelling sensations.

Immediately she was winging for height and position in the tricky thermals. She could already feel the rodent's fresh warm blood and flesh coursing down her throat, filling her belly. With a sudden fold of wings, she dropped, deadly and silent, the wind screaming at her passage.

Her talons clenched, snapping the sedgemole's spine on impact. Immediately she slashed the furry throat with her hooked beak, gulping down fur, flesh, and tendon. In six heartbeats the bird was laboring to her favorite fir tree snag to continue feeding.

The small animal's death filled Thera with horror. Her mind-scream had coincided with the sea hawk's victorious cry, and she now spun, formless, on the wind.

She tumbled in the violent winds off the shore, tattered, and about to be blown into nothingness.

"*Child! Thera! Think of the garden,*" Teacher's usually tranquil voice a strained mind-shout. "*See yourself in the garden. Remember, always, where you are!*"

It worked.

As soon as Thera remembered the garden, she snapped back into her body with such force, she thought surely she would break her bones. Her human body echoed with the sensations she had just experienced so intimately.

Thera heard Teacher say, "*I tell you, she is too young.*"

She fought the darkness now overwhelming her. "*No, I'm not!*"

Thera did not hear the Elanraigh forest-mind's deep-voiced response.

∾

THE ELANRAIGH FOREST quivered with deep unease. Forest-mind sifted the westerly wind and breathed its warning to the folk of Allenholme. Even the most practical fishwife in the market caught some aspect of its mood.

"Be a storm brewin'?" asked Alva, the Westharbour fish-monger. She paused in the act of slicing the dorsal fin off a large, spiny bluefish. There was heaviness in the air, similar to a pending storm, yet different.

"Aye," Mika drawled, "feels like." He continued to unload Alva's stock from his barrow to ice-filled bins, then straightened and shaded his eyes with his fisherman's rough hand, now glistening with scales.

"Aye. I'll be bringing the *Bride O' Wind* in, I'm thinkin', and snug her tight to dock this eve." Mika's brow furrowed slightly, causing a cascade of mahogany creases about his grey-green eyes. The sky out to sea continued an unblem-ished, cerulean blue.

"Tch," Mika was plainly disturbed. "Petrack, old barnacle that he is, be past due in." He shook his head, "He knows these waters well, crew be seasoned hands." He gestured west, out to sea, "The *one* thing that great flounder-brained nephew of his knows is his way about these islands. Old Petrack passed my *Bride* at dawn. Loaded to the gunnels, he was and flagged for home. He's not at dock yet and none's seen him since we sighted him at dawn's bless-ing." Mika rubbed knobby fingers through his grizzled head of hair. His concern was both as Fishing Guild Master, and as friend and archrival of Petrack, skipper of the *Grace O'Gull.*

Mika and Alva exchanged a long look. The old fish-monger was so distracted that she failed to notice a grubby hand that quickly filched a prime cod. So unheard of was a successful filch at Alva's booth that the youthful thief looked twice backward, then shivered and ran.

IN THE WEST TOWER of the Duke's residence, Lady Fideiya absently smoothed her fourteen year old daughter's abandoned needlework. The small piece of cloth was grubby and crumpled. Many of the irregular stitches in the unfinished piece were already frayed and pulled. Fideiya sighed.

"How long has she been gone *this* time, Nan?" asked Fideiya.

Thera's nurse paused in her tidying of Thera's chamber and her brow puckered, "Since I went to the cookhouse, my Lady, to fetch our noon meal."

Nan observed the worry written on Lady Fideiya's elegant features with mild surprise. Thera's habit of wandering off on her own was a grievance, true, but the child always turned up somewhere about the keep. Perhaps by the stable in company with the retired Master at Arms, old Sirra Shamic, or perhaps trailing after her father, Duke Leon, known as Oak Heart, and his captains.

"By the Dance!" exclaimed Nan, distracted again, as she gingerly lifted several small white-furred kirshrews from Thera's clothes chest. She sat back on her heels, "I swear, my lady, we've had such a clutter of kittens, birds, sun-lizards — and now kirshrews — all to be nursed and fed and then set free with the child's own special blessing, it's like she was a Salvai herself. Tch, tch."

The tautness of Lady Fideiya's features relaxed. She smiled to herself. *Thera like a Salvai?* Fideiya could not imagine her robust daughter leading the cloistered life that the child's Aunt Keiris chose.

"Yet Thera is nothing like my sister Keiris, is she Nan?" Fideiya was thinking of her sister Keiris' pale asceticism, her orderliness, and her precise manner of speech. No, Thera did not resemble her aunt. Fideiya smiled fondly as she brought her daughter to mind. Her hazel eyes shining like sunshine on the fast-flowing Spinfisher River when green with glacial spill, balanced with dark brows lofting cleanly against clear, olive skin. Her mouth was full and sensitive, slightly upturned at the corners, her chin strong, with a graceful jawline. Thera's long, curling hair was unruly, true, but was lustrous and thick. Overall, the child showed intelligence and a wildflower sort of loveliness that could soon blossom into sensual beauty. She was not *fashionably* pretty, but her appearance pleased Lady Fideiya.

Nurse Nan was sourly muttering under her breath, something about, "...there be no comparison between her Thera and Salvai Keiris."

Fideiya arched one brow.

Nan flushed, though her mouth set stubbornly. She had been a young chambermaid when Lady Fideiya and her older sister, Lady Keiris, were in their maidenhood home at Chadwyn.

Fideiya's eyes danced. "Yes, Nan, our Thera is *much* more trouble for you to mind, I realize, than were either Keiris or I."

Nan's blue eyes misted and she cast a warm glance over to Fideiya. "Oh, now, my Lady," she smoothed a nightgown into neat folds, "Thera is just as stubborn as my Lady Keiris," Nan's voice was earnest. "She's always doing before thinking. Truly, my Lady, her doings are meant well, and after the trouble she will admit honestly if she be wrong. She has a sweetness to her, does Thera that our Keiris never had, beggin' my lady's pardon for such plain speaking."

"My sister ever did wield her considerable intellect as a sword, Nan." Fideiya smiled ruefully, "Not the best way to win the love of others."

Nan paused in her refolding of Thera's clothes, her expression thoughtful. "The child has not been herself, this last quarter moon, my lady. She has been unusually quiet. Then, last night, she had a dream. She woke me as she cried out."

Fideiya carefully laid down her daughter's embroidery. She too had felt uneasy these last few days. Fideiya beckoned Nan up from her work, and gestured for the nursemaid to sit next to her on the carved bench beside the fireplace. Fideiya was carefully casual as she inquired, "A dream? Tell me of my daughter's dream."

Lady Fideiya felt an imminent focusing of the general unease that had been crawling over her skin all week. With pricklings of impatience, she watched Nan's blue gaze fidget over Thera's chamber, tallying work yet to be done.

"Nan, tell me."

"Why, my Lady," explained Nan, "Thera said she dreamed of black sails on the sea."

"Black sails!" Lady Fideiya exclaimed.

"Aye," affirmed Nan, her eyes widening as she observed Lady Fideiya's expression, "She said the forest *sang* to her and she saw black sails on the horizon."

Lady Fideiya pondered her gaze unfocused. It *could* merely have been that the chambermaids had frightened the girl with old tales of Memteth raiders. She sorted through possibilities. Could Thera have simply been dreaming *the forest sang*? Or could the child have the old gift, truly be in communion with the Elanraigh elementals, and be hearing at such a young age? Fideiya herself had only a vague sense of the forest-mind.

No, thought Fideiya, *surely not the old gift. Yet, Thera dreamed and the forest sang. Black sails! Could that vileness, the Memteth — monsters of legend and fireside tales — truly be advancing on Allenholme, and no warning!*

Lady Fideiya felt coldness, like a dark shadow, pass over her. Perhaps a child's dream *is* our warning from the Elanraigh. She strode to the casement. The salt wind, full of seabird voices, lifted her dark hair. Her grey eyes dilated, "What is it? What is it?" she murmured to the wind. Lady Fideiya shivered.

Warning. She sensed it, as if the wind had whipped a chill wave into spindrift against her skin.

"Blessings," Fideiya murmured. It must be forest-mind who sent these feelings. There must be very little time.

CHAPTER 2

*T*hera stretched sore muscles. Her eyelids felt heavy, reluctant to open, her skin was chilled and damp. She became aware of Nan's voice.

"Blessings," murmured Thera as she usually did upon waking.

"'Blessings' is it now, with the sun nearly set! And everyone be looking high and low for *Herself* this long day!"

Thera's eyelids flickered open, and she saw the worry in Nan's anxious face.

Dazedly Thera murmured, "Sorry, Nan...sorry." Her head lolled sideways and Nan's voice dwindled into the dark.

"My poor Button, what is it with the girl?" and Nan's arms pillowed Thera against her soft bosom.

THE NEXT MORNING Nan roused Thera as usual with a kiss and they exchanged murmured "Blessings." Then she alternately scolded and pleaded with Thera as she dressed her hair.

"Hear me, lass, I warn you well. Already you've been put on ration of crusts and water for today — alarming the keep like that!" Nan kept glancing sideways at Thera as she bustled about. She selected a grey wool gown with red smocking, "Here. This be warm and neat. What with half the household away from their duties searching for you."

Nan paused in her fastening of Thera's dress, "By the Sacred Hollow, child, you've grown four fingers since last this gown was worn." Nan tugged at the hem.

Thera's fingers pleated the material of the grey gown. Nan observed and worried. She plucked away the fidgeting fingers, "Do not crease yourself, Button, your mother will wish to see you soon. My lady was so upset, what with talk of black raiders, and you nowhere to be found!" Nan worried and prodded for response, "Does hear me, Button, when I speak?"

A sea hawk's shrill cry carried on the crisp morning air. Thera's head lifted to the window arch, where dust motes danced in the light. The kirshrews in their nest of cedar chips basked in the sun's warmth and groomed each other with rough pink tongues.

The sea hawk's clarion cry sounded again, closer, and insistent, as she soared on the winds around the residence towers. Thera ran to the window, its stone sill rough under her fingers. She felt the bead of existence that was the sea hawk strung as was she, Thera, on the web of all life. Thera smiled. "Blessings!" she called aloud, her arms flung wide, and projected joyously with mind-voice also.

Thera turned to Nan, who was dabbing at her eyes and smiling. "I always try to be good."

Nan crumpled away the plain linen hankie into a vast

pocket, and retrieved a scone from another. "Aye, Button; that I do believe. Here now," she handed the fresh scone to Thera and patted her cheek, "Lassies do not get roses in their cheeks on crusts and water," she muttered, as if to justify the lapse in the parental edict.

Nan straightened, her attention drawn to one of the maids who was tidying Thera's bed linens. "No, no, lass. We will air the cover outside today. It's blowing nice and fresh." She turned back to Thera, "Your Lady mother said she will be by to see you early."

Thera leaned on the window ledge, and nibbled at the fresh scone. "Is mother very angry with me?"

It was Lady Fideiya's voice that answered, as she entered the chamber with her maid, Rubra, following. "Yes, she is."

Thera turned quickly, her eyes wide on her mother's face. Though her lips were compressed, her eyes smiled. "You are getting too old for these tricks, my dear. You come of age, and have the duties of a woman, in a quarter moon."

Thera saw her mother's glance flicker to the hated embroidery sampler, and she flushed. Lady Fideiya's hand gestured toward the kreeling kirshrews in Thera's cedar chest. "Your knowledge of animal husbandry is second to none," she said, "but I doubt the young noblemen of Cythia's court will be as impressed with those accomplishments as your father and I. It would be well for you to persevere in learning some gentle arts as well." Thera opened her mouth to protest, but her mother waved her to silence, "Thera...I want you to stay with Aunt Keiris at Elankeep for a while."

Fideiya quelled with a glance the peep of protest that had squeaked out of Nan. Nan clapped her hand over her mouth, her blue eyes wide and worried.

Fideiya continued, "You met her a few times, when you

were only little. You described her, I think," Fiedeiya smiled, "as *still*, like a statue? She *is* the Salvai, and she can teach you much."

Thera felt as if she had suddenly been thrown into cold water. "You will send me away? Away from Allenholme? No, Mama, please! I'm so sorry I worried you. I won't do it again!" Her mother's hands clasped Thera's tightly. Thera breathed her fragrance, sea lily and cailia with a sense of anxiety overlaying all. Thera had taken instant dislike to her Aunt Keiris. Of course, she very properly hid her feelings when forced into her aunt's company, or even better, hid herself on those few occasions of Keiris' visits to Allenholme. Besides, the feeling was mutual.

Perhaps, she wondered, "Do you come too, Mama?"

"No, my dear; there will be much to do. I must stay and help your father, and the people will need us here. But I will send Nan with you." Lady Fideiya released Thera's hands with a little pat and swept from the chamber with Nan and Rubra in a flurry behind her. "I will tell Shamic to choose an escort for you," echoed Fideiya's voice from the corridor.

Thera returned to her window and, leaning against the sill, thumped her chin onto her arm. The last few days she had felt as if she were trembling at the edge of an abyss from which she would either fly or fall. There were the dreams of course. Also, all her senses were coming so much more alive. It was as if she saw, heard, and knew things through the medium of her spirit, not just the physical body. Of course she had been told that the ancient gift was hereditary in the female line of her family, though no one knew to what degree a child would be gifted. Mother said that from generation to generation it varied with the need of the times. The *least* endowed could at least vaguely sense the Elanraigh forest-mind.

Thera had not yet confided to anyone the extent of the gift she felt burgeoning within. For now she just observed with her new senses, waiting for what would unfold within herself.

So, Sirra Shamic will choose my escort, mother says, Thera thought as she reached down to a kirshrew that was chirping and scrabbling with tiny paws at her boot. She carefully lifted it, to cuddle under her chin. "Well, Little One, I can further Nan's happiness at least. I see how she and Innic look at each other. When Innic is pensioned, I am sure he will ask for Nan to be his life sworn." Thera pondered how she could manipulate the old Sirra into appointing Innic to be part of her escort party. It was not that she doubted her ability to finagle the old Master at Arms, but it would be a kindness to ensure that Shamic perceived it as his own idea.

Among Allenholme folk, the retired Master at Arms, Sirra Shamic, was Thera's second favorite person — next only to Nan. The gruff old soldier spoke seldom and sparely, but from her earliest days Thera had been content to be where he was. Thera knew that Nan feared the old soldier's abrupt manner, and scorned his crude speech. She also knew that the Sirra was gruffest where he loved the best.

Two mornings ago Thera had been out early by the stable. Her plan was to relocate a small nest of burrowing kirshrews who had chosen an unfortunate site too close to the horse trail by the fresh water cistern. Her father had clattered down the outside steps, followed by several of his warrior companions. The Heart's Own, folk called them.

Thera, and most all present, paused to bask in her father's bright, vivid energy.

Faces turned to him, greetings were called, "Oak Heart!" being the name his troops gave him in affection, as he stepped briskly into the courtyard and beckoned the stable boy. "Bring my hunter, lad, this pack of break-necks with me are restless this fine morning."

His piercing blue eyes scanned the courtyard and then his voice boomed out again, "Hail Shamic! Are you here to terrify my recruits into disgracing themselves?"

The startled recruits had indeed been uneasy recipients of Shamic's glare delivered from under bristling brows as the young Sirra, Maxin, put them through a basic equestrian drill.

That glowering eye transferred itself to the golden haired giant who stood grinning at him. His scowl deepened, "Aye, Oak Heart, mind who threw you on your first horse, when you be yet an acorn in short coats!"

Her father roared with laughter as he swung up onto Windgather, his roan horse. Controlling the fresh mount effortlessly, he waved the stable boy to safe distance and leaning down, bared his strong white teeth in a grimacing smile.

"Aye," he replied in Shamic's own broad dialect, "'een so, you grumping auld curmudgeon."

"Ha!" exploded the laugh from old Shamic's belly, "Ha!" and that fierce eye beamed with pride as he watched his young Duke spin the horse neatly and lead the Heart's Own to the Elanraigh foothills.

Thera felt the love between her father and the old Sirra like a poignant ache in her heart. The love was visible to her, like the golden glow of bright spring sun reflecting off the churned dust of the courtyard. It did not require the forest-mind murmuring of it to inform her.

Thera remembered many years ago her mother had said the Sirra lost his daughter. Even as a very small child Thera felt a reluctance to ask the old soldier how he lost his daughter. She had sensed she was not *misplaced* but something sad and permanent, like when Cook's son had fallen in the river when netting fish and never returned.

Not long after, when she was about five, Thera stood looking out over the undulating hills, toward the purple High Ranges. She was thinking of the Cook's boy and Shamic's daughter. "Nanny," she had said, "Where do people go when they die?"

Nan replied, "Folks go where they can have peace from children's questions, and they can sit resting with their feet in the cool river all day." Then, Nan always had sore feet. So Thera had asked the Elanraigh, using the inside voice Teacher had taught her, where people went when their bodies died.

In answer to this early childish request the Elanraigh sent her a feeling like a warm hug from Nan or Mama, but that was all it said.

Thera was aware of two distinct Elanraigh entities. She wasn't sure which one sent the hug feeling that long ago day.

One entity, the Elanraigh, had a mind-voice--deep and rumbling. This voice reminded Thera of Oak Heart when he would take her on his knee and speak just to her in the special voice he used only with Mama and her. His normal thundering tones would be softened, and burr in his chest like distant thunder. She could feel their resonant vibrations against her cheek as she laid it over the slow steady beat of his heart.

The other entity Thera thought of as the "teaching voice," or of late, simply as Teacher. Thera knew it was separate from the Elanraigh, yet part of it somehow. Teacher instructed her how to touch the forest-mind and how to be still. Being still was very hard for the small Thera.

Thera had once pushed rebelliously against Teacher's voice. "Not now. I do not want to be still! I'm playing with the kittens!" Thera had mentally shoved Teacher away and, tossing her hair defiantly, she bent back to Mouseripper's kittens. She chewed her lip, though, feeling her neck grow warm. This was very bad, she knew, and she waited with curiosity to know what Teacher would do.

Teacher had left quietly, and no matter how hard Thera called during the following quarter moon, Teacher did not return. Thera never defied Teacher again.

Now Teacher has taught her to join, only yesterday she had experienced the wonderful joining with the young sea hawk. Thera rubbed at her forearms where goosebumps raised as she remembered.

Yesterday morning Thera escaped Nan's vigilance and hid herself in her mother's private garden, back where the lace fronds grew high. She sat amidst the dry rustling branches and let their shadow-play against the stone wall lull her. Hours passed. All the small itches and buzzing thoughts settled like a cloud of gnats onto a quiet pond. She found her centre.

After a time — Thera couldn't tell how long — a small hunting bird had landed on the garden wall, its raptor's eyes focused on her as it ruffled sun-gilded plumage.

"*Take her, child,*" Teacher's voice had said to her. "*She is here for you...*"

CHAPTER 3

*R*eminiscing about her mystical union with the
sea hawk served only to make Thera all the
more aware of the constraints about to be put upon her.
Suddenly angry, she shoved away from her window,
replaced the kirshrew into its basket and ran into the long
hallway leading to the main stairs.

Slowing her pace, she solemnly acknowledged the
smiling salute of the guard stationed at the head of the stairway. Thera noticed there were more soldiers than usual
posted in the hall and main rooms. There was much coming
and going of guards, officers, and representatives from the
town. It was busy as a gathering for Mid Winter's Eve, except
folk looked solemn and preoccupied.

She saw Sirra Shamic and Horsemaster Harle near the
Main Hall entrance and she ran lightly down the stairway
past porters and messengers to stand near the Sirra.

Harle stood with his arms wrapped about his massive
chest. His brows were knotted over the high arch of his nose.
"Word has been sent alright, young Arnott riding Drummer.

Fastest we've got. Should get there by the time the sun twice blesses the Elanraigh."

Harle thumped his back against the wall. His eyes slanted toward her father's conference room. "It went hard with Oak Heart to ask for alliance with the Ttamarini. The Old Duke will be turning in his grave."

Sirra Shamic humphed, then spoke in measured voice, "Nah...Branch ArNarone ne'er thought a good thing to come out of Ttamarina till he fought over the Silver Toss border agin' em. *Then* he said they be an adversary to make a man proud. They fight like devils an' their horses follow their will like they be one body. Branch ArNarone would ha' made treaty with them too, if the filthy 'Teths had turned their bloody black ships to Allenholme in his day. Ttamarini or no, we share this good land, and no lizard-man...," Shamic turned his head as if to spit, glanced at Thera, and cleared his throat, "...will take it from us."

Harle's pale blue eyes shifted to Thera a moment. "It's on the dreams of a child that we base our knowledge? I would rather we'd had some confirmation from Cythia, or the South Bole caravaners," his heavy shoulders shifted with an audible creak of leathers.

Harle reminded Thera of a great brooding bird as he stood with his massive shoulders hunched and his pale eyes trained on her fixedly. She met Harle's look evenly. He was unconvinced of her abilities, she knew. Thera read his doubt, but did not take it amiss. She knew he could not hear the Elanraigh.

Shamic, too, regarded her. "You've the look of your Elder-Aunt Dysanna who was the Salvai at Elankeep years ago," Shamic's eyes were fierce as his large vein-corded hand rested gently on Thera's shoulder, "A beautiful, wise, woman she was." He slanted a look up to Harle, "Even if you feel

naught of warning, Horsemaster, the signs are there: there's
no word of any kind from Cythia since Beltidemas, and the
South Bole caravan be late...should ha' been here after the
freshet."

Harle's pale brows lifted, and then he snapped to attention as the double doors of Oak Heart's conference room
slammed open and Duke Leon, their Oak Heart, strode
through followed by his companions. Trailing more slowly
were the town's guild masters and marshals.

Oak Heart saw Harle and Shamic and he swung toward
them. "Well, the Ttamarini come then," he announced. His
eyes met Shamic's, "Not just the Chief, Teckcharin, but also
his cub, Chamakin."

"Chamakin," muttered Shamic as he rubbed at his chest
thoughtfully, "means 'Summerborn' in their tongue."

"I've heard tell of the lad, my Lord," said Harle. "If
rumors be truth, he is his father's Heir in all ways — a true
warrior."

Their Duke waved his hand, as if dismissing any doubts.
"He would not be Heir if he were not their best. The
Ttamarini will not tolerate an unfit leader, be he the chief's
only son or not." Restless, he waved the two to walk outside
beside him. "Come out into the sunlight. I've had enough of
council chambers."

Oak Heart breathed deeply the fresh morning air.
"Teckcharin comes with three hundred mounted and their
own supplies."

"My Lord," queried Harle, "how did you receive their
reply so soon? The messenger, *if* they grant him a fresh
mount, still could not possibly return before nightfall."

"They sent a carrier bird," Duke Leon replied. His bright
blue eyes crackled between Harle's puzzled gaze and Shamic's disturbed one.

Harle paused midstride, "I thought those birds had to have *been* to a destination before they could deliver messages there?"

Oak Heart smiled grimly. "Just so," was his bitten reply.

"There have been Ttamarini agents in the town, then," growled Shamic.

"Well," Duke Leon shrugged and smiled ruefully, "I also have had agents with carrier birds in Ttamarini lands."

The Duke turned to watch the dispersal of the town representatives, by foot and horse. Some few were sullen and muttering together, most appeared stunned or anxious, and some, such as the Fishing Guild Master, Mika ep Narin, looked purposeful.

"Was it bad?" asked Shamic, jerking his head toward the departing townsfolk.

"Much as I expected," replied the Oak Heart blandly.

Harle snorted, "Oh, I can guess. I remember two years ago when you told the town elders about an increase in tithe to strengthen the West Harbor breakwater and install a bastion there. What a howling there was!"

The Duke merely smiled.

In the small silence that fell, Thera used her gift to gently touch her father's thoughts. She was surprised to learn that many at the recent meeting in Council Chamber did not accept Fideiya's feelings of approaching danger, much less her own vision of Memteth sails.

Oak Heart brooded as he paced along, a small crease between his brows. "Peace has lulled Allenholme since my grandfather's time, except, perhaps, for the occasional high-blooded skirmish between the youth of both camps."

"Huh," grunted Shamic.

"The old ways," continued the Duke, "reverence for the Elanraigh, has faded. We've been enjoying this tranquil prosperity. The power of the Elanraigh is given lip-service only. We call upon it for the blessing of a tree for shipbuilding, the charming away of an inconvenient wind, or the finding of a lost child or beast. Over these years fewer and fewer Allenholme children have been born with the ability to even sense forest-mind." Duke Leon shook his head.

Harle stated, "They are merchants and craftsmen, that is what occupies them."

Thera felt her father's natural optimism assert itself.

He rested his hand on Harle's broad shoulder, "Do not judge them harshly, Horsemaster; they are a stalwart folk and when the time comes, they will give all they have to save this land."

He finally saw Thera behind them, and his expression lightened.

"Well lass, you go on a journey soon, I hear."

"Mama says I must go, Sir, but I would rather stay with you." Thera's heart flared with hope at the thought of reprieve from being exiled to Elankeep with her aunt.

Oak Heart smiled tenderly, "Ah, what a warrior lass you are!" he rumbled, and his arm clenched around her. "You're a lass to make a father proud, and too precious to risk to Memteth evil. If that's indeed what comes this way."

Thera leaned her head against her father's shoulder, and sighed.

"By the One Tree, Harle!" exclaimed Duke Leon, releasing Thera. "Those mounts of ours had best be prime if we're not to look outshone by the Ttamarini. Do we go to the stables and badger our recruits into becoming horse-masters in a seven day?"

Harle threw his head back in a basso laugh, "Aye, my Lord, that is a task to my liking!"

"And you, my girl," her father eyed her shrewdly. "Well

now — but keep out of trouble this morning, and at midday," he paused, "you may ride with me all the way to Kenna Beach." Oak Heart obviously expected her to be cheered.

Because she loved him, Thera smiled, and her father apparently was not deceived.

"Well now, *if* your mother agrees, perhaps we can delay the departure to Elankeep until after the Ttamarini arrive." He grinned. "Aye," glancing toward the keep, he nodded to himself as if rehearsing what he would say to his lady, "it would be a wise move, *I* think. The Ttamarini revere the Goddess, a girl-child with your gifts will give us status with them."

Thera watched her father and his companions continue on their way to the stables, Oak Heart and Harle towering above all the rest.

She saw young Jon strike a mock blow to Kertin's shoulder and they started a push and shove tussle which the older warriors laughed at.

Then came Sirra Shamic's unmistakable bellow, "You fribble-headed cockerels, any Memteth raider could split you from brisket to bowel with one blow, whilst you stood gaping foolishly." He clapped both recruits on the shoulder, with some weight behind the blow, "Save your bile for battle, lads."

"These Memteth, they be sharks. They make no truce, no parley. They will fight 'til they be dead, or we are."

Thera flinched at the frayed harshness of Shamic's voice. *Shamic is afraid! Afraid for us all.* She stood, transfixed, as the reality of what this conflict with the Memteth may mean for her people played across her mind.

She stood hearing and observing all about her; the clatter of servants' clogs as they ran their errands from residence to laundry building and kitchen to bake house; the longer paced step of the guardsmen's iron-cleated boots; the sudden skittering of the hounds nails on the cookhouse porch as they fled from some approaching terror.

Thera saw Cook, known for her hasty temper, especially since the death of her son, emerge from the cookhouse annex. Cook stood frowning, red hands propped on ample hips as her simmering gaze swept the courtyard. She spotted the Pot Boy, the same boy Thera had seen dropping a dead mouse into the servants' stew crock two days ago.

The oblivious Pot Boy lay belly down, playing penny toss against the granite wall of the residence. In a fury, Cook descended on him, her ladle smacking his buttocks in time with her words, "I-sent-you-to-the-smokehouse-an-een-since,-you-useless-grub!"

"Ow! Ow-ah. Ow!" The boy wailed and danced, hand clapped to his bottom. Cook eyed him, her foot tapping. The Pot Boy sniveled and bent, keeping a wary eye on Cook's ladle, to retrieve his two pennies.

Thera saw Cook throw her hands in the air and then take the Pot Boy by the shoulders. She made him face her as she spoke slowly and deliberately. She shook his shoulders as if in emphasis. The boy dredged under his nose with his ragged sleeve, smiling moistly, and nodded his straw-thatch head. Cook, still blackly frowning, delved into her pocket, retrieved a wedge of meat-pie wrapped in cheesecloth and slapped it into the Pot Boy's grubby hand.

The boy skipped off on the belated errand, and Cook watched his direction for a moment. Her look was thoughtful and sad. Then she turned in a business-like way and re-entered the cookhouse with majestic swagger, slamming the door on the various hounds whimpering at the threshold odors.

All these commonplace things and people that are my world,
Thera thought, *the Memteth will destroy if they can: the Cooks
and Pot Boys, Nans and Shamics, mothers and fathers.*

Thera turned and walked back inside, her steps as
measured and careful as if she walked on boggy ground. A
hot flame burned in her heart. Anger fluttered like a dusty
winged moth in her throat and chest. "No," she murmured.
"No!"

"You must teach me!" She sent to the Elanraigh, *"I will do
whatever I must to stop this from happening!"* Acknowledging
her pledge, forest-mind rumbled its fierce and gratified
response.

CHAPTER 4

*T*he fire crackled and snapped in the huge fireplace. The only other sound in her parents' retiring room was the rasp of whetstone against steel. Oak Heart's expression was thoughtful as he slid the stone down and over his dagger's edge. Thera's mother laid aside the scroll she was reading.

The amber glow of firelight held them all in its warm and fragrant circle. Lance, her father's deerhound, lay sprawled before the fire. His tail thumped in drowsy contentment. Thera lay languid on the thick woven rug, its exotic colors blurred before her eyes. She rolled her head which rested on Lance's ribs and furrowed her fingers through his silky fur. His tail thumped again.

"Leon..." her mother spoke softly, as if she called Thera's father from a sleep, "Leon...this alliance with the Ttamarini, if they agree, will it be enough...against the Memteth?"

Her father's brow quirked, "Oh aye, it will because it must. We will be a force to be reckoned with, the Ttamarini House of Chikei' allied with our House of ArNarone." Her father shifted his legs and stretched them toward the fire.

He nudged the dozing hound with a stocking covered foot. The dog cracked one lid and sighed gustily.

Leon's voice rumbled on, "Not since the time my great-grandfather held Allenholme, has there been a Memteth assault such as now seemingly comes our way. We must make sure that after this," his blue eyes flashed as he looked at Fideiya, "they will know our shores are bane to them."

"I was reading of those days," Fideiya gestured to the yellowed parchment, "they are fearsome fighters, Leon. Your ancestor writes of great hardships suffered by all to repel the attack, and *that* was only a few raiding ships." Fideiya's fingers lightly touched the vellum surface, as if she sought the very texture of the personality behind the spidery scrawl. "Maxin said that Lord Teckcharin and his personal guard arrive at dawn?" She paused, "Have you met him, Leon?"

The Oak Heart smiled ruefully at the fire, and stretched his arms behind his head. "Hmmm. You *would* ask, 'Deiya."

Thera sat upright and exchanged a quizzical glance with her mother. Nan who was quietly mending a stocking looked up in surprise at Oak Heart's comment.

Leon leaned forward, elbows on knees, "I was only sixteen. The truce had been in effect since my grandfather, Leif's, time. We were all forbidden to ride border raids, as were the Ttamarini fledgling warriors, no doubt." Leon's brow crumpled in sardonic amusement, "Though my father later told me that in his own youth there had been frequent skirmishes, equally forbidden, and as tacitly accepted.

"Ten of us decided to foray near the western Ttamarini grazing ranges, just north of the Silver Toss River. You understand, the idea was to collect some token, something of value which the Ttamarini would have to ransom back. I had in mind a particular colt I'd seen on a previous occasion."

The Oak Heart glanced brightly at his daughter, "Their horses are wonderful, Thera, graceful and strong." He continued, "If we'd been able to breed the young horse to our mares before the ransom was paid — well so much the better, it would have been a coup indeed.

"We were following the course of the Silver Toss, keeping fairly close to the border of the Elanraigh. We saw signs the herd we sought had passed, but not the horses themselves. It was enough, though, to draw us further into Ttamarini territory.

"After two days with no sight of them, we were deep in the foothills and with reluctance made ready to turn back."

Leon paused to lift a pewter tankard from the gleaming oak table beside his chair. He drank deeply and wiped the froth from his moustache and beard with the back of his hand.

"Was Sirra Shamic with you that day, father?" asked Thera.

Leon looked startled, "Blessings, *no*! He was a greybeard even then, with a dagger of a tongue, and a bludgeon for a fist. Somehow around my father and him I was always the stumble foot."

This last phrase her father had mumbled almost to himself, and he scrubbed at his beard with his calloused fingers.

His eyes twinkled as he scanned his small audience, "No," he continued, "this was to be *my* undertaking, so that when I came back with my troop and the colt as a prize, we would be treated as warriors. Hunnh. So.

"It was the third day and we decided we must return when we see the herd. There's the colt I want, driving northward on the high grass plain. There's no turning back now. We left the cover of the Elanraigh and pursued the herd.

"If I hadn't had the best horse in my father's stable, I doubt I would have caught up with that colt at all. I pull far ahead of the troop in my efforts to get a loop around the colt's neck. Once it was done, I look behind for my troops' congratulations, and then, what I see makes my blood run cold."

Nan gasped into the momentary silence and even Fideiya made a jerky movement of unease.

Thera saw that her father was flushed with the obvious success of his story. *Or perhaps,* Thera thought, tilting her head, *it was due to the memories he was reliving.* In any case he warmed to his story telling.

"The dust of a large troop of Ttamarini is on the eastern horizon; they are closing fast.

"Dougall, who rides a mare almost as fleet as my own, is now within voice range ... what he says to me," Leon drawled, "I'll forbear to repeat to my womenfolk's ears ... that he is fair bursting with rage let there be no doubt. They'd pledged to protect the Chief's Heir with their young lives, and I was making it no easy task for them, to be sure.

"Dougall and I ride back to the rest, who are milling about and undecided whether we fight or run. I can see there is no question...the approaching Ttamarini outweigh us in numbers, and are in the right. *We* are the interlopers here. So, we run and I have to relinquish the colt." Leon sighed gustily.

"We rattle down a deep crevasse. The Ttamarini plains are seamed with these deep gulleys, most running north and south. Riding two abreast we pound south for the Silver Toss and the Elanraigh.

"It's a credit to the horsemanship of my troop, that we

lamed no horses on *that* ride, either plunging down into the crevasse or riding hard along its rocky base. So, we make the Silver Toss all uninjured, but closely pursued by about twenty Ttamarini horse."

Fideiya suddenly interjected, "Leon, you have never before told *me* this tale!" Her tone was accusing.

Leon glanced up from under his brows, and said amiably, "Well, the mood to do so is upon me now, my own. In truth it has been the forthcoming meeting with the Ttamarini that reminds me.

"So, we swim our horses across the river and duck into the Elanraigh foothill trails. I split the troop, to better elude pursuit; Dougall, Lydia and I take the upper trail, it being the hardest ride and we the best mounted, and the others follow the river." Leon shook his head and smiled, "It was hard on them to leave me, even then they were my Heart's Own, but it was the only way. We'd rein in to a close trot, sure that now all will be well.

"Now, I had heard that the Ttamarini have an affinity with not only horses, but all manner of beasts. Some special linking of the mind and spirit...such as some Salvais have been known to have in the ancient days. I have no doubt of the Ttamarini gift, now."

Thera straightened, now alert and curious. This was something she had never heard. *The Ttamarini folk sound interesting*, she thought.

"Dougall, Lydia, and I ride a ridge that winds its way around the mountain base, some four pike heights above the river. The trail's drop-off side is all loose shale and any false move will reveal us to the Ttamarini who scout below.

"Above us is a small game trail that intersects our path some lengths further on. We see the Ttamarini leader hand signal several of his warriors up to scout the very trail we rode.

"I look up to the game trail, to see if we have an alternate route. It is then I see it — the largest hump-back bristlefang I've ever seen. He's loping easily along, hump swaying. We are downwind of him, so he is unaware of us, as yet. By some blessing our horses are also oblivious of the bristlefang.

"There is no chance of our reaching the trail intersect before the hump-back, and no turning back with the Ttamarini coming up behind us. We decide to try to descend the shale cliff to the river, and then run like our tails were on fire."

Leon shook his head. His fingers scrubbed again at his chin as his lips quirked in a self- deprecating smile.

"Obviously you escaped, Leon..." prodded Fideiya.

"Hmm? No, no; you see, at that very moment the wind changed. Our horses catch the scent of the bristlefang above, and start screaming and plunging on that narrow trail. My mare loses her footing on the loose shale edge and both she and I have a rough fall down to the river."

"Blessings!" exclaimed Nan, the mending completely forgotten in her lap.

Leon smiled and continued, "When I come to, an impressively strong old woman, all painted up and dripping feathers and bones, is raising my head to drink from a water-skin she holds to my mouth. About five other Ttamarini are seeing to my mare."

"Dougall and Lydia, I can see, are already remounted. They look pale but relatively uninjured. Lydia, who I've seen best lads four stone heavier than her in arms drill, is guarded by a formidable female Ttamarini warrior. This warrior may have grey braids, but she has a face like a granite cliff and corded arms covered in scars...I've never seen our Lydia look so subdued as then...and never since.

"The old woman giving me water, their *Maiya* I found out later, sees my eyes open and calls to a tall warrior standing nearby. I hear the name, Teckcharin.

"'Deiya, I hurt like a Cythian hell, but I get to my feet. I say to myself, *blessed if I am going to confront the Ttamarini Chief while lying in the dirt.*" The Oak Heart rumbled a laugh. "Ah, what a sight I must have been: a gawky, straw-haired lad, all knees and elbows."

Lady Fideiya murmured some protest and glanced fondly at her life sworn. He flashed a smile at his lady, "Oh, I'd matured much by the time *we* met, my own. Blessings Be.

"Lord Teckcharin, a seasoned warrior even then, wears his dark hair long, as they all do, one part by his face was braided with an eagle feather stuck through. His layered leathern hauberk was studded with shells and stones.

"We were of a height, I remember. Well, I meet that gaze and hold it, even though I am suddenly very conscious of being young and not at my best. I am covered in dust, dirt and scratches.

"That look. It was a long moment to endure. By the One Tree..." Leon shook his head, " ... my own father or even Shamic couldn't have burned me more with just a look."

"What is his appearance, Leon? I've heard they are a very...," she paused, "compelling race." Fideiya glanced at Thera, and lowered her voice, "I have told you of the rumor in my family," she hesitated briefly, "that my old aunts would whisper about Lady Dysanna and Lord Chemotin of the Ttamarini. It seems a very romantic and tragic story to me."

Duke Leon shook his head doubtfully, "As for old wives tales about a romance between Lady Dysanna and

Teckcharin's father, remember we were at war with the Ttamarini then. I don't see how such a union could happen." Leon shrugged dismissively.

"As to how Teckcharin looks, he has a powerful presence — a fine warrior's appearance. Most Ttamarini have high cheekbones, dark hair and grey eyes. They are a lean, strong folk of high ideals."

Leon snorted, "I'm sure those eyes were glinting of something like amusement as they inventoried me that day.

"Teckcharin speaks to me in our language, though in a rather antique and formal manner, 'You are young Leon Leif ArNarone.' It is more a statement than a question, you see.

"I bowed, don't think I *could* have spoken. 'Young ArNarone,' Teckcharin says, 'you are not yet a worthy rider of this noble horse.' He turns from me and listens to another Ttamarini who is waving his arms angrily, gesturing between me and my mare," Leon mused, "hopping with rage. Reminded me of Shamic.

"Then the Ttamarini Chief says to me, 'Tenatik tells me, young ArNarone, that your fine mare will recover with rest and care. It will be our pleasure to keep her with us. You also, will remain with us, until you may be safely returned to your father. Your companions have my leave to return to Allenholme now.'

"At this point, I must suppose Lydia can no longer contain herself, 'The Heart's Own do not leave him in enemy hands!' she says, 'We remain with our Lord.' She gets all that out without a quaver, though her cheeks were very red.

"Dear Lydia!" exclaimed Fideiya, "I do love her."

"Just so, my own. Well, the stony faced woman guarding Lydia regards her steadily a moment or two, then speaks to Teckcharin... I *believe* she calls Lydia a *hissing cub.* I don't have confidence in my knowledge of their tongue.

"In any case, Lydia's outburst didn't do her any discredit with the Ttamarini. Teckcharin gives her the benefit of the friendliest expression I'd seen on his face so far. He spreads his hands and bows to her, warrior to warrior, 'I hear a warrior's words,' he said.

"Then he turns again to me, 'A man who can command such loyalties, is a man to be reckoned with, your warrior companions return honor to you, young ArNarone. Your companions may remain at your side.'

"This is all smooth as silk, mind, while maneuvering me onto a spare horse and preparing to get his troop underway. Before we heel our horses eastward, Teckcharin paces away from us several strides and stands with arms raised, facing the Elanraigh. His demeanor is both reverent and proud. He chants some blessing or thanks, and as he finishes, we all hear the unmistakable roar of a bristlefang from deep in the forest.

"You think the beast responded to him, Leon?" asked Fideiya skeptically.

"I truly do not know, 'Deiya." Leon cracked his knuckles, his expression thoughtful. "I suspect they have a bond of sorts with animal-kind, as I have said."

"And reverence for the Elanraigh, it would seem," said Thera, alert.

Leon nodded silently and then continued, "Our ride to their encampment is much of a blur to me. I don't recall all that I answered to Teckcharin as we spoke, but I must admit, in spite of everything, I found myself warming to him. He was skilled at drawing a young man out. We talked of hunting and horses. He was interested in my father's method of governance in Allenholme, and whether we were

closely allied with Cythia. I was treated with so much courtesy I was scalded with it.

"Naturally father was informed of my *rescue*, and in his
'*gratitude for my safe return the Honorable Chief Branch
ArNarone would surely wish to offer the Ttamarini Chief,
Teckcharin, the injured mare as gift.*'"

"Needless to say, the mare stayed to greatly increase the
value of *their* herd, and I was returned two months later to
face my father and Shamic."

Fideiya was pensive, "I'm surprised, Leon, that the Elanraigh permitted you to be captured virtually within its
boundaries. The Elanraigh's bond with us is so strong."

Thera stated wonderingly, as she prodded forest-mind,
"The Elanraigh cares for the Ttamarini too."

Both parents and a startled maid regarded the girl a
moment.

Oak Heart nodded, "Hunnh. Our little Salvai here is
correct, I think. The Ttamarini have great reverence, for the
world in all its aspects: forest, plains, sea, and sky. The Earth
itself is Mother, Bride, and Wife.

"My brief time with them was not an unhappy one,"
Leon mused. "It is strange, the Ttamarini expected us to be
very insular and narrow minded. As soon as they saw our
open interest in learning of their ways, they responded with
an open hearted enthusiasm." He leaned back, "Teckcharin
himself instructed us in the bow. My improvement in
archery *almost* reconciled my father to my adventure.

"The female warrior, whose name was Chertai, taught us
much about tracking. I would say she had taken a special
liking to Lydia.

"Their Horsemaster, Tenatik, worked to improve our
horsemanship. He took special pains with me, I must add.
No, in truth, the two moons we were "guests" of the

Ttamarini were happier than I would have dreamed. I like to think that it is as a result of our deportment during that "visit," that the Ttamarini are willing to parley with us now."

"Well," smiled Fideiya, "here you are now, years later, a man full grown and leader of your people, about to meet the leader of all the Ttamarini once again, now perhaps to be declared ally and friend."

"Aye." murmured Leon with rueful smile, and he scrubbed again at his beard. "Aye."

Thera sensed something that caused her to study her father. It seemed she was seeing much these days in the adults around her that she had never noticed before. She was amazed to see that her father, the Duke, Oak Heart, could feel nervous about anything.

CHAPTER 5

Thera woke in the velvet shadows of predawn light. The stone arch of her window perfectly framed the pale new moon, and the dark spine of the distant High Ranges was touched with opal light. She stretched sleepily, sliding her arm over the soft cover of her feather quilt. Then she remembered.

The Ttamarini must be here. They may already have set up camp on the North Field, west of Kenna Beach.

Swinging her legs over the edge of her bed, she rubbed with brief irritation at her shins. Her bones ached lately. Nan said it was because she was growing so fast. She ran to the window and the cool silkiness of morning air caressed her skin. She massaged her chest, Nan insisted she wear a binding now. One restriction after another, it seems.

Nothing was visible yet in the courtyard, though she thought she heard boot steps and voices in the stable yard. Anticipation flickered along her nerves as she danced her feet on the cold stone floor.

She dragged on the green gown Nan had set aside for this day, but her long, sleep-tangled hair caught in the buttons. Nan came in to find her half dressed and jigging in frustration.

"Lass! What be you doing out of bed at this hour?"

"Are they here, Nan? I want to see them."

"Hold still now, you're all a-tangle, I should have braided your hair last night, but a more sleepy lass I've never seen."

"Ouch! Please hurry Nan."

"You may as well hold your breath, Button. I will see you properly dressed and fed before you leave this chamber, does hear me, lass?"

Thera recognized the tone of Nan's voice and with a great effort of will, forbore to fidget. *Elanraigh Bless. I don't need a nursemaid! Nan's fussiness is so annoying. Mother should have had other children for Nan to lavish her care on, then I could be left alone.*

Thera cast a sullen glower at Nan's profile as the maid turned slightly to unravel a knot of Thera's hair. Nan's fair brows were puckered in concentration, a pink tip of tongue protruded past the compressed lips.

Thera sighed at her freakish irritability and contritely took back the wish. She loved Mother, of course. However, it was Nan, with this very same look of concentration on her face, who had plucked out slivers, crooned over scrapes or cuts as she bathed them, or simply cuddled and rocked her whenever she needed the closeness. Nan always knew when those times were — that was Nan's gift.

By the time Thera washed, there was constant movement and voices beyond her chamber door. Nan's deft fingers subdued Thera's curls into a head-molding braid.

"I was with your mother this morning, early, lass," Nan's hands rested a moment on Thera's shoulders. "We be leaving at dawn's blessing tomorrow for Elankeep." Thera twisted around, aghast. Nan continued quickly, "Now, now, lass. You be knowing your lady mother only agreed to let you stay long enough to see the Ttamarini arrive. 'Tis just for the now, 'til it be safe again to come home."

Thera simply said, "I don't like to leave, Nan, not when there is trouble. They needn't treat me as such a child — I could help."

Nan's voice was thick as she pulled Thera to her. "You're getting so grown-up, Button." So tightly did she clench Thera to her bosom that Thera's cheek bore the imprint of Nan's apron button for some time after.

THE EARLY MORNING light shone bright, burnished by a brisk wind blowing inland off the sea. Dew still sparkled on spider webs and on the tossing cedar branches.

Thera stood with her mother and the household guards. Oak Heart was mounted in front of the Heart's Own, the guards, and the town dignitaries. Thera could not recall ever seeing the front courtyard so crowded with people. Representatives of the guilds and town marshals stood to one side, resplendent with polished badges of office. Their murmured conversations lapsed into silence. Soon the cracking of banners in the wind, the creak of leather, and the scuff of shifting horses was all the straining listeners heard.

Thera watched her father. *He is a heroic figure*, Thera thought. She watched the light reflecting in the amber hue of his link mail and the clean wind drifting the white plume of his helm. Grandfather Leif's square-cut emerald broach gleamed at his shoulder.

Thera mused on her reading of her father at the end of his tale last night. She had learned that Oak Heart had a fear he could barely bring himself to acknowledge — that he would become as a callow youth, a "stumble foot," when once again face to face with Lord Teckcharin, Chief of the Ttamarini. Thera was bemused to find that her father, a warrior, could harbor such an anxiety.

The Heart's Own — Dougall, Lydia, and all the rest — were in formal military dress, their faces stern behind the nosepiece of their helms. Horses had been groomed meticulously, leather tack was buffed until it shone, "Like a maiden's blush," as Shamic said. Every bit of brass, silver, and steel gleamed.

From the North Gate finally came the sound of many horse hooves on paving stones. Cheers echoed from the folk of Allenholme lining the roadway outside the gate as they greeted their new allies.

Thera felt a welling of anticipation and wanted to cheer too. But she was very conscious of her woman's crown of braids and full-length green gown. She glanced sideways at the stiff formality of the guildsmen and town representatives ranged alongside, and encountered a smile from one grizzled man who wore the badge of a fishing guild master. His grey-green eyes held hers in friendly rapport a moment, and then he turned with a show of restoring his face to decorous dignity.

Thera could read the welcome in townsfolk's' voices. She was sure anyone could. Dread of the Memteth was as great a part of the mythology of her people, as was respect for the prowess of the Ttamarini warrior.

The drift of music came with the approaching troop; drum, tambour, and pipe. They played, not a martial air, but a song to move feet and lift spirits. Finally the Ttamarini riders turned through the gates.

Thera strained to see the Ttamarini leader, Teckcharin. She saw a regal stallion to the front of the approaching company that must be seventeen hands tall, its black coat gleamed and rippled in the sun. The beast danced into the courtyard. Teckcharin, it must be he who rode this horse, seemed almost familiar to Thera. Her heart thudded behind her ribs.

He was as she'd known he would be from her father's recounting of his adventure the evening before. He sat tall and straight, it hardly appeared he needed to guide his mount at all. The long straight hair, only lightly streaked with grey, was bound off his brow with a brightly woven band. An eagle feather was attached to the single braid that hung beside his face.

That face was proud and stern, yet as he locked eyes with Oak Heart, Thera detected a glimmer of smile. She read no smugness or mockery there, indeed, Thera read a considerable affection for her father.

Once through the gate, Teckcharin's warriors fanned out behind him. Their horses stepped high, with much jingling of decorations, sea shell chimes were braided into the horses' mains and tails. Next came acrobatic dancers, *Song Dancers*, she'd heard they were called. Thera smiled and clasped her hands. Energies swirled about the courtyard, bright and chaotic, full of life.

At a sign from Teckcharin, the music ceased and he rode forward alone. The Oak Heart heeled his horse ahead of his assembly. For a moment, in complete silence they regarded one another. Her father extended his arm, palm up, in the warriors' greeting, and Teckcharin smiling openly now, grasped it with his own. They met and held each other's eyes as their troops cracked the sky with the thunder of their approval.

CHAPTER 6

*T*eckcharin spoke into the last echo of their cheer. "You must be Leon Leif ArNarone." His voice was as Oak Heart remembered, deep and melodious. His greeting was an echo of their first meeting fifteen years ago.

"Well met, Lord Teckcharin," rumbled Oak Heart. His smile encompassed the Ttamarini entourage as well.

Windgather jibbed at the proximity of Teckcharin's stallion. The Ttamarini watched as Leon placed his hand on his shoulder and spoke a soothing phrase in the Ttamarini tongue. Windgather subsided with a white-eyed toss of his head.

Teckcharin's tone was pleased, "So, you do not despise our ways?"

"Indeed not, my Lord," replied Leon. "If the Elanraigh was so determined to put such a lesson in my path, it was my duty to remember it." Leon glanced over at the Ttamarini riders. "In fact, I have good memories of the two moons I spent in your camp — your people were generous with their time and diligent with their teachings."

Teckcharin smiled. He looked over Leon's mount, "It is a

fine animal, Duke Leon, but..." Teckcharin turned in the saddle and gestured to a warrior that Leon had already recognized as Tenatik. The Ttamarini horsemaster heeled forward, leading another stallion. Several of the Allenholme folk murmured their admiration.

Tenatik, whipcord lean and grinning broadly, spoke to his leader in animated accents.

Teckcharin turned to Leon with raised brows. "Tenatik says that he hopes you fall from your horse less frequently now."

Leon snorted and quirked his brow. "Did I not have the finest of instruction while I guested at your camp," he replied to Tenatik with a bow, "to cure me of any such ineptness."

When Teckcharin had translated this, Tenatik laughed in turn. Tenatik had a long-featured, jester's face, but the eyes that appraised Duke Leon were shrewd. His lips pursed, and the smile lingered in his gaze. He spoke then to his chief and passed over to him the reins he held on the led stallion. With a salute to Oak Heart, he heeled back to the warriors' formation behind Teckcharin.

Teckcharin, in turn, ceremoniously handed the reins on to Leon. "A gift from my people to yours. From the very colt that caught the eye of a rash young warrior, some years ago."

Speechless and with shining eagerness, Leon swung down from his mount. He back-handed the reins to the closest guardsman. Removing his gauntlet, he reverently smoothed his hand over the stallion's glossy russet chest, deep and well muscled. Murmuring Ttamarini endearments to the horse, he ran his hand down a canon bone like iron. The horse whuffled down his neck interestedly.

"His name?" Leon asked.

"His name is Leishtek, after the flame-red tree that grows near the sea."

"Ahh." Leon gusted out his breath and looked up at Teckcharin.

"My Lord Teckcharin, the magnificence of this gift humbles me. Truly. I have nothing in my stable to match this horse. The best of my hunting birds will be yours to choose from, indeed, anything I have that delights your eye it will be my pleasure to gift to you."

Teckcharin's eyes glinted, but he merely nodded his head. "It is well, my friend, it is well."

The Ttamarini chief swung gracefully off his mount. As he faced Leon, his expression sobered. "It was time for this ancient bitterness between our peoples to be finished, my friend. Our Maiya, Ishtarik," he gestured respectfully to the Priestess/Dream-speaker that Leon remembered from years ago, "has seen visions of black sails in her dreams." The old Maiya came forward to join them.

"Aye. So has my daughter. She is only a child, but my Lady tells me she comes into her gifts young. She promises to be a great Salvai, Lady of the Elanraigh, you understand."

Leon saluted the Dream-speaker, Ttamarini style, both hands to forehead. "Goddess guard your peace, Maiya."

The old woman smiled, showing teeth that were surprisingly strong, white and even, though the eyes in the craggy face were dimmed with the chalky whiteness that sometimes comes with old age.

"Goddess guard the fruit of your loins, Duke Leon," she intoned.

Leon flushed a bright red. He pushed back his camail hood and scrubbed at his beard and neck. His bright blue eyes squinted at the Ttamarini chief. Teckcharin's features held only an elaborately bland expression, but as he met the

Oak Heart's look, his eyes danced. "Our Maiya is a Dream-speaker and walks always with one foot in another land, Duke Leon. Even I, Chief of Ttamarini, can only accept her blessings with the same wonder." Teckcharin looked down at the top of the Maiya's head, a wry smile twisting his lips. "She will never deign to elaborate."

The old woman laughed appreciatively.

Leon found himself wishing Fideiya was at hand. He scrubbed at the back of his neck again and then gestured toward the assembled high folk of Allenholme waiting to receive the Ttamarini leader. "You will permit me now to introduce my people?"

The Ttamarini chief placed a hand lightly on Leon's arm. "If *you* will permit, Duke Leon, there is one other I would have at my side for this."

"Of course, Lord Teckcharin." Leon eyed the assembled Ttamarini with amiable conjecture. No doubt the man had certain of his retinue to whom he was close, as he, Leon, was to the Heart's Own. It was Leon's opinion that Teckcharin would call Tenatik, the horsemaster forward.

The warrior who heeled his horse in response to his Chief's signal was not Tenatik. It was a youth, the image of Teckcharin, who galloped his mount to the waiting Chiefs, reined and dismounted in one easy motion, to make a profound obeisance at Teckcharin's feet.

Teckcharin's voice thrummed with pride. "Duke Leon Leif ArNarone, I present my son and Heir, Chamakin Dysan Chikei'."

The youth surged to his feet with supple grace and bowed his head to Leon, who rested astonished eyes on the young warrior in front of him.

"Chamakin," he breathed. "I know this youth. He was a toddler still when last I saw him. I remember making him a small reed pipe to play, which he then played incessantly all over the camp until Tenatik threw it for the dogs to chew."

Oak Heart observed the flush that crept over the youth's face and mentally kicked himself. He had equally disliked old soldiers' recollections voiced about *his* childhood once he was grown and considered himself a man. Leon cleared his throat.

"This is a warrior I see before me now. I give you a warriors' greeting, Chamakin Dysan Chikei, be welcome to Allenholme," and Leon extended his arm palm up to have it firmly grasped.

The youth has muscles of iron, thought Leon. For a brief moment Leon wished he too had a son like this, then, resolutely, pushed the thought away.

The horses were given over to a retainer's care and the small party turned to walk together.

"Your Salvai is here?" Teckcharin asked, "Perhaps she and our Dream-speaker will jointly bless our alliance."

"Nooo." replied Leon, slowly. "Our Salvai Keiris never leaves the Elankeep sanctuary. Though long ago, in different times, I understand, a Salvai did more frequently commune with the folk."

Teckcharin was silent for several strides, then spoke. "Your Salvai, a position of great importance — like a Maiya, or Dream-speaker — is Goddess appointed. Is it truly your tradition for her to be unmated? To keep herself apart?" There was disapproval in his voice.

"Yes." Leon's voice was thoughtful. He had often wished that Keiris would interest herself more with the people of Allenholme. There should be more gifted people than there were. He personally thought Keiris hoarded her gift, though he would not wound his Lady to speak so of her half-sister. "That is how Salvai Keiris explains it." He continued, "She,

the Salvai, is the chosen one of the Elanraigh. An interme-
diary for the people of Allenholme with the elementals of
the forest, her devotion cannot be divided. That would be to
insult the Elanraigh." Leon glanced at the Ttamarini chief,
whose expression still expressed, what? Distaste?

The Oak Heart felt obliged to explain further. "The
Salvai Keiris is the chosen of the Elanraigh, her interpreta-
tion of its wishes could not be in error."

Teckcharin looked disturbed. "It is our way to guard and
express our love of the land by way of union between man
and woman; priestess and warrior. Anything else denies the
Goddess, and belittles her gifts."

The Oak Heart sighed, it was the Old Faith. Leon felt a
strong wish for the friendship and trust of this man. He
spoke slowly, turning to face Teckcharin. "This will be a
time of learning and sharing ideas between our people, as
well as fighting the common foe. May we follow wisely the
path the Elanraigh," he nodded respectfully to the Dream-
Speaker, "and the Goddess, show us."

The party stopped in front of the granite steps on which
were arrayed the Oak Hearts' family, officers and guild leaders. "Lord Teckcharin Rys Chikei," said Leon formally, "I
would present my Lady Fideiya Ned'Chadwyn, who is sister
to the Salvai at Elankeep."

Lord Teckcharin studied with focused concentration the
countenance raised to his. Fideiya's brow crept upward as
she forbore the scrutiny.

"Blessings, My Lord," she greeted him, a trace of
austerity chilling her voice.

Teckcharin blinked and the tension in his features
relaxed. He smiled with great warmth. Taking Fideiya's
hand, he placed it over his heart. "Goddess bless, *Chaunya*."

Leon's brow rumpled as he pondered the greeting.

Surely Teckcharin had used the Ttamarini word for *kinswoman of high birth*. His glance caught Shamic's. The old soldier, he saw, had flushed hotly. Leon, himself, was not inclined to take offence. It was obvious the Ttamarini chief meant only to convey respect to the life sworn of his ally.

Oak Heart noticed the old Dream-Speaker was staring at Thera. Indeed, so now were all three Ttamarini.

These Ttamarini are all so intense in everything they do, Leon thought. He observed that his daughter did not quail under the regard of such powerful personalities. Though slightly flushed, she returned their measuring with a searching look of her own.

"My only child and Heir," rumbled Leon in introduction, "Thera ep'Chadwyn Ned'ArNarone."

To the Oak Heart's surprise, Lord Teckcharin gently took both Thera's hands in his own, and stood quiet a moment before folding her hands over his heart in a greeting similar to that he'd given Lady Fideiya. The words he murmured to her were lost to Leon, though he saw his daughter smile in return.

Thera's voice rang sweetly clear, "My Lord Teckcharin, I know your heart. Goddess bless."

The Dream-speaker turned in surprise to Leon. "Where did this *enoiten* child learn of our ways?"

Leon's brow rumpled again as he ruffled through his memory of Ttamarini speech. *Enoita*, he believed, described both an igniting beauty of soul, as a lit candle will shine through fine porcelain, and one who acts in harmony with all things.

Leon did not immediately answer as he was frowningly observing the young Chamakin's reaction to his daughter; the youth was obviously struck by her beauty. The Oak Heart felt alarm.

"My daughter, though well grown, is but a child yet," he spoke ostensibly to the Dream-speaker, but intending Lord Teckcharin and his son to take heed, "and has seen only fourteen summers."

"My Lord," interposed Fideiya, "Thera will celebrate her woman's rites in a quarter moon." With an enigmatic glance over her shoulder at the Oak Heart, Fideiya led Lord Teckcharin and his Heir to meet the waiting dignitaries.

Leon gaped after his life sworn. "By the Sacred Hollow," he murmured, "the girl is as tall as her mother." He felt a presence, the Dream-speaker, Ishtarik, still stood beside him.

"When in the Goddess's hand, Lord ArNarone," she said, "a blossom may unfold out of season." Her blind eyes rested on Leon with a certain pity.

CHAPTER 7

The great hall was a sea of voices. Sound washed like waves — rising, falling, occasionally lapping around the sharp rock of a shouted laugh, or clank of goblets clashing in yet another toast.

Thera's face warmed as she remembered Chief Teckcharin's words and gestures from this morning on the steps. 'Your beauty is great, as foretold,' he had murmured, and placed her hands against his chest. Such intimate touching fanned the heat in Thera's face again, although she read that this contact, this touching and gesturing with the hands, was as important to their way of speech as voice was to her folk.

Thera had smiled uncertainly and searched his eyes to see if he teased her, the way adults will patronize youth. *No.* She saw that this was a man to whom falsehood would be foreign.

She had not received many compliments from men. Her father, to be sure, called her 'his pretty lass.' Shamic had said she resembled the Lady Dysanna, who had been wise and beautiful.

Thera had read that Teckcharin saw strength of character and spirit in her, and this pleased him as much as her appearance.

The Ttamarini had bent closer, his long hair swinging with the movement. "You are but a young *Maiya*, yet," Thera had not known that word, "*Maiya*," he repeated in explanation, "in service of the Goddess. As is our *Maiya*, Ishtarik. Know this, young one, my warriors will strive to save this land." He had pressed her hand between his warm, calloused palms. "It has been foreseen that no real victory over the darkness that comes will happen without compliance to the ways of the Goddess."

Thera pondered his words. Chief Teckcharin's command of our language is good, Thera thought, though he speaks it with a formal ceremoniousness. Past the Ttamarini chief's shoulder stood a young man watching her with a strange, stern intensity. She felt her face and ears burn, and suddenly it was difficult to read the people around her. These strangers expected something of her, and she felt buffeted by the forces they exerted on her.

As if sensing her turmoil, the *Maiya* reached her hand to briefly touch Thera's face. "Do not worry so, *Chaunika*," she said with a smile, "for it has also been foretold, that all you will need to do is heed your heart."

With the touch of the *Maiya's* hand, Thera's swirling thoughts settled. She suddenly felt rooted and acutely aware; aware of her skin on her bones, the beat of her heart, the moistness of her eyes, the impact of sound on ears, and heat of the fire on her skin. Never had she felt so intensely alive, except perhaps once--when she had lived briefly in hawk form. Before her eyes formed a vision, Ttamarini, root and sinew of the One Tree, Allenholme, leaf and branch. Both are loved by the Elanraigh and the Goddess.

Following an instinct born of that moment, Thera placed her hand on the Ttamarini's chest and ritually replied, "My Lord Teckcharin, I know your heart. Goddess bless us all."

THE FEAST GREW raucous and loud, dinning in her ears. Even the Harbor Master who had been so pompous in his welcoming speech was now blowing froth off his beer into the laughing face of a burly stave smith. She glanced at her father, who was engrossed in his conversation with Lord Teckcharin, Captain Dougall, and Sirra Maxin. Their animated discussion involved much drawing of lines on the table planks with wine-dipped fingers.

Thera could not help but be aware that each time she turned her head to her right, in her father's direction, the young Ttamarini, Chamakin, would fix his attention on her.

For a while, the Ttamarini *Maiya*, Ishtarik, had been seated on Thera's left, and Thera found herself able to direct some shy courtesies there. The elder woman radiated warmth that Thera felt very attracted to. It felt natural to tell the dream-speaker about the family of kirshrews she had rescued who now made a comfortable nest in her bedchamber cedar chest, and of her care of the negligent Mouseripper's kittens. She had even confided how much she loved sea hawks, though that mystic joining she did not feel ready to share. The old woman had listened to all. In fact, Thera felt herself being held in the bright light of the *Maiya's* inward vision.

Thera had, at first, found the *Maiya's* blind eyes disconcerting, but the face with its strong, weathered features was vital and animate. The *Maiya's* energies pulsed warmly about her and Thera leaned with pleasure into their nimbus.

Dream-speaker Ishtarik ate sparingly, soon rising to leave. Placing a dry kiss on Thera's brow, she whispered into her ear. "When you fly as an eagle, child, then will you be fully fledged."

The *Maiya* left with her escort to return to the Ttamarini encampment. Thera, bemused, lapsed back into her awkward silence.

So much poetic speech and imagery, mused Thera, *yet I wonder if she knows how close to the actual truth she came with that particular image.* Thera hugged the memory of her hawk flight to her.

I can't eat. This surprised her, for usually her appetite was hearty. Thera eyed the trencher before her — tender roast fowl with crisp golden skin and cooked grains with mealy nuts. Her mouth watered, but her stomach clenched. Tentatively she took a bite of crusty warm bread, chewed determinedly and swallowed with what she was sure must be an audible sound.

Finally, Thera glanced sideways at Chamakin. He ate slowly, chewing with deliberation. His face was flushed with bright color along the high cheekbones. Her eyes slid along the table to where her companion's arm rested. His arm was long, and smooth muscled, the hand broad with tapered fingers, calloused much like any warrior's. His body, clothed in artfully decorated leather garments, was lean and his chest showing through the lacings of his shirt was hairless with the skin shining smooth over the ridges of his muscles.

Most Allenholme men were built tall like her father, with heavy muscles and broad-shoulders. Oak Heart's arms and chest were covered in fine red-gold hair. Chamakin had no beard to detract from the firm clean lines of his mouth and jaw.

Suddenly the hand she had been observing clenched upon itself tightly, and then slowly released as if by a needed act of will. Chamakin cleared his throat.

"The weapons displayed on the far wall," he said and gestured toward them. "They are the preferred weapons of your people?"

Thera glanced at his face. *Is he speaking to me,* she wondered? His voice was deep, without the hoarseness that edged her father's voice.

At least his face had at last relaxed somewhat from its usual expression of sternness. Thera very carefully placed her two-pronged fork beside her trencher.

"Um. The two very long swords were my great-grandfather Leif's weapons. It takes a strong man using both hands to wield them. The cross-bows — I don't know who they belonged to. My father prefers the long bow. He says a powerful bowman can discharge six arrows to the cross-bow's one. However, it takes strong men to keep up that kind of fire. Sirra Maxim has charge of our archers and they train and practice constantly.

"As for swords, my father uses a shorter sword than Great Grandfather's, one that he can wield one-handed and use a shield with."

"The Ttamarini also," affirmed Chamakin with a slow nod, "our sword is shorter again, and curved. They are called *Kyphim* and each warrior's is forged for them at a time agreed upon as auspicious by the *Maiya* and the adult warrior who sponsors him or her on their Oathday." Chamakin's hands gestured in a relaxed manner now and a smile warmed his eyes.

Finally Thera could observe Chamak as she wished. She

was fascinated by his elongate grey eyes, thickly fringed with dark lashes. *He is very handsome, if exotic in appearance, and so different to any Allenholme youth.*

She realized she had become distracted from what he had been saying to her about the Ttamarini swords...*Kyphim?*

"...their making is an art known only to the clan's *Kyphimitat,* the forgers of steel. The making of each warrior's *Kyphim* is part of a rite that will bring life to the blade with the strength and protection of that warrior's spirit guardians."

Thera nodded, "Our custom is similar," she said, "A soldier will proudly inherit a sword handed down from generation to generation. We believe that such a sword will acquire characteristics of its own, almost as if they absorb some of the spirit of each person wielding them."

Thera lowered her voice and Chamakin leaned closer. "When I was young, I once came alone to this Great Hall and tried to lift my Great-Grandfather's sword from the wall." Thera gestured to the broadsword.

"As soon as I put my hand to its hilt, I felt that I should not. Then, then I saw a vision. Before me stood an elder warrior, with a grey-brindled beard and the emerald broach my father now wears was on his cloak. He too wore a red cloak over mail and surcoat, and his voice when he spoke, was similar to my father's. The vision spoke to me. He said that so unwieldy a weapon was not for me, and that when the time came, 'I would be my own weapon.'"

Thera's voice was subdued. "And then he raised his hand as if in blessing and was gone.

"I do not lie," she said, rearing back, for Chamakin's expression was again grave.

"That I do know, *Chaunika.* It is just, the young of my

people often have such visions when their bodies and spirits prepare to make the passage into manhood or womanhood. My people revere these visions, and they are always of importance to the life path of that person."

Thera gazed at Chamak a long moment. *How is it that we understand each other so well?* Aware she must be conspicuously staring, Thera broke the silence. "You speak our language so well. How is that?"

Chamakin toyed with his knife a moment. "My father has always spoken your tongue, and he taught me. Our *Maiya* also speaks the language of the coast, and some few of our warriors."

"How ashamed I am that we are so remiss, although my father does speak some Ttamarini. I'll try to make up for my ignorance by learning quickly."

She read instantly that she pleased him with her willingness to learn the Ttamarini language.

Flustered, Thera blurted, "How long ago was your Oath Day?"

A slight austerity smoothed Chamakin's face. "I have been a warrior of the clan since last summer."

He is eighteen years, then, Thera realized.

"I am fourteen," said Thera, squaring her shoulders. Her eyes met Chamakin's squarely. "I shall celebrate my woman's day very soon."

Chamakin laughed, and his gaze warmed her. "*Chaunika,* you are already formidable."

Thera knew many things in that moment, that she was deeply admired and that he had an almost overpowering desire to touch her, but he leashed the wanting. She fled from this reading. The emotions it stirred in her were as chaotic as they were compelling. Some of the sensations she felt were reminiscent of her experience as a hunting hawk, tautness and anticipation, fluttering just under her skin.

Thera craved quiet and time to think upon all that had happened today. Held in place, she gazed at Chamak. "I leave to go to Elankeep soon. My mother wishes it."

The smooth calm of his features is deceptive, Thera thought, *for his eyes burn and flicker with his emotions.*

"Please excuse me," she murmured, rising suddenly. A young page in her father's service rushed forward to move her chair back for her. As Chamakin also stood in courtesy, a page rushed forward to his service also.

Thera curtsied quickly. "I have much to do to prepare for my journey tomorrow," and she fled the Great Hall, the heat of Chamakin's gaze scorching her back.

CHAPTER 8

*S*lamming the door to her chamber behind her, Thera paused, then ran to her window. The soothing night air, full of the scent and feel of the Elanraigh, fingered her brow.

Coyotes raised their voices to the moon rising pale over the serrated edge of the dark foothills. Closer at hand she heard a laughing exchange between two soldiers on guard duty, their voices echoed off the courtyard walls before their booted steps dwindled into the dark.

She turned and her gaze travelled over her chamber. The grey stone walls were enlivened with brightly woven tapestries. Some had been bequeathed to her by her grandmother, others, portraying the trees and animals of the Elanraigh that Thera so loved, had been worked by Fideiya. There were the carved wooden horses from Shamic and the jewel-colored bed throws knitted by Nan. Bright copper bowls were full of the spring flowers that she had gathered herself. She loved the way they would shine like gleaming pools of color in the sunlight.

Thera realized it might be long before she slept here again.

HER TRAVEL TRUNK was closed and belted, ready to be carried away in the morning.

The clutch of kirshrews lay mewling on a knitted blanket at the foot of her bed. Their white fur gleamed iridescent in the moonlight. Thera sat with them a while, her fingers absently stroking their silky pelts. Their small trilling sounds soothed her. The kirshrews' pink tongues lapped at her fingers and tiny-fingered paws kneaded in gentle contentment at her palm.

"I've neglected you," she murmured, "I must find you a new home now, because Nan and I leave early tomorrow." She looked around, then reached for a woven basket from her dresser. Thera dumped the contents, various hair ribbons and ornaments, onto her bed and gently placed each kirshrew inside the basket.

She glanced out her chamber door. No one was visible in the hallway, but Thera remembered there was a guard at the top of the main stairway. Moving swiftly, but quietly, she turned off the corridor and down the servants' stairway.

Thera was certain it would be hours yet before Nan sought her cot in her room. She had seen Nan and Innic seated together, their hands clasped. Nan's fair skin had been rosy with happiness. Thera smiled to recall how Innic's moustaches fairly bristled with pride. With all her heart Thera wished them well, and sincerely hoped they may make a night of it. It seemed likely they would at least stay to hear the balladeer, and *he* would sing as long as there were those who wished to listen.

When finally she reached the ground floor, she

cautiously opened the outside door. The cookhouse was still brightly lit. Dark figures flit between it and the Great Hall. No one looked her way.

Crooning under her breath to the kirshrews, Thera darted along the walls where shadows hung. She decided to relocate the kirshrews near the top of the bluff that over-looked Lorn a'Lea Beach, to the south of the keep. The problem would be getting past the sentry who would certainly be patrolling the southwest gate.

The granite wall gleamed in the bright moonlight as Thera warily made her way toward the gate opening. Holding herself still and listening past her heartbeat, she heard the rhythmic scrunch of gravel as the sentry paced. A moment's distraction would be all she needed to pass through the gate and into the shadows cast by the tall sitka trees.

"*A small distraction,*" she sent her plea to the Elanraigh. She searched, not really knowing whether the Elanraigh would hinder or help in this case. The Elanraigh seemed, usually, to pursue only its own obscure purposes. Thera had noticed, however, that where she was concerned, it did frequently act just like another parent. The Elanraigh might not approve of her night excursion either.

"*For the little kirshrews' sake,*" she sent. "T*hey need a home.*"

Almost immediately, Thera sensed a thread of inquiring thought. Animal thought, not human. Out from the Elan-raigh trotted a lone coyote. Thera sensed the almost jovial greeting it sent.

"*Blessings!*" Sent Thera with a smile to both the Elan-raigh and her four-footed volunteer. The coyote barked, close at hand, and soon appeared within the circle of light cast by the torches mounted either side of the gate.

The guard halted his pacing. "Gee-it!" he yelled, gesturing broadly with his arm. The coyote skittered, then returned, tongue lolling and eyes dancing, to stare at the astonished guard. This time the soldier bent to the ground and picked up a stone.

Thera quickly skipped through the gate and running light-footed over the loose shale, sprinted to the shadow of the trees.

"*Run!*" Sent Thera. She got a sense of laughter back from the coyote as he danced away from the soldier's widely flung stone.

Laughing with the audacious coyote, Thera turned away and placed her hand gently on the bark of a tall sitka. This was what Thera had always called a grandfather tree, because it felt benign and wise. It rose twenty-five pike lengths above her head. Its bark vibrated with energy. Inside her head, Thera heard it thrum her name with familiar affection.

Moving onto the rocks high above Lorn a'Lea, Thera inhaled deeply of the salty air. Teacher had told Thera that sitkas thrived where the ocean spray could splash to the ground and feed their roots the salt they loved. It was their wood that was especially sought by the Allenholme mariners. The fisherfolk's spirits and that of the sitka were akin. An Allenholme fisher, who in ancient times had his or her ship's timber chosen and blessed by the Elanraigh through their Salvai, knew their boat lived and sang beneath their feet.

The moon's broad path on the ocean was chopped and scattered by a brisk wind. The tide was rising quickly. The shale beach ground against itself, slipping beneath the waves with a rumble like the purring of a great cat.

Thera glanced back toward the keep. She shivered to

think of her parents' fear and anger if her absence was discovered. It was one thing to fall asleep in her mother's garden, but it would be another to be discovered outside the gates at night.

The kirshrews' trilling, however, reminded her of other responsibilities and Thera turned to scan the forest edge for a likely nest site. The rising wind whipped her hair into flying tendrils. She loosened her coil of braids, sighing as her crimped hair relaxed.

There. A cozy hollow sheltered between two large granite outcroppings. Picking her way with care, Thera inspected the site. It was mossy and protected from the wind by both rocks and trees. A small trickle of water wove through flower-studded moss and cascaded down the cliff to the beach. Food was plentiful for the kirshrews, for bunch-berries abounded.

Thera hummed one of the balladeer's lively songs as she pulled shallow-rooted moss away from a deep and narrow crevasse. *The perfect nest site.* She began placing the furry kirshrews inside and watched fondly as they sniffed about, trilling their satisfaction. With their tiny hand-like paws, they began rearranging the moss to their own liking.

Along with a curious prickling sensation on her skin, Thera was suddenly conscious of being watched. She looked up and gasped.

Seated on its haunches above her was a large dark wolf. Moonlight silvered the tips of guard hairs on his thick pelt and his teeth gleamed moistly white.

Thera's heart plunged and then rose to a rapid staccato in her throat. She had been so sure no harm could come to her, here on the very apron of the Elanraigh. Almost immediately, however, she realized that there was nothing threatening in the animal's posture. It sat at ease regarding her; its smoky, almond-shaped eyes beamed with uncanny intelligence.

Deliberately relaxing her rigid muscles, she took a deep breath and opened herself to knowing. The contact was made instantly, as if the beast had been waiting patiently for her to collect herself.

This is completely different than with the coyote, was Thera's first thought. She quickly understood, with some amusement, that the wolf was indignant at being thought of in the same breath as one of that foolish clan.

The wolf gaped his massive jaws in a toothy yawn. He stood, and Thera realized his shoulders could reach her waist. He was a male in his early prime. Slowly he stretched, flexing spine and haunch in an assured, yet seemingly careless, display of musculature. Thera relaxed into the knowing she had been invited to extract.

"*I am Farnash.*"

Thera was aware of a strong, if alien, intellect. Farnash, Thera realized, was able to gather information with senses not unlike some of her own. Farnash is a vital being who lives wholeheartedly in the moment he is in. Humankind's howling after the past or cringing in fear of the future is not for him. *Running in circles. Trying to catch a scent in a windstorm*, is how he dismissed it.

Farnash's loyalties were not easily won, but he gave respect where he felt it earned. "*Clanship*" is the feeling he sent to Thera. It was both a challenge and an invitation.

Thera sent a grateful, "*Blessings, for this knowing.*" She had to repress a smile and try her best to shield her thoughts at the moment, for most of this *knowing* had come about as a result of the wolf's *sending*, and his tone was as arrogant as a newly promoted squire's.

Farnash tilted his head, and his jaws gaped again. Arrogance as a concept meant nothing to the wolf. "*I am what I am.*"

Chagrined, Thera sent, "*Apologies, I do not mean to offend.*"

"*No offence possible between us, fledgling. Eagle and wolf are clan.*"

Thera was nonplussed. "*But I am human.*"

"*I see wings unfurling about you, and sky in your eyes.*"

Thera pondered. It had, fleetingly, crossed her mind to reach for a joining such as she had shared with the sea hawk. She knew instinctively that this would have been an unforgiveable intrusion on this proud and solitary being. He was not for her, not that way. His true bonding lay elsewhere. Yet he had approached her, and offered her the knowing.

Farnash's ghostly eyes gleamed in the moonlight as he regarded her, then he turned, glanced back to Thera over one massive shoulder.

He gaped his jaws again. "*Farewell.*" The wolf disappeared, quiet as smoke, over the granite rocks.

CHAPTER 9

*T*hera's fingers plucked at the soft moss as she pondered this latest encounter. Again she sensed a presence and thinking Farnash had returned, she quickly looked up to the granite spur. *Chamak!* Chamak stood where the wolf's energies still lingered. *Yes. There are similarities between Chamakin Dysan Chikei and Farnash, grey wolf of Elanraigh.*

Chamak's features were limned in moonlight as he watched where the wolf had blended into the trees. One hand clasped the amulet which rested on his chest and his lips moved. Then the young Ttamarini's eyes turned, gleaming, to rest on Thera. His expression was inscrutable.

Thera felt her heart beating strongly as he leapt, soundless, to land beside her.

He clasped her arm in a strong grip and turned her toward him, searching her face for a long, breathless moment. His expression relaxed, he released her and lowered himself to sit beside her. Thera felt a comfortable awareness that no wordy social salutations were necessary between them. He wants to be with me, Thera read. *Perhaps he can read me also.* She flashed a glance at him; he was waiting for her to speak first.

"Chamakin, you said to me that at your Oath Day, you received the protection of a spirit animal. Would it be incorrect for me to ask about this?"

Chamak made a gesture of opening a clenched hand, palm up.

"I would share this knowledge with you, *Chaunika*, but I think you already know the answer."

"Is Farnash, *your* wolf?"

"*I* have not yet been given his name, but that grey wolf did come to me on my Oath Day, when I was in *Nu'asee*, the Trance. Sometimes from the corner of my eye I think I see him pacing beside me, but if I look straight, he is gone.

"Our spirit kin choose us, the honor is ours." Chamak made the Ttamarini gesture of reverence, hand to forehead. He then clasped his hands together. "I will tell you a thing. When I was but a young hunter, I was gored by a bush-slasher. Before my spear freed its spirit, it ripped me with its horn. Here," Chamak pulled the neck of his vest sideways and Thera saw a thick scar angling from collar bone to underarm.

Thera shivered. She could never see such scars without imagining the terrible pain their bearer must have suffered.

"My hunting companions were still far afield," Chamak continued, "I did not expect they would even begin to look for me until the moon rode high." He rubbed at his right side absently, his gaze unfocused as he remembered. "The bleeding from the wound was profuse, but not the bright red that springs straight from the heart." Chamak paused, "All hunters know how to treat wounds. I knew I must stop the blood flow, or I would soon lose consciousness. I padded the wound. Working one-armed, I made a fire — already I felt myself becoming chill and weak.

"It was full dark when something woke me. The fire was almost out. I became aware a coarse fur pelt lay warm against me. It was the grey wolf. I thought I must be dreaming, yet his breath was warm on my face. He lay beside me as a clan brother, to keep me warm." Chamak shifted, his eyes looked to the forest again, where Farnash had gone. "I think I spoke my thanks to him, though my thoughts and words were not clear. It was as in a dream. However, he replied to me and I understood him then, though I cannot remember now what we said.

"My companions told me when they came upon me, that they had followed the call of a wolf. The grey one had appeared near them, and Zujeck, my closest companion, knew something had befallen me.

"How my spirit brother could be in two places at once, both leading my companions to where I lay injured, and lying close by my side, I do not understand. But I know him for friend."

"Chamak, you would surely have died if he had not helped you," said Thera.

Chamak eyes rested on her and he nodded. "My song would have been sung at the next great gathering, Chaunika, and we would not be here together." He flushed slightly and regarded the kirshrews with elaborate interest.

Thera eyed him with much the same expression. She watched him study the new nest site, the fresh water source, and plentiful bunchberry vines. Chamak turned to her with a raised brow.

"They are your pets?" he asked.

"Blessings, no. I had always meant to return them to the

forest. It was pleasant having them by me, and they seemed content, so I put that parting off — until tonight."

"Ah. I wondered," he said, "if they were accustomed to being handled."

"Oh, yes," murmured Thera, "they thrive on affection and are very responsive." Unaccountably, she felt a heat in her face.

With singular care, Chamak reached toward the nest. Laying his hand, palm up, he purred rhythmically deep in his throat.

Thera felt strange stirrings within herself. She was easily able to sense his strong sendings of *caring* and *safety-warmth* to the kirshrews.

I can't help but feel a kinship with this young Ttamarini, she thought, *he is the first person I've met with gifts similar to my own. I wonder if he, too, can hear the Elanraigh?*

Two of the kirshrews sat back on their haunches, whiskers twitching, and regarded Chamakin with their pink bead-like eyes. Then both scrambled into the hollow of his palm and began trilling and kneading at the flesh under his thumb in utter contentment.

Thera smiled to see both the kirshrews' trust and Chamak's obvious enchantment with the small creatures. His hands were gentle as he held them up close to his face to better examine them.

As he continued to thrum deep in his throat, the kirshrews' tissue-thin lids began to close, the tiny paws slowly coming to rest. Thera felt her own lids drooping and bemusedly registered an urge within herself, to curl contentedly under Chamak's free arm. Thera slanted at look at Chamak's profile, the strong, clean lines of his face. His firm lips were curled slightly in a tender smile. Never before had she seen a warrior use such gentle care with a creature, other than a favored horse or hound, of course.

Chamak's voice roused her from her study. "We have a small animal on our plains that is much like these little ones." His finger gently stroked the small heads and a muffled trilling resumed. "They are called krilltics, but *they* are very shy, nocturnal creatures. To hear their delicate song is considered a blessing from the Goddess.

"When I was a very young boy, my friends and I attempted to catch one. Not meaning any harm you understand, just to see one up close and hold it like this. But we were loud and rough, and it was terrified of us."

Chamak paused and Thera saw his brows knit in a troubled expression. "I caught it finally, after much dodging through the tall grass. Even as I held up the krilltic for the others to see, its rapid heartbeat stilled and its body lay cooling in my palm."

Thera quelled the immediate urge to lecture. Such lectures had earned her the acerbic title of "Her Holiness" from some of the keep children she had played with when younger. There was pain enough in Chamak's voice at the retelling. Thera looked aside and plucked at the moss beside her. "I have noticed that boys will often do cruel things," she said slowly, "but it is usually because they are careless or curious, not that they mean to do evil."

Actually, Thera thought as she looked at him, *I can't imagine you possessing any of the same traits as the Allenholme youths I know. You are so different.*

"Ah." Chamak nodded. "What you say is true. I should have known better. Both my father and the *Maiya* trained me to use my gifts to be one-with-all-life — *Enoita*. I had chased the small creature far from its burrow against its desire, and did not spare the time to soothe or reassure. It died of fear, in my hand.

"I was in misery over the manner of its death. I was sure that the Goddess would reject me for what I had done so thoughtlessly to this favored creature of hers."

"So what did you do?" whispered Thera. Her hair blew across her face as she turned to him, and plastered itself against Chamak's shoulder. With his unoccupied hand, he lifted the strand and inhaled its fragrance. Lapsing into silence, he lifted his eyes to hers, his gaze as warm as a hand stroking her face.

Thera felt pricklings of sensation, and was strangely nervous. "Chamakin? What did you do?" she repeated.

The young warrior's hand trembled as he released the strand of her hair.

Now this is a strange, heady, power I have over him. Is this what it is to be a woman? Immediately Thera remembered a lesson of Teacher's, *There is nothing so damaging to the soul as the seeking and abuse of power.* Teacher's voice had been very solemn as it had spoken to Thera about this.

It seems Chamakin and I have been taught similar lessons.

"I buried it on the prairie where I had found it," Chamak finally continued. "I prayed to the Goddess to forgive my irreverence, and then I went and told the Maiya what had happened and how I felt."

"Did she understand? Was she very angry?"

The corner of Chamak's mouth drew down. "Once she understood that I had not used my gift of calling to capture the krilltic against its giving of self, her anger lessened. She bade me fast and meditate on *Enoita,* the oneness of all living things. I have never forgotten what I learned from that day."

Thera thought the Maiya sounded *very* like Teacher.

He had mentioned the gift of "calling." Thera stored that away, to speak of at some future moment.

She was thoughtful as she remembered the death of the sedgemole. "But, your people *do* kill for food, don't they?"

"Yes, of course. However, it is as your folk harvest a tree for some worthy purpose. It is done with the blessing of the trees themselves, and the gift of the tree is accepted with reverence." He spread his hands. "It is done with *Enoita*. This is correct, is it not?" he asked.

Thera was quiet as he placed the sleeping kirshrews back in their nest. *It used to be*, Thera thought.

Thera knew from histories that a Salvai's calling was to commune with the Elanraigh, and use her gifts for the people as does the Ttamarini Maiya for her folk. Yet her aunt, their Salvai, keeps herself apart, a recluse in her refuge at Elankeep.

I want to be like the Ttamarini Maiya and bring my people back to feeling the Elanraigh in their hearts!

The Elanraigh thrummed gently along her nerves and senses.

Chamakin took Thera's hand in his. He examined it, as if he'd picked up a curious shell on the beach.

The pounding of the waves seemed very close now. The sound of them filled Thera's ears. The tide is full, Thera thought. The moon was high and dazzled her eyes.

Very gently, Chamak placed his hand along her face, sliding his fingers down her neck. His eyes blazed, dazzling as the moon and stars that tangled in the spruce trees.

"You are so beautiful, *Chaunika myia*." His thumb traced her lips, then smoothed the small pucker between her brows. "Do not worry, *myia*," he murmured, "for I swore to the Goddess, I would never again take anything against its desire."

His hand rested on the pulse beating wildly just under her jaw. Thera *wanted* his lips to touch hers. She closed her eyes and tilted her head, her whole body yearned toward Chamak.

His kiss was light, at first, but a wave of feeling like a multi-voiced, triumphant shout flooded Thera's body, engulfing them both. The muscles of Chamak's shoulders clenched and shook under her touch.

Thera parted her lips, and with a small sound Chamak pressed her body against his.

Apart from the fiery sensations radiating from his touching, Thera was conscious of an echoing sense of recognition and joy.

The Elanraigh's voice rumbled approval in the swirling of her mind.

Superimposing itself over the Elanraigh's rumblings came Teacher's voice, " *I tell you, she is yet too young. It is not time.*"

"*My beloved Entities.*" With a mental groan, Thera sent, "*Not now. Please.*"

Both voices immediately lapsed back. They were left alone, and with a sigh, Thera willed herself to sink back into that sweet turmoil she had been experiencing. Chamak's skin smelled of the fresh night wind, with a slight scent of smoke from the leathers he wore.

Suddenly Chamak drew in a deep, shuddering breath, and with both hands gently held her away.

Astonished, Thera stared at him. She struggled to read his expression in the darkness.

A muscle pulsed at the corner of his jaw, and the hand he raised to stroke her cheek trembled. Yet he said, "The time is not yet, *myia.*"

This was not Thera's opinion at all, nor, apparently, was

it the Elanraigh's. *Can Chamak hear at all? Ah, but there is yet so much for us to learn of each other.* Thera rubbed her forehead head against Chamak's vest, welcoming the scratching of its beadwork against her skin.

"What then." she whispered.

"If it is your wish, Chaunika *myia*, I will ask your father to consent to our union, and we will 'Become of One Heart.'"

"Life sworn, we call it," Thera whispered.

Chamak's warm hand both stroked and pressed her head against him. As she continued silent, he pressed his lips against her hair. Chamak sighed, and continued, his voice resonating in his chest. "*We* believe the soul chooses but one companion, *myia*.

"Does *Maiya* Ishtarik have a life sworn? Asked Thera. "Tell me of her life sworn, who was he?"

"Lehatin. He was a tall man of great girth, and our clan's storyteller. He loved life. He loved all the Ttamarini people. Lehatin could talk even the most quarrelsome into seeing reason, without resentment. He knew all the children by their names. You will see our *Maiya* smile when she speaks of Lehatin, and I've heard her say she loved him so because he would make her laugh. She mourns for him still."

Chamak paused so long, Thera thought he had finished speaking. Eventually he finally continued, "A wolf mates for life. *I* have met my soul companion, my *myia*. I will look no further. If you do not feel as I do, *Chaunika*, tell me..."

Thera sat up and hugged her knees to her chest. She felt sure she did love, yet she was troubled. "Oh...my father...he will never..."

Thera flushed. *What does father really think of the Ttamarini, aside from this recent alliance to fight the Memteth.*

What would my people say to the Allenholme Heir cleaving to a Ttamarini. Are the old hostilities truly put aside?

Thera continued, "You see, I have the gift, there is no one else. I *must* train to be the next Salvai."

Chamakin's voice was urgent and eager. "I knew it — I felt it within you! *Chaunika*, this land needs us..." He gestured toward the forest.

Thera's neck hairs prickled as the Elanraigh voices sounded, sweet and sudden, an arpeggio of crystalline notes. *Doesn't Chamak hear the Elanraigh? His expression doesn't alter.*

"...not to be hidden away in a wilderness shrine, but to be leaders and teachers. To build a strong land by teaching our people to be *Enoita* with the land." His expression was earnest as he looked into her face. "I do not mean to anger you about the beliefs of your people, *myia*, but do you truly believe retreating into meditation and prayer is what is needed now? Is that what the Goddess wants of you?"

"The Elanraigh? Nooo," replied Thera slowly, "I have reason to believe the Elanraigh would approve our bonding."

Chamak stood to pace the narrow confines of the crevasse. "A *cloistered* Salvai," his lip curled, "What perversion is that? It has not always been that way, Chaunika. It need not be that way." He smacked his fist into his palm, his lips compressed. He turned to her and sighed, "this is not my story to reveal to you — the *Maiya* forbids — but had things happened the way they should have in our grandparents' time, we would now be a united people and Allenholme today would be filled with *hearing, seeing* folk, instead of ..." Chamak groped for a suitable word, "...blind-hearted merchants and fisher folk." His voice was scathing.

Thera's tone was icy, "Truly you do not know the folk of Allenholme, Ttamarini."

"I wish to know only one resident of Allenholme," he replied soothingly. "Chaunika, you *know* I am right. In your heart you know. We are *Enoitun,* you and I."

Thera felt as if she had swallowed a vile brew as his bitter words against her people curdled within her. *What story? What secrets?* She turned from Chamakin and began to climb the small path, back to her father's house.

CHAPTER 10

Thera reached the giant sitka tree by the Southwest Gate. She walked stiff-legged with anger, her footsteps jarring her spine as if she were a landlubber walking a storm tossed deck. She was very aware that Chamakin was a few paces behind her. She glanced back. He watched her, his expression was concerned, but he did not attempt to speak. So. She paused to get her breath and collect herself. Dawn bloomed red over the High Ranges. The sun would soon bless the Elanraigh.

As Chamakin caught up to her, she heard a clamor of agitated voices at the West Harbor Gate.

"What is it?" demanded Chamak, his body tense and alert.

"Shhh...," Thera placed her hand on his arm. She strained to hear. "Something ..." Thera picked up her skirts and ran down the road, Chamak running easily beside her.

As she rounded the corner of the southwest wall Thera was caught up in a small crowd of folk, mostly mariners by the look of them, all gesturing and speaking at once to the guards on duty.

Thera pushed her way forward. She addressed a man-at-arms, authority in her voice. "Guard, what has happened?"

"My Lady," he saluted and gestured with his pike toward the keep, "I've sent a recruit for my Lord." He gestured to the crowd gathered before him, "It seems the fisher folk have found something he should see."

Thera swirled around and scanned the faces waiting for her father. "You, guildsman, will you tell me what you've found?"

The old fisherman turned his liquid gaze on Thera. The hollows of his features were mauve hued in the predawn light, "Oh Lady," he shook his white head, cap in hand, "they've found the *Grace O'Gull,* she that's been missing at sea four days now."

At that moment her father and his party, accompanied by footmen bearing torches, approached the gate at rapid pace. Chief Teckcharin strode beside Oak Heart.

"What's amiss, Colis?" her father demanded of someone in the crowd.

The young mariner spoke up, "My Lord, a fishing vessel that went missing some days ago has been found. Guild master Mika epNarin said there is that which you must see and asks that you come to the harbor, my Lord."

Her father's brow rose, but without further word he gestured for the mariners to lead on. His gaze travelled the crowd, resting on Thera and Chamakin. Thera held herself erect and met Oak Heart's eyes with a demand in hers. "*Do not treat me as a child,*" she sent, even though she knew her father was unable to hear sendings. Anger still throbbed in her. "*Secrets and more secrets. They treat me as a child.*"

His lips parted as if to speak, but even as Thera read his intention to send her inside, he clamped his lips and his jaw tightened.

He glanced from Thera to Chamakin, who was standing at her shoulder, and his expression briefly conveyed some pain that Thera was unable to read. Then he curtly nodded. Thera and Chamakin joined the company as Oak Heart turned to stride the stone paved road.

Lord Teckcharin was contemplative as he glanced at the averted face of his son, and the rod stiff posture of Thera's back as she swung after her father. Chamakin followed Thera, placing himself at her left shoulder. Everything about his son declared *his* choice had been made.

The Ttamarini Chief's mouth curled in a small smile as he fell in behind the young ones. He murmured an ancient Ttamarini saying that was both blessing and reminder, "The Goddess' voice is the wind that both hollows the rock and sways the grass."

The road was steep, and at its foot was the harbor. Thera could see a cluster of folk gathered on the wharf. The torches they held cast eerie shadows over the water and roared in the wind as the people stood silent, waiting for Oak Heart's party to approach. One man, the grizzled Guild master Mika, Thera remembered, stepped forward.

The sun began to lighten the sky over the amethyst-hued mountains behind them as they reached the wharf. The small birds of the Elanraigh raised their voices in clamorous greeting, yet Thera felt a dreadful oppression bearing down upon her.

It was then she saw what was left of the *Grace O'Gull*, the most graceful fishing ketch in the fleet.

The *Grace O'Gull* listed in the water, her decks charred, the wood slashed and breached. Gruesome dark stains spattered the pilothouse and deck alike. Thera's gaze moved to the four canvas covered bodies lying on the wharf. One of the still forms was that of a huge man. Tears filled her eyes. This could only be Master Petrack's kindly nephew, Bren.

Her childhood friend, Bren, had been a gentle giant even as a lad of twelve years. In her company he had become less shy and awkward, and she had learned from him about the sea and its creatures. Bren had sailed her up and down Kenna beach. Together they had laughed at the playful antics of sleek-coated sea-pups, and Bren had fed them fish from his uncle's catch. Thera and he had ridden the wind in that small swift boat, and raced the tide accompanied by singing opal-finns.

Oak Heart, Lord Teckcharin, and Captain Dougall were examining the markings on the ruined vessel. Her father's face was mottled with anger. "Where was she found," he demanded of Guild master Mika.

Mika's voice was strangled and hoarse, "My crew and I found them, my Lord, aground off Ripsail Island."

There were many exclamations at this. In the vast archipelago of islands off Allenholme's shore, Ripsail Island was only one day's sail to the northwest. Duke Leon chopped his hand abruptly for silence, his gaze adjured those around him, and then centered once again on the Guild master.

Mika epNarin swiped angrily at his eyes with the back of a chapped fist. "They might have had some warning, my Lord — perhaps the ship herself had time to warn Petrack. They made a strong defense by the look of things." Mika's throat convulsed, "There is too much blood to be theirs alone. I think they did not give up their lives easily."

"Any weapons left behind?" asked Dougall.

"Nay, Captain. Not much but some arrowheads embedded here and there. The Memteth must have gathered up all that fell."

Oak Heart had dropped to his knee beside the shrouded crewmen. Gently he lifted back the canvas from their upper bodies. His features stiffened. Hissing imprecations through gritted teeth, he flung the canvas back, fully exposing the still forms.

A gasp and murmur rose out of the small crowd of mariners and soldiers there. Some women folk, clustered together, cried out at the sight of the crew's mutilated bodies with bloody runes carved on each man's forehead and chest. Captain Petrack's eyes were gone, and gaping, bloody sockets were all that remained. Thera felt her consciousness retreating as if to distance her from what she witnessed. Though furious with her weakness she couldn't help swaying, and she felt Chamakin's hand in the small of her back, unobtrusively supporting her.

"Aye, my Lord," Mika almost sobbed, "they fought hard enough to mightily upset the filthy 'Teth, it seems."

Chief Leon carefully replaced the sheet. "Did you see any sign of Memteth ships as you returned, Guild master?"

"Nay, my Lord. Blessings Be."

"Dougall, I want word sent to all those on lookout, especially the coastal watches. Guild master, how many vessels are still out?"

"Only one crew, my Lord. They were spotted off Kenna North and flagged to return home. They will be here before noon."

"That is well, then," murmured Oak Heart. "Guild

master, what do you want done with the *Grace O'Gull* crew? They will have any honors we can provide."

Mika shook his head. As Guild master, he was aware of each mariner's death-rite wishes. "All, captain and crew, wished only the Lament and their ashes scattered on the sea."

"We shall launch the *Grace O'Gull* then, a final time, with the ebb tide," said Oak Heart.

Mika bleakly nodded his agreement, and mariners and soldiers worked silently together placing the bodies of the crew back onto the deck of *Grace O'Gull*.

Thera was startled to suddenly realize Guild Master Mika EpNarin was standing before her.

"Lady, will you free the spirit of the wood with blessing and thanks." His voice grated out the request and grief flooded the smoky grey of his eyes.

"*What Mika asks of me, is the office of a Salvai. Here? In front of all? Will the Elanraigh permit?*" Her chin came up. "*Well, the Salvai is in a fortress far away. I, Thera, am here. I will do what I can,*" she sent. The Elanraigh thrummed its approval along her nerves. She was hardly aware of the small crowd parting for her as she moved forward down the wharf, to lay her hand gently on the prow of *Grace O'Gull*.

A sad and gentle resonance vibrated under her hand. *Grace O'Gull* had been created from a yellow cedar. The tree had gifted itself to Petrack's grandfather with blessings of the Elanraigh. It had been shaped by the elder Petrack's skilled hands and they had sailed together for thirty years before she passed to the next Petrack's care.

Thera felt herself seeming to sink into the wood, oblivious to everything except comforting the elemental. The Elanraigh elemental, utterly grieved and wounded, surged to meet her. Thera offered what comfort she could. "*We share your grief, wounded one. May you find solace and peace with your own kind. Blessings.*" Gently, the grieving elemental embraced her there, where they met in spirit. Then, turning, it yearned to the Elanraigh. Thera gasped at the force with which it was drawn through her. After a moment, she lifted her hand from the bow and examined it. Strange. She felt sure her flesh had joined with the very substance of the wood.

Becoming aware again of the gathered folk, of the dawn wind on her face, she gusted a shuddering sigh. "It is free," she said quietly.

The Guild Master bowed profoundly to her, and each mariner also, as they passed by to form an honor guard about the dead. The women kin first and then folk of the town filed by to make their respects to the dead. A young lad in apprentice garb raised his sweet tenor voice in the Lament, "*Elan-rai-aigh Bless-s. Beneath the sea may they rest.*" Other voices joined in." *May their voices sing to us on the waves ...*"

Thera's throat felt too tight to utter sound.

Still singing, the mariners made ready to tow the *Grace O'Gull* and her crew to sea one last time. They scattered oil about her deck.

Thera's eyes swam. She had no wish to witness the burning. She wondered if it would be expected.

One of the elder wives left the cluster of women where they stood and hobbled toward Thera. She bobbed her head in a courtesy. Her rheumy eyes searched Thera's features, "It be good to have you back with us, Lady," she whispered under the song. She reached her gnarled hand toward Thera's face.

A young woman ran forward, curtsied to Thera and drew the old woman away. "Beg your pardon, my Lady. Old

Gram gets confused some nowadays, lives in the past she does."

Thera watched after them a moment. The elder woman's voice carried back to her. "It be the Lady Dysanna, Nora, come back to us. The forest will sing to us again."

Thera felt a frisson lift the hairs of her neck. She glanced at Chamak. He returned her look somberly.

Oak Heart came up to her, his face both proud and sad as he offered her his arm. The party from the keep walked back up the hill, some wrapped in their silence, some in song. Behind her the pipes skirled their notes to the lightening sky.

CHAPTER 11

*T*wo sturdy porters left Thera's chamber carrying her trunk. Thera scraped a fingernail back and forth across the rough stone ledge of her window. Gloomily she observed the final preparations underway for her departure to Elankeep. She felt as dismal as the morning's overcast skies. A few fat plops of rain spattered the sill and she flared her nostrils at the scent of dusty stone dampened with the first rain in six days.

She thought she might feel better if she could talk to Chamakin, but *he* had apparently returned to the Ttamarini encampment with his father. She didn't want to stay angry with him, but his disdain of her folk seemed destined to flaw their relationship.

Thera turned and paced the room. Her hands scrubbed at her scalp. *What is* wrong *with me!* She sprawled into a nest-chair in a graceless manner she knew Nan would deplore. *Well, perhaps I'm being unfair. Most likely Chamakin will make an effort to see me before I leave. It must be the events of this morning and the overcast sky which oppress me so.*

Thera had tried to sleep after returning from the harbor

with her father, but the ravaged faces of the murdered crew haunted those restless hours.

Someone scratched at her chamber door.

"Enter," said Thera, hurriedly sitting up and arranging herself. *Oh. It's only Rubra.* The maid carried a leather satchel.

"My Lady," whispered the girl in her soft voice, her cheeks flushing, "This is a gift for you. His Lordship commanded me to bring it to you."

THERA STOOD before the polished copper mirror and studied herself in the new riding costume. *Guilt Gift. My father knows I do not wish to leave.*

She smiled, however, looking back at her reflection over one shoulder. Oak Heart had obviously made effort to please her particular taste, conventions aside, for this was not the standard riding dress of a noble lady. It was styled Ttamarini fashion, a soft cream colored kid-leather shirt with hood, and leather pantaloons. Over this she wore a long tunic of rowanberry colored wool. The tunic was trimmed in black jet, and slit high on the sides for ease in riding. On the tunic breast, worked in black and amber, was the face of a wolf. On the tunic back was an eagle in flight. Thera lightly, thoughtfully, traced her fingers over the wolf pattern.

She looked up as Rubra exclaimed over the riding boots, "Oh, my lady, here. Just feel the softness of them!"

They were finely worked boots, also cream colored leather. Rubra helped her pull them on. They fit her feet perfectly and rose to just below the knee. She cinched her waist with a wide black leather belt. It was a Lady's belt, not a weapons harness, but there was a ring to hold a dagger sheath.

Rubra quietly let herself out, as Thera continued to preen in front of the copper mirror.

Startled and embarrassed, Thera suddenly became aware of her mother standing in the doorway.

"May I enter, daughter?" Fideiya asked.

Thera was surprised at her mother's formality. Then she flushed as she realized her mother was treating her as an adult, to whom that courteous inquiry would be due.

"P-please. Blessings." Thera stammered.

Fideiya carried something wrapped in fine cloth.

"It is your Woman's Blade, my dear one," Fideiya said, presenting Thera with an emerald-jeweled dagger. "For your coming of age birthday. Did you think I would forget?"

Thera reverently reached her hands toward this emblem of both her new womanhood and her noble birth. The *Sha'lace*. Her hand clenched above the flashing hilt.

"It is not actually my birthday until the sun twice more blesses the Elanraigh."

Normally, Thera and her mother would make a pilgrimage to Elankeep at this time. This was a journey of only two days, when the Elanraigh roads were open, now they faced at least five days travel. There they would properly celebrate Thera's coming into womanhood. She would have been presented to the Salvai and the Salvai would ceremoniously Name her to the Elanraigh.

Thera *had* thought her womanhood day would be forgotten in the furor of recent events, and her eyes welled in surprise and gratitude.

Fideiya hugged Thera, "You have proved yourself a woman, these last days. Both your father and I agree in this." Fideiya tilted her daughter's chin, "Be only safe, my dear, and your father's burden will be eased."

THERA WENT DOWN to the courtyard to join her small caravan. The rain seemed more a heavy mist now, and fog huddled in the folds and hollows of the landscape.

Her entourage would be small; a pony for Nan, a pack mule, the two soldier's mounts, and Thera's own mare, Mulberry. Swordsman Innic was head to head with the House Steward and Sirra Maxin, no doubt discussing the requirements for their journey. Young Swordsman Jon was checking Mulberry's hooves.

She glanced about the crowded courtyard for her father and then heard his rough edged voice calling to Captain Dougall. He looks tired, Thera observed. *I'm sure he has not slept this night either.*

At that moment a horse and rider clattered onto the granite-paved apron by the South Gate entrance. The rider called his name to the guardsmen at the gate, with no abating of his headlong pace. The horse was darkened with sweat. The horseman, Arnott, slid to the ground before his mount had stopped. Harle ran forward to catch the reins, his startled admonition about manners and protocol unheeded, as the young rider ran to where Oak Heart stood alert.

He quickly saluted and gasped out, "My Lord! It's a me...message from *Cythia*. It came by ca..carrier bird to the lookout posted at Spitting Rock Point." Arnott shoved his sweat- dampened hair from his eyes, his gaze fixed on his Duke.

"Thank you, Arnott," replied Oak Heart calmly as he took the missive and examined the direction written on the sealed note. Frowning over the florid script, he glanced up at the variously eager or anxious company gathered around him. His brow arched, "Messages from Cythia are rare, I grant." he drawled.

The Heart's Own traded chagrined smiles.

Young Arnott blurted, "But my Lord, it may be about the Memteth!"

Chief Leon smiled, "It may be, or it may be a notice from Duke Lammert Perrod that they urgently require bluefish roe for Virdenmas Festival."

Seeing Arnott's crestfallen countenance, Oak Heart clapped the young rider on the shoulder. "The vagaries of the Cythian royal house aside, you did well Arnott, for the direction is to bring this to my attention immediately. Now go warm yourself in the barrack hall." Chief Leon nodded to the house steward, "Steward Valan will see you well fed."

"Thank you, m-my Lord. If you please, I will see D-Drummer cared for first."

Horsemaster Harle beckoned a stable boy to take Arnott's mount in hand. "Do your Lord's bidding, Arnott," his voice was gruff as his gaze skewered the stable hand. "We've idle men enough standing about who can care for the beast." Harle pointedly handed over the reins to the flushing stable boy, then strode over to the group surrounding Chief Leon.

"Arnott's a good lad, my Lord," said Harle surveying Oak Heart's expression.

"I do agree," affirmed Oak Heart, unaware he was frowning at the missive in his hand.

Arnott was led away by the amiably chatting Steward Valan. The Heart's Own, with Thera close by, waited expectantly as Chief Leon finally broke the seal and read the missive.

"*Is* it dire news, my Lord?" asked Lydia finally.

Oak Heart handed the message to Lydia and Dougall to read. For the benefit of the others he summarized its contents, "A troop of Cythian guards found the remains of the South Bole caravan two days ago, by the bank of the Spinfisher River. It is, unquestionably, the work of Memteth raiders." The Heart's Own shifted and murmured. Captain Dougall muttered a curse.

"Our Ducal neighbor also, 'regrets that he cannot send troops to aide us, as the Elanraigh forest roads are storm torn and impassable and the Coast Trail is impossible for troop movement. *His* ships will be needed to protect Cythia and his own royal person.'"

Oak Heart cocked an eyebrow as he regarded his captains. "He bids us be wary, as some of his informants have told him that the *Ttamarini* also seem to be on the move." Oak Heart's own wry expression was reflected in more than one face as they envisioned the effete Cythian Duke fearing Memteth raiders on his western doorstep and Ttamarini riders possibly moving south. The Cythian Duke reportedly feared the 'strange magic's' of the Ttamarini almost more than the legendary ferocity of the Memteth.

"Ha!" exploded Shamic. "It be a wonder he does not demand that we send our troops down the coast trail to assist in the defense of his precious self."

"No doubt he would, except he undoubtedly thinks that Allenholme is all that stands between him and the approaching Ttamarini hordes."

The assembled warriors laughed heartily, but Shamic shook his head, his voice and expression sour. "Huh. I'm thinking we've acquired better allies than Cythia could provide."

"Yes. Blessings to the Elanraigh on that account. But...,"

Chief Leon scrubbed at the back of his neck, "it seems I must send a message to Cythia's Duke and inform him of our new relationship with the Ttamarini. I can only imagine the consternation ..."

Thera moved forward to take her leave of her father. The Heart's Own parted to let her through, as many hands patted her shoulders with rough congeniality.

Thera was very conscious of the *Sha'Lace,* hanging in its scabbard at her side, and the flattering berry colored tunic that emphasized her woman's shape. She was elated, yet anxious to look accustomed to her woman's honors.

Captain Lydia was flushed with empathic pride. She had tutored Thera in the rudimentary use of dagger for defense. Though arms play had never proven to be a gift of Thera's, she had struggled to learn adequate skill to please Lydia. A broad grin flashed white in Lydia's suntanned features.

Captain Dougall's eyes sparkled.

Shamic frowned.

Her father's bright blue gaze travelled the length of her, not missing the treasured *Sha'Lace.* He advanced to take her hands in his, then raised each and kissed it in turn. "Truly, truly," he spoke the father's ritual words to all, "I am a proud man today, who is the father of a *woman* both lovely and learned."

They turned, her father's arm hugging her to his side as he walked her toward the waiting horses, and the Heart's Own crowded around them.

Harle massaged his chin thoughtfully. "How will they travel, Sir, if the Elanraigh be closing all roads."

"Well, Thera? Shall we tell Harle what the Elanraigh told you?" said Oak Heart.

"The Elanraigh will provide passage for *this* small party,

Horsemaster. We will travel the fringes of the forest, near the coast, yet close to the safety of the Elanraigh."

Harle's brows shot upward. "Oh. Aye." He nodded and cleared his throat.

Soon all were murmuring advice and admonitions, "... careful of the log bridge over Thunder Gorge...dangerous if wet...wary of fog..." and so on. But as they all spoke, Thera read the love and concern for her in their words. As she said her farewells, her father patted her shoulder and moved away to join Innic and Maxin where they conferred about the pending journey.

Thera still believed she should stay, but she was aware of, if still annoyed by, their vulnerability where she was concerned. She had to stiffen her resolve to be strong at this parting, as the general outpouring of their love nearly overwhelmed her.

Lady Fideiya came out with Nan. Her smile trembled at the corners as she embraced Thera again.

Her eyes swept over her daughter. "How exotic you look, my dear one." Her fingers smoothed the softness of the leather hood. "No one does leathers or bead work like the Ttamarini. He would have given them to you as a betrothal gift, you know. But your father forbade it — told him you were too young to be life sworn yet." Fideiya observed Thera's shocked expression. She tweaked Thera's chin. "You must have seen how the Ttamarini admired you, my own. I have told your father that he must be prepared to receive many such offers for you. Someday you will be presented at the Cythian court and..."

"Mother, I beg you," Thera's hands twisted upon themselves, "tell me, Chamakin spoke to father, and it was *he* who gave me these leathers?"

"Why, yes. As I have just said. However, your father told

him you were too young, and made him promise not to approach you until such time as he has given consent for you to be courted.

"The youth, I must say, made no promises, but he considered your father's words very gravely. Then he offered the leathers to your father once again and asked that they be given to you only as a gift from one chieftain's Heir to another's. 'The patterns are traditional,' he said, 'the spirit animals represented are protective.' He also told your father that the beaded tunic once belonged to a lady of his family, known for her...what was the word," Fideiya's brow creased, "ah, yes...*Enoita.*"

Fideiya placed an arm around her daughter's waist and steered her toward the waiting caravan.

Thera felt dazed, her ears were hot and roaring. She became aware her mother was still speaking.

"...so different from us, my dear. Admirable, noble, but have many strange ways about them, and you must remember that we were at war with them in grandfather Leif's time. Some of their ways are not compatible with ours."

Fideiya hugged Thera to her side and pressed a kiss to her temple. "It worries me that you have seen so little of the world as yet."

She slanted a glance at her daughter's face. "My own, if he truly cares for you, he will wait as your father asks."

Almost before she knew it, Shamic threw her to her saddle, with a pat on the knee and a gruff admonition, "Keep well, lass, you be the heart of many of us you know." He then cast an angry look around him, finally focusing on Swordsman Innic. "Do you be waiting for the tide to turn before you lead them out? You navigate by the stars then, is it?"

Swordsman Innic knew well enough what spurred the old Armsmaster's temper. The old man's doting love of the Lady Thera was legendary in the keep. He saluted the retired Master at Arms, and then patted Nan's hand reassuringly, for she had startled at Shamic's angry voice. Innic swung himself into the saddle.

They rode out, with the keep's folk calling farewells after them. Swordsman Innic in the lead, followed by Thera, Nan, and at the last, Jon leading the stolid mule.

In the quiet first hour of their travel, Thera's thoughts returned to Chamakin, and what he'd said last night, *'...had things happened the way they should have in our grandparents' time ...'*

She sent a query to the Elanraigh, *"What is it Chamakin knows of our history and was told not to tell me?"*

As moments passed, Thera worried she would receive no answer. *"No more secrets,"* she pleaded.

It was Teacher who finally responded, *"What were you taught of those times, Thera? How do you think the Great Peace was finally established between the people of Allenholme and Ttamarini?"*

"Blessings be. The Great Peace between Allenholme and Ttamarini was established when my great-grandfather, Leif ArNarone, was Duke, and my grandfather, Branch, was Heir. Peace was negotiated because it was agreed to be fruitless to continue to raid and pillage each other and the merchant caravans." What she said was almost rote repetition. Thera had also had more prosaic teachers than the Elanraigh.

"No...!" After a moment, Teacher continued, *"It was Salvai Dysanna and Chamakin's grandfather, Lord Chemotin, who ended the fifteen year war. Their union, their love, was to have healed the land and brought peace.*

"Allenholme's ruling house suppressed widespread knowledge

of their union. To the folk, they announced Dysanna was dead. Her line of lineage was broken and her name was struck from the Royal House records.

"Lady Dysanna was exiled to Ttamarini lands. The Elanraigh mourned the stubbornness of Allenholme's Duke and Council, who publicly celebrated the treaty, and took credit for the Great Peace. Lord Chemotin was killed five years after, when his hunting party came upon a Memteth raider ship at the mouth of the Fleetride River. Lady Dysanna saw him buried with honors, gave her infant son into the care of the Maiya, and then walked into the Elanraigh, never to be seen again."

IT WAS mid-morning halt before Thera roused from her reflections. Chamakin, she knew, would wait for her.

CHAPTER 12

*T*he driftwood fire crackled, redolent of seaweed and salt. Thera leaned back comfortably. Long, rolling waves washed ashore — the expended fury of a storm far out to sea.

The sun had set as they finished their meal and now crimson cirrus clouds swept across the darkening sky, reflecting their hue in the ocean. A cozy air of contentment wrapped the small group from Allenholme.

The first day of travel, the Coast Trail took them through the forest edge, always within sound of the crashing surf. Though it rained all day, they were sheltered under the rainforest canopy. The second day, the trail descended steeply through banks of blooming yellow gorsgrass to the ocean shelf where the sea wind refreshed them and they tread crackling seaweed underfoot.

When taking halts, Thera insisted on helping Jon with the animals. He was frustratingly diffident and full of platitudes as to what noble ladies did and did not do. His patronizing ways grated at her nerves and she couldn't help

comparing his insufferable attitude to Chamak's easy accep-
tance of her abilities.

Sighing, and minding Lady Fideiya's constant admonition to be always gracious with the folk, she continued to
help with steadfast, cheerful insistence. As Thera displayed
a great degree of competency in handling even the fractious
mule, Jon finally fell silent. *How different, though*, Thera
thought, *than when working side by side with Captain Lydia or
Sirra Shamic. Jon acts as if he is indulging a precocious child.*

Thera humphed as she slid Mulberry's saddle off the
mare's sweating back and laid it over a log. Huh. Well, *she*
may be constrained by her mother's training, but she could
imagine the results if a young cub of a swordsman ever
dared to condescend to Captain Lydia or Swordswoman
Nerla.

Ha! Thera chortled to herself.

She swiped at her horse's sweaty hide with a coarse
cloth. Mulberry grunted and rolled her eyes at Thera. She
laughed again and patted the glossy shoulder.

Nan and Innic had set up the cook-pots and Jon the canvas
shelters. Thera was thoroughly enjoying her second bowl of
the savory stew Nan had put together. Steward Valan had seen
that they had a plentiful supply of dried meat and tubers. Nan,
it seems, had thought to pack her own cache of dried herbs.

Innic settled back against a log with a contented sigh.
His heavy brow over deep-set eyes was relaxed in an
amiable expression of pleasure. Thera watched as Innic
reached into his pocket and withdrew a pipe, and then
reached into a finely tooled leather pouch dangling from his
belt. His movements were deliberate, almost ritualistic.
Tamping down the aromatic leaves into the pipe, he lit them
with a taper from the fire and drew in deep breaths that

sucked at his cheeks. The sweet smoke drifted past Thera and she sniffed experimentally, her nose wrinkling.

Innic's eye brightened as he watched Nan bending over the fire. "Ahh. Come here my little pigeon and sit by me." He patted the ground beside him.

Thera smiled, delighted. *Little pigeon! Yet it suits Nan so well.*

"Did you have enough to eat, now, my lad?" asked Nan, archly ignoring the invitation.

Innic patted his lean belly. "Oh. Aye, lass. Enough to march a ten-day span, I swear. You be a fine cook, my dear."

Nan smiled, "Oh now, that was nothing so much."

"You be such a modest lass," adjured Innic fondly, "and the best cook in the keep, to think. Better even than Goodwoman Tannis that's been Cook these many years."

"Oh? Do you think so, then?" Nan asked, her tone thoughtful and considering.

Thera's jaw dropped. Nan's reputation as an excellent cook was well promoted by Nan herself. The rivalry between Nan and Goodwoman Tannis had often reached epic proportions. Thera remembered recovering from a childhood illness and while having to be tempted to eat, their rivalry in creating savories and possets had almost done her in.

This type of dissembling was foreign to Thera. She had certainly seen her mother being playful with her father, and Fideiya did have a particular smile that was for Leon alone. However, Thera could not recall any occasion when her mother had pretended to be less than she was. *Certainly,* Thera thought, *no man ever loved a woman more than father does mother.*

Turning her head, Thera considered Jon as he was unpacking the night rolls. *Beyond doubt he is a handsome* boy, but he is so very vain. Also, he has very peculiar ideas of what kind of treatment is pleasing to me.

Thera sent grateful thanks to the Elanraigh, *I would not wish to be the daughter of a poor man, with a duty to go with whoever contracted the most bride price. My happiness,* Thera vowed, *will never depend on how well I configure myself to suit some man's wishes.*

Yawning, she paused, mid stretch. *Perhaps if I become the Salvai, I could work to change such things.* She propped chin on fist as she thought about this. *An impecunious young lover should be able to obtain a bridal price for his loved one from — who? — oh, the township perhaps. Or, even better; I, when Salvai, will establish a fund.* Thera smiled, *Yes, that's it. The grateful young couple could then repay the bridal debt by services to Allenholme and Elanraigh.*

It would be a departure from tradition, but it felt right to her.

At present, guilds that accepted a promising female apprentice would usually provide the girl's family with a reasonable equivalent of bride price.

Captain Lydia's case had been different, though. There was no such thing as a soldiers' guild. Lydia had told her she had to put aside half her pay for five years before she was able to pay her father the same amount a chandler merchant had offered for her.

Thera considered this. *My Salvai's fund will also provide for women who do not wish to marry, the financial means to placate their families.*

Satisfied with her idea, she smiled and briskly dusted the gritty sand off her hands. She paused as she remembered Chamakin's vision of *Maiya* and Warrior working together with their people as teachers and leaders, and nodded to herself. It could be a useful and fulfilling life.

Yawning mightily again, Thera stood and said her good-nights. She doubted if Nan and Innic particularly noticed.

As she lifted the flap of her tent, swordsman Jon approached her.

"Is there anything I can get for you Lady Thera," he asked, "some water, or an extra blanket?"

"No. I thank you."

"I will be right here, then. You needn't fear," he smiled, even as he saluted.

Feeling her face flush, Thera nodded, and with consider-able irritation, dropped the tent flap in his face.

THERA CAUGHT herself nodding in the saddle. It must be near our noon halt, she thought muzzily, as her stomach rumbled. The drone of insects and heady scent of broom had lulled her.

Their route today had humped up and down ever since the tide last changed. In some places they had to dismount and walk the horses around the rocky outcroppings. The trail was becoming rougher. Some of the ancient crude-carved stone benches were crumbled, and whole segments had been broken to rubble by storms.

Nan was not an experienced horsewoman, and Thera read her increasing fear of the high black rocks cantilevered out over the surf. Thera cleared her throat, about to suggest another dismount as if at her own need to Swordsman Innic.

Before the words were out of her mouth, however, Innic with the clear perception born of caring, rather than gift, was helping Nan off her pony.

"We'll rest the horses and walk awhile," he called back

to Jon. He turned to Nan, clasping her hand, "Now lass, the trail goes down to the ocean again after the next bend and is a nice sandy beach for the next day's ride. Will you be alright?"

Nan merely patted his arm and nodded. She turned to walk on, mopping at her brow with a piece of white linen.

Innic watched after her a moment, waiting for Thera and Jon to pass so he could tie Nan's pony and Thera's mare behind the pack mule.

The swordsman walked beside Thera. "Our Nan be weary, my Lady, but she doesn't like to show it. Once we're around yon bend, the trail descends to Shawl Bay." He squinted skyward, "It be early yet, but by chance you wish to take mid-day halt there?"

Thera studied Innic a moment. He had the rough features of the veteran foot soldier he was. Thera could remember seeing him during festival games, wielding his sword with cool precision. He would distort his features into a rictus grin, meant to disconcert his opponent. It succeeded in its purpose with the novices, and was loudly admired by the other veterans.

The old soldier looked transformed, however, when his thoughts were of Nan. He need only speak her name, to gentle the craggy terrain of his face.

Thera blinked out of her reverie. She nodded in answer to his question.

"Indeed." She smiled as she placed her hand on her midriff. "In truth my stomach has been growling like a bristlefang since Opal Fin Point."

Innic's deep carved features relaxed and he laughed, bearing strong yellowed teeth, and strode forward to assist Nan.

Thera strolled along, admiring the colorful variety of

starry flowers growing on the vines that netted the lichen-blackened rocks. She glanced back-trail, and laughed to see Mulberry dancing at the end of her lead and nibbling at the pony's rump.

Their small party rounded the bend; the trail now steeply descending toward the roar of surf. It twisted past some sitka spars and turned to drive its way through more gorsgrass.

Thera *sensed* something. *A chill*...she looked up to see if a cloud covered the sun. *No*. The sun's light ignited the washed blue of sky and she shaded her eyes from its brightness.

Clenching her hand on her dagger she pivoted to look back again. Jon appeared as usual, he had removed his skullcap helm and was wiping his arm across his forehead, but nothing altered his swinging stride or easy demeanor.

Thera's gaze narrowed. The horses were uneasy. Mulberry's ears twitched and her skin flinched, as if she were bothered with flies. Jon's mount tossed its head, eyes rolling.

Ahead, Swordsman Innic walked alone, as the path was narrowing. He frequently turned, though, to talk to Nan. Thera could not make out the words they said, their voices were strangely muffled to her hearing as if spoken through heavy layers of cloth. Neither Nan nor Innic appeared alarmed.

Thera shook her head. Now she suffered a sense of smothering, of struggling to draw breath into her lungs. She sent her senses out groping for an answer.

It was the Elanraigh.

The Elanraigh was immensely angry.

Thera felt a sudden silence like an indrawn breath held ominous and tense, then rage gusted forth. Her hand rose to her throat where her pulse leaped under her thumb. Never had she felt such as this from the Elanraigh before.

It was as if an advancing army trod the air with pounding footsteps.

Her throat tight with fear, she tried to cry out a warning. At the same instant, hundreds of crows burst voiceless into the air where they swirled in their unnatural silence, as if they feared to alight.

They must have seen each other at almost the same instant, the Memteth raiders and the party from Allenholme. The Memteth crew were bent over a freshly fallen sitka spruce they had dragged down to the beach. Their bright-bladed axes hewed away its branches and skin. Their gibing joviality indicated no awareness or regard for the spirit of the deeply shocked sitka. Their black-sailed ship lay at anchor some several horse strides from the beach.

The apparent leader stood to one side. *His* manner was both brooding and watchful. The armored head swung from side to side as he scanned the beach and his partially scaled hand clenched an amulet that hung around his neck.

The Memteth leader's strident yell and Swordsman Innic's clashed in the air as they both cried out alarm.

CHAPTER 13

*I*nnic spun on his heel. He grabbed Nan about the waist, half lifting her off her feet as he doubled back-trail to where Jon and Thera were attempting to control the panicked animals.

Sweat prickled out of Thera's pores as she twisted her hand in Mulberry's reins. The mare, her eyes rolling, attempted to spin around, dragging Thera with her. Her arm felt as if it would be pulled from its socket. Belatedly Thera realized Mulberry might be responding to her own terror — she had forgotten Teacher's lessons.

Thera drew a deep breath, and visualized rain falling on a still pond, the water rippled and smoothed, rippled and smoothed. From this calm centre within herself, she sent soothing feelings to the mare. The mare's eyes still showed white, but she settled enough for Thera to turn her. Nan's pony biddably followed, *Blessings be!*

Jon turned the mule and with a swack on the rump, sent it back the way they came. The young soldier ran to join Innic, his sword ringing as he unsheathed it.

At Innic's abrupt hand signal, Jon halted in his headlong

run. He strained to see down the twisting path. A clamor of harsh commands and shouts reached their ears.

Innic swung Nan round in front of him, his hands clenching her upper arms. "Now, love," his voice grated, "you listen close. You and Lady Thera run to the trees. You be safe in the Elanraigh, I vow."

Nan's face was ghastly, and she clung to him. "What do you think to do? You foolish man, you must come with us! They are too many!"

"I have my duty, as you have yours to Oak Heart's Heir," he said, shaking her slightly. The soldier's features contorted in the grimace Thera remembered. "I will show those scum what they face from the men of Allenholme," his voice softened, "and I will buy *you* time. So 'tis not in vain, this."

He pulled Nan to him, kissed her hard, then spun her up to Thera. "To the trees, my Lady," he shouted, "and Elanraigh protect you."

"And you," choked Thera.

She stood erect, her hands gripped Nan's. Thera braced herself as Nan cried out to Innic and flung herself toward him. Thera's eyes met and locked a moment with Innic's, then Jon's. The soldiers bestowed on her the swordsman's salute to Liege.

Then once again Innic flashed his fighter's grin, and both soldiers turned to position themselves somewhat down trail, to where it steeply descended past two rock formations towering either side of the path.

Thera turned, and continuing to grip Nan's hand she pulled her stumbling up the path. Nan was gasping. Thera heard her moaning Innic's name. Thera focused only on the distance to the tree line. She too cried out, a litany of anger and pain, pleading with the Elanraigh, *"Oh save my two brave men who face odds of six to one."*

Thera felt the Elanraigh respond with great frustration, it chaffed like a tethered and tormented beast at the tree line demarcation.

With an ice-water chill, Thera realized the Elanraigh could not affect the event about to take place. Though its anger built like the towering front of a thunderhead, it was held powerless at the exact edge of the forest.

The last segment of the twisting trail was the steepest. Thera had one hand wrapped around Nan's forearm and used the other to grasp hand-holds on the rocks. Her shoulder muscles burned and her hand was soon scraped raw and bleeding. She paused, her breath rasping in and out.

The final bench of rock was just above them. Then it would be about twenty horse-strides distance to run, before they would reach the first stunted shore pines of the Elanraigh.

They both heard the clash of arms begin below them. The battle cry of Allenholme's soldiers rang out.

Nan moaned and collapsed to her knees.

Wild eyed, Thera pulled Nan to her feet. "Just a little farther. Come Nan, Innic wished it."

Nan slipped constantly. Her feet pained her much of the time anyway, and she was not wearing boots like Thera's. Thera saw that Nan's ankles were swollen and scraped.

Finally reaching the level shelf, Thera shifted her arm to around Nan's waist and supported her as they stumbled on toward the first wind-twisted pines. To her inner vision, the barrier of the Elanraigh's anger rose like a towering wave ahead. Like the still silent and anxiously circling crows, Thera almost hesitated to enter.

However, she heard her name urgently thrummed. This

was a voice that would brook no discussion, and she was driven where the Elanraigh wished her.

As they entered the shelter of the trees, all sounds from behind them were cut off--as if a heavy curtain had dropped. All Thera could hear was Nan's gasping. Her pasty color alarmed Thera. They needed a safe resting place. *Now.*

Thera patted Nan's arm, her gaze searching, her senses alert. There would be time for words and grief when they were safe. Forcefully, the Elanraigh drove her on toward a large hemlock. The old tree giant was split some two pike lengths up its side and Thera could see a hollow niche beyond the very narrow opening. It was just large enough for the two women.

"Blessings," murmured Thera, near exhaustion. Yet, she hesitated. She stared back toward the direction of the sea, where her men fought. Nothing was visible. It was like trying to see through a heat wave mirage. The air shimmered.

She felt an impatient pressure at her back, as if a hand insistently pushed her. Beyond any further resistance, Thera dropped to her knees and crawled through the narrow opening. The oppressive air weighed heavier and heavier upon her.

"Nan?" Thera's vision darkened around the edges. "Hurry Nan."

Nan held to the sides of the opening, she licked her lips, and sweat ran in rivulets from her temples. Her eyes pleaded with Thera. "I wanted only to see you safe, Button. Here, in the Elanraigh's care. Blessings be. Nevertheless, I must see my Innic again. I'm going back. As you love me, do not try to stop me."

Thera scrambled back toward the tree cave opening,

"No! Nan! This is madness, you must not — the Elanraigh can't protect you there!"

Thera grabbed at Nan's skirts, but the tree cave aperture had so narrowed that even her slender form could not now slip through. "Nan!" she screamed. She clawed at the old tree like a wildcat in a trap. She raged in soldier's speech at the Elanraigh. A warm weight inexorably pushed her down onto the deep humus of the tree cave. Darkness poured over her.

CHAPTER 14

*O*nce, Thera dreamt she awakened in the dark. She murmured Nan's name and rolled her head. Night wind redolent of wild mint blew onto her heated face. She imagined quicksilver eyes watching her from the tree's opening.

"Farnash," Thera whispered. His glistening teeth shone. Then, either she simply closed her eyes, or the darkness was forced upon her again.

It seemed to Thera that she awoke weeping several times. Each time the Elanraigh and the old hemlock drove her back into the darkness.

Finally she was freed from sleep. She became aware of the weight of her arms spread out upon the carpet of needles, her fingers curled over her palms like fronds of baby fern. Her shoulders burned from long immobility. She licked her lips. Her mouth was very dry.

Outside the tree cave was the riotous birdsong of early morning, and a brisk, soughing wind tossed the evergreen boughs in the forest beyond.

Thera moaned out loud, trying to sort dream from reality. She was here, and she was alone. *"You could have stopped her,"* Thera accused bitterly. *"Nan was weak and tired. You stopped me readily enough."*

The Elanraigh offered no explanations. It waited, silent, at the edge of her consciousness.

Thera was surprised that she could close out the Elanraigh voice by her own will, but she had never before been angry at the Elanraigh. It was a bitter satisfaction; cutting off the Elanraigh was like losing a part of herself.

Thera could now easily crawl through the opening of the tree cave. She found a trickle of water that fed the hemlock's roots and bent to moisten her lips. The water tasted of green fern and moss, greatly satisfying her thirst. Slowly, painfully, she stood erect, her eyes squinting in even this soft, ambient light.

Thera refused to allow her thoughts to alight yet on the thing she must do.

She moved several lengths away from her tree den to relieve her bladder. Methodically she brushed at her clothing. She became aware that tears were tracking along her cheeks and she brushed those away also. Kneeling, she unbraided her hair, ran her fingers through it to remove leaves and debris, then rebraided it. The familiar motions were comforting to her.

After all the small rituals of personal grooming were attended to, Thera faced seaward. No sound of waves. The tide must be in.

How much time has passed, she wondered. It is obviously now just past dawn. Clenching cold anger like a warding amulet, she sent terse words to the Elanraigh. *"Do not attempt to stop me this time,"* and began the walk back to the coast trail.

She paused at the fringe of shore pines, listening for any

sound. Thera lightly touched the forest mind. The Elanraigh was emanating anxiety, but Thera perceived it to be concern for her peace of mind rather than fear for her physical safety.

In spite of her present mood, the Elanraigh risked the sending of a small air elemental, which skittered about her, bursting in its zealous duty.

She absently noted the air elemental and remembered that legend told of the Elanraigh having an ability to influence the winds. She remembered that Teacher had said, however, that elementals of wind and air were flighty and temperamental, and when asked for a gentle breeze, were just as likely to produce a considerable storm.

Thera moved out into the open, paused, and then continued on to the rocky ledge. There was no sign of the others. The small breeze attempted to buffet her back from the cliff edge. She moved back, but only because she intended to descend the cliff path.

She soon found Jon and Innic. They lay piled one upon the other like broken jackstraws. Thera felt her body shaking. She clenched her teeth, swallowing hard against the grief that rose like bile in her throat, and sank to her knees beside them. They lay on the rocks where she had last seen them at the narrowing of the trail. Jon's body was on the bottom, face down. The rocks and sand below him were stained dark with blood. Jon's arm was out-flung with the sword still clenched in hand. Probably his plain weapon had not been of interest to the Memteth who slew him.

Innic lay face up, the swordsman's famous grimace intact. He had many wounds. He had probably weakened from loss of blood, Thera thought, and then taken his fatal blow. Innic's sword was gone, as were his leathers. Some Memteth had carved a bloody rune on Innic's forehead.

Thera placed a shaking hand on his brow and murmured an ancient blessing. No curse of theirs could keep Innic's soul from finding its rightful place.

Innic's skin was cold and waxy. The eyes stared.

A cold sweat broke out on Thera's forehead and her stomach heaved sickeningly. The Elanraigh's small breeze caressed the sweat-dampened tendrils of hair off her forehead. Past the thunder of her own blood in her ears was the far off mewling of gulls.

Scanning the area around them, Thera saw other dark patches staining rocks nearby. Her lips curled in a snarl. She observed the ground more closely and saw the swath of overturned rocks. This must be the way the Memteth had hauled their own dead or injured back to their ship.

She turned her face back to the bodies of Innic and Jon. "We will raise you a cairn here, swordsmen, and at my father's house your names will be entered in the Scroll of Honor."

Thera flashed a question toward the Elanraigh.

She didn't believe a soldier's soul was as likely to yearn toward the Elanraigh, as would that of a woodwright, hunter, or Salvai. However, it was possible Innic and Jon had chosen so.

In a strange, subdued voice, the Elanraigh replied, *"Their spirits were welcome to come to us, but have chosen another place."*

So. Thera stood again. *There was the Lament to be sung, but that must wait.* She looked down trail. She had yet another to find.

At the foot of the trail, she stood where she was screened by tall yellow broom. Thera looked out upon the vast crescent of Shawl Bay. The Memteth ship was gone. Her hands clenched as she saw the remains of the fallen sitka — only its boughs, branches, and shavings —thrown into a heaping pile. Nearby were the remains of a fire. Her brow puckered. *They had been ashore long enough to have a meal and some comfort, it seems.*

How long did I sleep in the tree cave, she wondered again.

Thera walked onto the sand. The butchered remains of a horse lay some lengths ahead. Thera sighed shakily, it was not Mulberry, it was Jon's mount. Sand fleas covered the decapitated head and the poor beast's gelid eye gazed skyward. Large bones lay cracked in the remains of the fire.

Past the pile of sitka branches Thera glimpsed a flicker of white blown by the wind. She began to walk toward it, stumbled, then ran. Her foot slipped on a sandy rock. Quickly outreaching her arm, she slid to the other side of the sitka's branches.

Nan's garment. It's Nan! Her white petticoats spread like the wings of a fallen gull. Thera fought for breath as the nausea and horror threatened to overwhelm her. She moaned deep in her throat.

"Ahh. Nanny ... !" Sobbing a litany of old nursery endearments, Thera dropped to Nan's side.

Her fingers gently touched Nan's pale limbs all mottled with bruises. She straightened Nan's splayed body and tidied the white dress about her. Nan's face was grimy as if she had fallen in the dirt, though a cleaner tear track ran from the corner of each eye to her tangled hair.

Thera pressed her face to Nan's cold flesh, the tears she had thought to forbid until all was done, poured down her face. She wept, in gut-wrenching sobs as she had not done since she was a very little girl, and her fingers tightly clenched the folds of Nan's dress.

Finally she lay still, hiccupping and empty.

"*She is not here, Thera. She is with her soldier now,*" sent the Elanraigh, its inhuman voice resonating with sorrow.

"*They could have had a life together!*" Thera straightened and moistened a corner of her tunic on her tongue to wipe gently at the grime on Nan's face.

Thera sat back on her heels. The corners of her lips jerked downward as she gazed at Nan's face.

Her expression smoothed and hardened as she tilted her head to the sky. "*How long did I sleep?*" She demanded of the Elanraigh.

Silence.

"*How long, if you please,*" Thera repeated.

"*Two days.*"

With fluid swiftness Thera rose and strode to the fire pit. She bent to feel the rocks surrounding it and frowned. "*The rocks are cold.*"

"*How long have the Memteth been gone in their ship?*" She demanded.

A silence again, before the Elanraigh finally responded, "*They sailed on the evening ebb tide yesterday.*"

"*Thera, what do you think to do?*" It was Teacher's voice.

"*Teacher,*" murmured Thera with a small curl of lips, unlike her usual smile. "*You are here? Were you here, then?*" Thera gestured to Nan's still form.

Teacher's voice was mournful. "*There was nothing we could do for her, Thera. Nothing you could have done, except share her pain. Her spirit was not there, at the end, my child. She had already left. You must continue on to Elankeep. We will see you there safely; we will not be caught by surprise again.*"

"*I have a thing to do first,*" stated Thera, and closed her mind to their dismayed murmurings. She remembered Chamakin had spoken of "calling." Thera had no idea if the ability to call was part of *her* gift, but with mind-voice Thera projected a request for the sea hawk to come, to join with her again.

"Thera!" Alarm rang in Teacher's mind-voice, but Thera already heard her hawk's response, and felt a sense of feral joy as the sea hawk recognized her, followed by a faint but eager query.

Thera formed a picture of herself standing on the wide white crescent of Shawl Bay with the sun in morning position over her left shoulder. She detailed the image in her mind as clearly as she could.

The sleek raptor sent recognition, and a sense of fervid acquiescence. Thera smiled. The young bird could not verbalize like Farnash, but the sensations and images she sent Thera could understand very well.

Thera returned to Nan's side, and ignoring the queries of Teacher and the Elanraigh, composed herself to sing the Lament.

CHAPTER 15

*I*t was some time before Thera was roused from her watch at Nan's side by the strident greeting of the sea hawk. Thera placed a last evergreen bough over Nan's still form and rose to her feet. Gazing northward, she shaded her eyes. The young raptor was flying very high, though already beginning her characteristic spiral descent. Her ardent, piercing call to Thera scattered raucous gulls from her flight path.

The wind elemental, to Thera's surprise, was still by her, mindful of the duty the Elanraigh had laid upon it. It began to skitter and dance between Thera and the sea hawk. The wind elemental greeted the sea hawk like kin.

"*Welcome,*" Thera sent as the hawk settled on the topmost branch of the pile of sitka remains. She composed herself for the joining, and then paused to send, "*Is my friend hungry or tired from her flight?*"

The young raptor ruffled, and with impatience, she flared her wings.

Thera responded to the sea hawk's eagerness with a

grim smile. "Indeed, my friend, I feel the same," she murmured.

Teacher's anxious voice inserted itself into the moment, *"Thera, wait! You must safely conceal yourself..."*

Thera did not delay to heed it; she was aflame at last to *do* something. She reached for the joining, just as gently as the time in her mother's garden, but with more sureness of touch. The joining was immediate with no disorientation.

Screaming her defiance, she stroked upward, swift and strong. As before, her hawk body felt buoyant and wondrously light. Wind fingered through her feathers with a slight hissing.

Already high above the white crescent of Shawl Bay, she looked down upon the long, rolling curl of surf. Nan's body lay under the criss-cross of branches and evergreen boughs that Thera had placed over her with the blessing of the Elanraigh.

There was her own body lying crumpled beside the green mound. Her red wool tunic was a splash of vivid color on the beach.

Oh.

She keened softly in chagrin. *That* is what Teacher meant — to make sure her physical body was secure and safely hidden before the joining.

The hawk circled twice, there were no ships on the horizon, and the sun was not yet high. She clashed her beak and screamed once again, then banked westward out to sea.

The air elemental whispered to her that its name was Sussara, and then frisked in her wake like a hound pup just out of kennels.

From this height she could see the first islands of the archipelago on the horizon. The dense chain stretched a four day sail north of Allenholme and eight days south. Thera was told by the mariners of Allenholme that it was a six day sail west, through often treacherous passages, before open ocean was reached again. This was one reason the large warship from Cythia had never been much use against the Memteth raiders, whose smaller ships could skim through the maze of islands, defying perilous shoals and rock-strewn passages.

As she neared the islands, she saw a small herd of sea pups emerge from the water to clamber up a kelp-covered rock. A flock of orangebills landed nearby to feed on limpets. The sea hawk circled and then continued her search for a black sail. She swung between the vast cliffs of West Rednape and Carver Islands. While passing through the cool mist of a waterfall she shrilled, and her voice echoed off the steep rock face.

She continued flying west using the snowy spire of Banner Mountain on Lastmer Island as her westerly lodestone. Then she saw a Memteth ship below her.

Her neck feathers fanned, but Thera hushed the hawk's defiant scream of challenge. *"Hush! Not yet,"* she soothed, *"not yet."*

That they were Memteth was beyond doubt. However, they might not be *her* Memteth. She circled down. She was either unnoticed or disregarded. The crew's attention was on their ship as they prepared to negotiate a riptide passage between islands.

A small exclamation escaped the sea hawk as she recognized the raw sitka spar lashed into place as main mast. She circled closer.

"Sussara, can you get close enough to see how the sitka's elemental does? I need to know if it yet clings with its tree, or if it has...left."

Sussara whirled downward to circle the Memteth mast,

meanwhile playing havoc with the sail. The hawk keened a wicked laugh as the Memteth leader roared out commands to the scrambling crew. Thera counted only seven Memteth. Five body shapes lay under canvas near the stern.

"*Sleeping.*" Came the reply from the air elemental to Thera. "*Sitka sleeping.*"

Thera suspected the sitka elemental was either still in shock, or had deliberately gone dormant. She pondered as she wove the air streams above the ship. If it could be awakened, the tree elemental could perhaps be transported home to the Elanraigh with Sussara.

The wind elemental circled and danced around her in its eagerness to be of service.

"*Sussara help the poor cousin--yes I will.*"

"*Blessings.*" Thera thanked the elemental with a mental smile, and bent her head once more to check on the activities of the 'Teth.

The depleted Memteth crew were encountering turbulence now where the tidal streams met around Dog Leg Island. Thera decided to risk alighting on the sitka mast. Her eye on the Memteth leader, the young hawk tightened her circling, until at last, furling her wings she gripped the sitka with her sharp talons. The sitka's elemental, not so deeply submerged after all, must have sensed her as a friendly and familiar presence, for almost immediately Thera was aware of a poignant query from it.

"*This is Sussara, sent by the Elanraigh. It will carry you home, if you agree to release yourself and be joined with Sussara?*"

With a small trill of gratitude that tickled through Thera's light avian bones, the sitka's elemental agreed. Once again Thera felt the resonance of an Elanraigh life form vibrating under her touch, and then it was gone.

She, too, lifted gratefully back into the air. The Memteth had paid no attention to her.

"*Safe? Together?*" inquired Thera immediately of both elementals.

They replied with satisfaction, "*Safe!*"

"*Blessings be!*" The young hawk sensed Thera's joy and screamed its challenge.

The black-sailed ship was fast approaching the narrow bend in the passage, yet something in the hawk's cry caused the Memteth leader to glance upward.

Thera studied him, as he briefly directed his attention to her. The Memteth was tall and lean. He stood spraddled-legged on the heaving deck, his posture practiced and sure.

She saw long, hooded eyes, amber colored with ovoid pupils. Human-like, yet something reptilian about him, with glinting amethyst scales forming a widow's peak below his helm.

Prominent bony plates of forehead and cheekbones shone smoothly taut. The thin, sharp nose ended in flaring nostrils. There was a honed symmetry to his features, and a presence both shrewd and dangerous.

From her high spiral the hawk saw him look away, dismissing her. When he shifted position, placing his hand on his hip, her raptor's vision clearly saw the leather pouch suspended from the 'Teth's leather belt. *Innic's tobacco pouch*!

Rage consuming her, she closed her nostrils against the drive of wind into her lungs, folded her wings and dove, straight for the Memteth's face.

Warned by a shout from an alert crewman, the startled Memteth leader threw himself backward, falling onto the canvas covered bodies of his dead. He flung one mail-covered arm up over his face and with the other reached for dagger or sword.

The hawk screamed. Her wings cracked the air as she slashed at him with talons and hooked predator's beak, opening his face to the bone.

Livid flesh gaped, pouring dark-hued blood.

The Memteth made no outcry. His yellow eyes glared into hers, then his sword was free and he stabbed upward at her, meanwhile levering himself to his feet.

Frenzied by the smell of his blood, Thera beat her wings for height, intent on renewing her attack.

A hoarse shout, and intense pain followed. An arrow struck her left pinion.

She tumbled over the end of the boat. The young hawk recovered awkwardly, able only to skim the rough waves. In panic, she labored to uplift.

It was Sussara and the sitka's elemental who inserted themselves between the drenched sea hawk and the clashing, pike-high waves. Carrying her, they spun themselves into a small thermal and she rose awkwardly.

It was a long, laboring flight to a bleached bone of a snag on Dog Leg Island. Even though exhausted, her talons gripped the branch with instinctive strength. Her injured wing she held aloft a moment, then gently folded it. The crossbow bolt had torn flesh, but the damage would heal.

Yet she trembled. She mantled her feathers, and mantled again. Her beak opened and she panted slightly. The pain was nothing compared to Thera's remorse. She, Thera, in her anger and lust for revenge, had driven the young sea hawk almost to its death. What would the Ttamarini Maiya have to say to her for such abuse of this trust?

She received the young hawk's vigorous assertion of life. Thera sensed also, that the hawk had thoroughly absorbed her human friend's hatred of the Memteth. Strangely, this grieved Thera.

The Memteth ship was holding course through the white water of the passage. They would soon be clear of the rip. Thera shifted nervously. She had an idea.

CHAPTER 16

*S*he must leave the sea hawk. The young raptor would need to feed, rest, and heal. Thera would not risk her again, yet she was uncertain how to go about what she planned. The last time Thera had left the joining, she had almost lost herself upon the wind. Of course, then the rupture had been sudden and unexpected, and this time Thera would prepare.

Thera took time to compose herself, and then projected herself outward. Quick as thought, she was borne far above the wind-bitten trees of the island, loose upon the wind.

The hawk on her branch keened after her, and Thera sent warm reassurance and thanks.

Thera could sense that the elementals were intrigued and excited about her change of form. She too, was fascinated with this disembodied state. There was danger, however, as already she could feel the urge to dissolve as a warm lethargy washing over her. She must hold to her purpose or she would be lost.

She moved out over the water, faster and faster through the air, as if she were an air elemental herself. With hissing speed she passed the Memteth ship, the elementals so close they were almost joined with her. She marveled at the speed of her flight in this state.

She continued east, back toward Shawl Bay, skimming as far across open sea as she could from the Memteth ship, then slowed and turned. The Memteth sail was a small black speck against the white water of Dog Leg passage.

Teacher had long ago explained to Thera how waves were actually energy moving through the water. Master Petrack's nephew, Bren, had told her that fearsome furies are unleashed when tidal currents happen to cross the path of waves, or move in opposition to them.

"*The tide is ripping at full flood through the Dog Leg now.*"

She demanded of Sussara, "*Have you ever played on the water, to make waves?*"

"*Yesss!*" Was the wind elemental's response, "*We play to see who can make the biggest wave crash on the rocks.*"

The Elanraigh tree elemental sent Thera the equivalent of a grunted laugh. Thera sensed the tree elemental already knew what she hoped to achieve, and it thrummed a grim satisfaction with her plan.

The small wind elemental swirled eagerly, "*Therrra, what is it you and tree cousin plan?*"

"*We are going to make a wave,*" Thera explained to Sussara. "*As big a wave as we can. I will enter the water, you and tree cousin will stay as close to me as you can, skimming the surface. The riptide is running north through the passage and we will strike the rip and the Memteth ship as they pass in front of the rocks at Dog Leg Island's north end.*"

"*But we are so far away from the black ship,*" complained Sussara.

Thera swirled thoughtfully a moment. "*We are not a very*

big energy front, little one. We need *the distance to gather as much wave as possible. You will see."*

"*Sussara,*" Thera continued, "*are you good at this game you play?*"

The small elemental puffed, "*I am the bessst!*"

Thera expanded with approval. "*We must hit the rip, just as the Memteth ship passes in front of those jagged rocks. You must judge for us when is best to start our run toward them.*" Thera's mind voice expressed worry.

The small elemental buffed itself against her and whispered reassuringly, "*I can do thisss, Therrra.*"

The three of them swirled silently in place, watching the agonizingly slow progress of the Memteth ship toward the tangle of dark rocks that marked the end of Dog Leg passage.

Finally, Sussara hissed, "*We go, now!*"

Thera dove beneath the water, trusting the two elementals to keep close by her at the surface. Her speed in the water was only slightly less than it had been in the air, though she could now feel a resistance building ahead of her.

"*Ssoon now.*" Sussara urged her on, keeping their course true. Then their wave hit the riptide, and Thera was thrust into the air on impact. She reunited with the two elementals and they boiled together with excitement.

"*Hush now,*" urged Thera. "*Let us see what we have done.*"

The Memteth ship was trapped in an eddy which quickly became a whirlpool, whipping the seven pike-length ship end for end, and tumbling the crew helplessly on the deck. A huge dead-head log breached from its watery grave and crashed down upon the ship. The Memteths' cries were lost in the groaning and splintering of the wooden hull. As if in death throes, the prow heaved skyward on a swell, only to sink silently into the wave interval.

Thera spiraled over the place. Debris from the deck bobbed in the turbulence. She could hear gull cries again.

"*By the One Tree!*" Thera's mind-shout sent Sussara and the tree elemental spinning. There was the Memteth leader, clinging to a remnant of the shattered sitka spar, kicking for the shore of Dog Leg Island. "*He lives!*"

Thera dove again, but disembodied, and at this close range couldn't affect his progress in any way. The Memteth spasmed in a shiver, glancing briefly below the water, and then resuming his efficient, thrusting kick, he swam toward the shore of Dog Leg Island.

With horrified fascination, Thera studied him; his teeth clenched, his face in a twisted grimace as he fought to survive. The slash her sea hawk had torn in his face ran from brow bone, past the corner of his eye, to his upper lip.

"*It will be a very ugly scar. Could anyone be so tenacious of life!*" She swirled closer. He grunted with effort as he kicked behind the log, his eyes steadily fixed on the rocky shore of the island.

Riptide might accomplish what she could not. He may never make shore. It must be enough.

Suddenly, Thera felt an extreme lethargy. *So tired.* Feeling frayed and thin, she wove slowly upward.

"*Therrra! You must not sleep. Stay with usss, and we will take you home. Yesss?*"

Her two elementals were worried and swirled around her, creating an eddy to keep her in one piece. She felt them buffeting her toward shore.

When she was once again above Shawl Bay, she saw her body just as she had left it lying on the beach and with the sighting, she experienced again the stunning force of rejoining with her own body.

Her physical pains quickly prodded her to consciousness. Wiping sand off her face, she flinched in pain. Her skin was afire with sunburn on the left side of her face, her lips were so dry and cracked. And oh, the thirst!

Thera moved her stiffened limbs, dragging herself upright. Startled crows fled squalling from their perches on the sitka remains. She swayed dizzily a moment. With her first deep breath, she gagged on the odors rising from the beach.

Nan, Innic and Jon, my dear friends, I do not have the strength just now to build you stone cairns to honor you as you deserve, but it will be done. Tears filled Thera's burning eyes.

She must get into the shade and the protection of the Elanraigh. Nausea boiled up from her stomach and burned at the back of her throat; she fell to her knees and vomited. Her head pounded. Slowly she rose, and one foot in front of the other; her progress halting and meandering as a drunken soldier's return to barracks.

As the trail steepened she was on all fours more often than not. The throbbing in her head worsened and her vision blurred. At the last part of the climb, she collapsed, pressing her aching forehead against the seeming coolness of the granite rock.

However, the Elanraigh would give her no rest. "*Rise. You Must!*" The Elanraigh sent her visions of her dark haven, the hemlock tree cave. The rivulet of cool green water that bathed the hemlock's roots would soothe her forehead and burned cheeks. It was an irresistible argument. She rose and climbed the last few feet.

Sussara caressed her, twining about her like a cat. "*Ther-*

raa! Tree cousin is home again, you are home again. Just a little farther."

Thera remembered nothing more of her staggering progress until she became aware that the tree cave was before her, and with a groan of pleasure she slid forward, elbow deep in the fragrant humus, and buried herself in its darkness.

CHAPTER 17

"*T*hera. Thera, wake up!*"

Thera groaned and licked dry lips. "*Unn.*" Teacher's voice in her head. *Head hurts.*

"*She's slept too long, we must wake her!*" Teacher's voice was anxious.

"*Did you not teach her the Bear's Sleep?*" rumbled the Elanraigh.

"*No. How could I? I hadn't time; she had just done the first joining. I kept telling you she was too young for all this. Look at her now, poor child. Help me to wake her.*"

"*We must teach her the Bear's Sleep,*" replied the Elanraigh.

BETWEEN THEM, the Elanraigh entities prodded her awake.

Thera's eyes felt swollen. She opened them just enough to see as she crawled from the tree cave and lay belly-down by the rivulet. Its sweet water was balm to her dry mouth and throat. With a small groan of relief she laid her face on the cool moss.

Thera returned to her tree cave and slept.

A wolf howling or perhaps she dreamt it. Perhaps it had howled a long time ago, and she just now remembered it. Thera slitted her eyes open. Her head felt clearer. Dappled light fell across the tree cave's floor.

The air was alive with bird song. She heard bush robins, tree pipers, and waxwings, all mingled with the harsher counterpoint of crows and jays.

Thera came rigidly alert, a chill wave of alarm washing over her. She also recognized the distinct sound of booted footsteps and the creak of leather gear very near her tree.

Remaining absolutely still, her heart pounded as she reasoned, *Surely no Memteth could penetrate the Elanraigh, certainly not without her receiving a warning.* She sent a quick question to the Elanraigh and received no sense of alarm or an answer.

Thera crept cautiously from her cave and found herself facing the boiled-leather shin greaves of a soldier. Her startled upward glance quickly took in the green-brown dappled cloak with hood, worn over a layered leather breastplate and green kilt. The dappled cloak should have identified the person as a forester, except this person was heavily armed with sword and dagger, as well as bow. There were others, dressed as the first, and they came swiftly toward her.

A suntanned hand was extended down to assist her.

"My thanks," Thera murmured. The soldier's grip was warm and dry. With the swift movement to her feet, her vision suddenly darkened and dazzling sparks swam before her eyes.

She must have wavered or looked stricken, for there was a sudden furor of voices and she felt herself carried swiftly to where her hemlock's rivulet joined a tiny creek. She was lowered to the ground and someone splashed her face and wrists with cold water.

Thera felt humiliated by her unexpected weakness and struggled to steady her vision. Though still blurry eyed, she could make out the several figures standing about her. Their postures and voices indicated concern for her well-being. Their accents, though different than hers, were of the coast. If these soldiers were not known to her, they were at least not hostile. Thera became aware she was supported against a soldier's knee propped behind her back.

She straightened.

"Lady, are you injured?"

Thera could finally focus her sight and she examined the soldier's features. A woman's visage--tanned, scarred, and rough as bark. The eyes that returned her regard so steadily were the color of coppers.

"No." Thera croaked, though she felt a feverish sort of sweat break out over her clammy skin.

The soldier nodded to one of her company and she was handed a water skin. "Drink. Not too much."

The soldier made as if to hold the spout for her, but Thera took it, though her fingers shook, and drank gratefully.

She handed the water skin back, wiping her mouth with the back of her hand. "I thank you."

Thera rose to her feet, this time with no ill effect. The company about her came to a loose attention. Their leader was a head taller than Thera, and Thera was tall for a woman of Allenholme. The soldier pushed back the hood of her cape, revealing grey-brown hair pulled back to a single thick braid. She wore a headband; its silver disk badge proclaimed her a Sirra, Master at Arms. Embossed on the badge was a cedar tree emblem. The workmanship was very fine.

"Lady, I am Sirra Alaine of Elankeep, and these others are of my command. We serve the Salvai."

"Sirra," Thera's nod included the company. "I am Thera ep Chadwyn Ned'ArNarone." Very little change of expression showed on Sirra Alaine's face, but Thera read relief. "My party was on route to Elankeep, when we were set upon by Memteth. I...I alone survive."

"We found your party, Lady Thera," the Sirra's lips compressed and a scar at the corner of her mouth paled, "and built a cairn above their remains."

Thera dropped all formality, and clasped the Sirra's rough hand in both of hers. "Blessings on you! I thank you all." Her voice shook with emotion. Tears threatened to spill over and Thera felt ashamed to seem so weak in front of these soldier women. She withdrew her hands and wrapped her arms about herself, rocking slightly. With effort, she firmed her voice, "I was not able to build a cairn, and I thought I would have to give them to the fire. However, after I returned from the joining I was weary and sick. I don't know how long I have lain here in the Elanraigh's care. I have lost all account of the days."

"'Joining,' Lady?"

"Yes." Thera suddenly felt the time was right to reveal her gift. "It is my gift from the Elanraigh. The joining. You see, first I joined with the sea hawk, to pursue the Memteth who killed Nan, Innic and Jon, but the hawk was wounded by an arrow." Thera paced a bit. "It was my fault she was wounded. When I saw the Memteth leader with Innic's tobacco pouch on his belt, this terrible rage came over me."

Thera suddenly became aware she must seem to be gabbling. She felt her cheeks flame.

A sturdy woman at the Sirra's shoulder, murmured something to her companion. The Sirra flicked her a quelling glance.

Thera saw the sturdy soldier appraise her. Her cheeks warmed under that scrutiny. She squared her shoulders and stopped pacing to face the Sirra. "I left the hawk on Dog Leg Island, where she could rest and mend, and set out again in disembodied form, like the wind," she added, wondering if they understood her at all. "Of course I couldn't have done it without the help of Sussara, a wind sprite, and the tree elemental. They saved my life more than once." She clenched and moved her hand demonstratively, "We made a wave, the three of us, and sank the Memteth ship." The clenched hand smacked her other palm.

The Elankeep troop shifted, and some exclamations were uttered, which the Sirra hushed with a wave of hand.

Thera continued. "I left my body lying on the beach, and when I returned to it, well, I think I suffered from heat stroke as well as the usual weariness I seem to experience after a joining. I don't know how long I lay ill."

Thera's voice dwindled as she took in the varying expressions around her. Then she blinked. Though the Sirra's face was as stolid as stone, Thera read a fierce exultation barely held in check.

"You speak the truth," declared the Sirra. The sturdy soldier on the Sirra's right eyed Thera in surprise.

Thera knit her brows at the tone of the Sirra's assertion, "Do you have the gift of reading hearts then, Sirra Alaine?

"No, Lady, my gift is small compared to the gift of reading hearts, but from the day I swore to the Elanraigh that I would serve its Salvai, I have been able to *feel* truth when it is spoken."

"That is a great gift, Sirra," said Thera, regarding her in some surprise.

The corner of the Sirra's mouth tipped upward. "Aye. Blessings be."

The soldier to the Sirra's right side grinned openly. She and the Sirra exchanged a speaking look.

"Lady, I suggest we make a night camp here and proceed at dawn to Elankeep."

The Sirra hung on her heel apparently waiting for some sign from her. Thera nodded agreement. Sirra Alaine swung her gaze around the gathered troop, who, Thera now saw, were all women, quickly dispersing to duties.

The Sirra walked Thera back toward the more level ground at the hemlock tree. She gestured toward the sturdy soldier at her side, "Lady, this is First Sword, Alba NedArywn." The swordswoman saluted Thera, hand to brow. Alba was a younger, shorter version of Sirra Alaine.

"We will have a fire, Elanraigh permitting, and some food..." the Sirra paused to appraise Thera's appearance, "... you have the look, my Lady, of one who has marched over-long on short rations."

Thera allowed them to cosset her. She leaned back against the hemlock, with a warm blanket between her buttocks and the damp ground, the ends wrapped over her legs. The Sirra's troop had a camp quickly in order, with a small boulder-ringed fire pit dug, and a crock of stew with dumplings bubbling over the cheery flames. Someone handed her a steaming mug of herbal brew. Thera inhaled its fragrance with pleasure. The moist steam soothed her sunburned skin as much as its taste pleased her. The women spoke softly to each other. Their voices were homey and pleasing to her. Duties done, they came to gather about the fire. The sky had darkened to deep violet. Stars flickered between the waving branches of the evergreen trees. Nocturnal insects creaked in the bushes. The Elanraigh itself purred contentedly along her nerves.

Someone awakened her. "Lady, you should eat."

Her stomach growled in true feral greed and she reached for the cup. She paused, aghast at the lapse in her manners, "I thank you!" said Thera, spoon poised before her lips.

"Indeed!" laughed the young woman who handed her the bowl. Her laughter was rich and warm, making Thera feel as if a friendly arm had been thrown over her shoulder. "You will find no dainty appetites, or formal manners, in *this* group, Lady. Blessings on you!"

Sirra Alaine hunkered down beside Thera. She was already mopping up gravy from her bowl with a heel of bread.

"I would hear your story from beginning to end, Lady, if you will tell me."

Thera glanced round the faces, firelight reflected in their eyes and a hush came over them as they waited.

"Yes, Lady," prompted the young woman who had given her dinner. "What weapons do the Memteth use?"

"I would know what it is like to fly as a hawk," said another wistfully.

"I wish to hear if it's true that Allenholme has made peace with the Ttamarini," came the Sirra's prosaic voice, "and whether they be all legend has them. So, let the Lady speak."

Thera placed her empty bowl beside her and rested chin

on bent knees. She decided to begin with the first joining in her mother's garden ...

THE MOON HAD CLIMBED FAR past the topmost branches before all but the watch took to their bedrolls.

CHAPTER 18

"Sirra Alaine, how did you find me? Did the Elanraigh show you where I was?"

The Sirra continued to pace her troop single file along a forest track that twisted through the mossy rainforest. Alaine had told Thera that they had a two day journey ahead before they would reach the fortress of Elankeep.

Sirra Alaine shifted her shoulders. "The Elanraigh does not speak to *us* as it does to a Salvai, Lady. No." She slanted a look to Thera, and then studied the ground as she walked in silence a moment. "The Salvai sensed something was amiss in the Elanraigh, and surmised it must be your party in trouble."

Alaine's brows lifted, "Hnnh. It was a grey wolf who led us to you." She shook her head. "We felt strange and uneasy at his seeming to seek us. He showed himself soon after we set off to find you. We wondered if he might be half tame, perhaps the friend of some forester or hermit. However, though he shadowed us, he would not come close.

"We soon learned he had his own idea of the direction we should hold to. His howls would lift the very hairs on our heads if we moved other than the way he wished us to go. We felt finally that he must be sent by the Elanraigh."

Grief, like wind across water, stirred the Sirra Alaine's features. "We came upon your dead, yesterday, and feared you were lost or taken, Lady. But the wolf stayed near us as we gave your folk their death rites, though he would pace restlessly and then disappear from time to time. Immediately after we had sung the Lament, he appeared again to lead us to the tree cave where you lay."

"Farnash." murmured Thera, and her heart swelled with thanks.

THE PALE SUN shone through the cloud cover on the second day of their march. Thera had to push herself to continue. She had thought they would surely have taken a rest stop at that last small clearing, but the Sirra had pressed on. Her head was beginning to pound from the mugginess of the overcast day.

I am hot and tired. Nan would have noticed and cared, but Nan is gone. The corner of her mouth jerked down. *So. So stop whining like a...a...what was it Shamic called the recruits' complaints? ... the squeals o' the last suckled piglet!*

Thera grinned at the memory. She began to hum an old marching tune that Captain Lydia had taught her. Her stride lengthened to match that of the Sirra's ahead of her. Sirra Alaine's brown, muscular legs worked steadily — ever surefooted, stepping easily over twisted roots and deadfalls. Thera admired her strength as she mentally tallied the weight the Sirra carried. A bulky pack as well as her sword, bow, quiver, and dagger.

Thera sighed and shook her head, *"I thought I was strong enough to be a warrior. A boyish hoyden, Nan always called me."*

Her steps faltered as she remembered. Nan's many sayings would be with her all her life. *"Blessings be, Nan."*

Thera hoped Nan's spirit would know she was remembered with love.

Swordswoman Alba, marching just behind Thera, must have heard her sigh. "Be you tired, Lady? We *run* a path worse than this daily, as part of our drill."

Thera turned, and met Alba's droll grin.

The Sirra responded without looking around, "You braggart, Alba," she drawled, "and mightily do you complain about it daily, also."

"WE SHOULD BE at Elankeep before dusk," said the Sirra after they'd marched long in silence. Her voice startled Thera out of a meditative calm induced by the rhythm of their march.

"We will rest here," continued Sirra Alaine, slipping her pack from her shoulders and flexing them. "We have made better time than I thought we would." She bestowed on Thera her almost-smile which was little more than a shimmer of light in the eyes.

Thera flushed. She was glad she had not held the troop back, though now that they halted, she could barely stand on legs suddenly wobbly as a loosely strung puppet's.

Alba, wiping at the sheen of sweat on her brow, passed Thera a water skin. Damp tendrils of Alba's dark hair corkscrewed around her face.

"The forest leans close today. I would you had the gift of calling breezes, Lady."

Though Alba spoke in jest, Thera paused, water spout halfway to her mouth. *But no,* she decided, *it would not be right to call on the elementals just for personal comfort.*

After Thera finished drinking and returned the water skin to her, Alba sluiced her neck and poured the tepid water over her head.

"Cythian Hell!" she sputtered, "I'm going to peel off my skin an' rest my bones in the coldest, deepest part of Elankeep's springs..." Alba abruptly stopped speaking.

A great sense of urgency caused Thera to tense, uttering a small sound under her breath. Sirra Alaine was quickly beside her.

As movement and speech among the troop stopped, Thera strained to read what she yet only sensed. She heard the water dripping from Alba's hair onto her boots and the sudden cry of a bush skree streaking past them, its wings snapping the air.

The Sirra, her hand clenched on her sword hilt, whispered hoarsely, "Lady, what is it?"

"The Elanraigh," Thera said. "Something's wrong! I've felt something like this before. It was the Memteth, then."

The Sirra was gone, moving down the line of her troop. With a hushed efficiency, weapon harnesses were retrieved from the discarded packs; the women shrugging into the leather straps and buckled iron-studded belts. Silent as smoke, four of the troop disappeared to scout the forest around them.

Thera stood, as if bespelled, awaiting word from the Elanraigh. Alaine, Alba, and four others formed a protective loop around her. Then like the approaching rumble of an earthquake, she felt the Elanraigh's attention turn to her. A wind bent the top branches of the trees.

"Memteth! At Elankeep!"

The Elanraigh's anger made its words an almost unintelligible burr in her mind.

Thera was struck with horror. "*Elankeep! How many?*" she asked.

The ground shook. "*Two ships anchored in the Spinfisher River. They climb the rock face at Bridal Veil Falls.*"

Thera's mind worked furiously, "*How long before they are in position to attack Elankeep?*"

"*Before sunset.*"

"*Can you stop them?*"

A silence. Thera hung, waiting.

"*Water elements rule there, at the falls. However, they must pass through a grove of Old Ones to reach Elankeep.*"

"Lady, does the Elanraigh speak to you?" Sirra Alaine's voice penetrated Thera's preoccupation.

She grasped the Sirra's leather-cuffed forearms with the strength of urgency. "It *is* Memteth! Memteth are preparing to attack Elankeep!"

A hissed curse broke from someone in the troop.

The Sirra's amber eyes locked on Thera's face. Like wind-tossed flame, they flickered from Thera to the troop behind her, and back to Thera.

Thera remembered her father's words, 'A leader is both heart and head of the people.' She drew a deep breath and in calmer voice, continued, "The Elanraigh tells me they climb a rock face alongside a place called Bridal Veil Falls. The Elanraigh can do nothing against them there, it is the domain of a water elemental apparently, but they must pass through a large grove of ancient trees before they reach the clearing around Elankeep.

"What can the Elanraigh do exactly, Lady, to help us?"

"I do not know," murmured Thera, dropping her grip on

the Sirra's arms. "I do not know. It pains it to do harm, but it will do what it can."

A breeze swirled around her, "*Therra. Therra, I will help.*"

"*Sussara! Blessings be.*" Thera smiled, deeply touched. How fond she had become of this childlike elemental.

She searched, but could not touch the mind she sought.

"*Sussara, could you find Farnash, the grey wolf?*"

Sussara swirled joyfully. "*Yess! Wise wolf keeps nose to wind.*"

"*Tell him we need him. Tell him our clan is in battle against the Memteth.*"

The women's yellow longbows were strung and strapped across their backs, as were the short, curved swords. Some stretched and flexed, some shifted restlessly, though their eyes continually returned to their Sirra and the young Heir of Allenholme.

Alaine drew on a tapered leathern helm, reinforced with iron bands. Her eyes glittered at Thera from behind the nasal, as she buckled the waistband of her harness.

"There are usually a dozen Memteth to a ship. Is that how many you encountered at Shawl Bay, Lady?"

Thera's voice flattened. "There were ten on *that* ship, Sirra, unless they had lost some crew before they encountered us."

"Well. So..." Sirra Alaine continued, "The odds be not so bad, providing we get there in time. We are ten of us here and ten at Elankeep. Some of the Salvai's ladies can draw bow."

"We run," she said to the troop at large. "Our companions' lives depend on our getting there in time. Pace yourselves accordingly. Remember too, you must arrive with breath to swing a sword."

She turned to Thera, "Lady Thera, we cannot wait if you

fall behind, or spare any to stand guard over you. We must again entrust you to the Elanraigh."

"I will come with you and I will not hold you back, any of you." Thera's voice was muffled as she was pulling her red wool tunic over her head. She dropped it beside Alba's pack. She turned back to the Sirra, her jaw set. "I have fought Memteth before."

Thera watched the Sirra's glance slide over her kidskin Ttamarini garments and touch at the graceful emerald-hilted Sha'Lace dagger at her belt. Heat crept up Thera's neck under that scrutiny.

Some emotion Thera could not read, worry or doubt, shadowed the Sirra Alaine's eyes.

Feeling impelled to do so, Thera spoke the Liege Lord's Oath, "I defend this land and those pledged to my care with my heart, my blood, and all gifts granted of the Elanraigh."

Blessings be, her voice had not quavered though her heart felt as if it had been wrung.

Of their own accord, the troop drew blades and with the traditional cry of affirmation, their swords clashed in a salute to Thera.

Alba cleared her throat, "By the One Tree," she muttered to Alaine, "it makes me maudlin as an old Sirra at a troop review."

"Aye." The Sirra's rare smile twisted on the pale scar that crossed her lip.

Sirra Alaine gave the signal for the troop to move out at a quick march. Alba positioned herself behind Thera. The Sirra observed them all as they passed. A snap of fingers and hand wave sent her four scouts back into the forest. Then their Sirra ran easily to the head of the column, and the small troop lengthened their stride into a steady jog.

CHAPTER 19

*T*hey ran in silence. The trail switch-backed upward now and the air was blessedly cooler. Far below, on her left, Thera could hear the rushing of the Elanraigh River. She *had* fallen behind, even though the women kept to what had first seemed an easy jog. Thera tried not to think of Elankeep and what might be happening there. Yet, there came the memory of Nan's body at Shawl Bay. Her chest tightened. "Oh, Nan!" The last Elankeep soldier glanced back at her.

So, run then. Focus only on breathing, mind carefully empty of thought. Soon she could see the troop ahead of her, stretched along the upward-climbing trail. The Sirra Alaine and Alba must already have topped the crest of the hill.

When Thera turned the last bend before the hillcrest, two of the Elankeep soldiers were waiting for her. One offered her a hand up a final tumble of rocks and shale, while placing a finger to her lips in a signal for silence.

Bracing her hand against a cedar tree, Thera struggled

to catch her breath and waited for her vision to clear of dancing sparks. Sirra Alaine saw her and beckoned.

She crept to where the Sirra and Alba lay at the cliff's rough edge. They were several horse strides past the edge of the tree line, on a high rocky promontory.

For the first time, Thera saw Elankeep. It rose above the black sea cliffs like a natural formation of the rocks. Around the keep was boulder-strewn pasture. The grassy apron lay at least five pike lengths below the cliff edge where Thera lay. What Thera had thought were scattered grey boulders, she now saw the bodies of sheep.

Dark smoke rose from a huge rolled bundle of wood the Memteth had piled against the iron plated oak of the main gate.

A faint rumbling from the east was Bridal Veil Falls, where the Elanraigh River plunged to meet the Spinfisher. West of the plateau was a sheer drop to the ocean below. At the base of that black-rock cliff, white plumes of surf broke, dissolving into mist and foam.

She caught glimpses of Elankeep defenders crouched at arrow loops, both in the high round turret of the western wall and spread thinly along the battlement. Two Memteth lay dead or injured beyond care near the main gate. Another twelve or so continued to shoot fire arrows at the pitch-soaked wood piled at the gate and at the defenders on the walls.

Thera noted grimly that the Memteth avoided taking shelter in the trees.

They relied on the smoke from the fire to confuse the defenders, and their shields to protect against arrows as they kept to the clearing around the keep.

"I count only twelve raiders," whispered Alba. "Where be the rest?"

The Sirra shaded her eyes against a sudden glare of sun as the clouds broke overhead. "There *are* only twelve. Lady, does the Elanraigh speak of the others?"

Thera communed with the Elanraigh, then relayed, "There are ten raiders dead in the ancient grove by the falls."

Astonished, both the Sirra and Alba swiveled their heads and stared at her.

"Ten dead?" Alba's jaw dropped, and then snapped shut. "Cythian Hell!" she muttered.

"The Elanraigh says the ancient tree elementals are very powerful and are roused against the Memteth." Thera added, "Blessing Be."

"Hnnh." Sirra Alaine returned her gaze to the besieged keep. She watched as several arrows shot from the western turret fell abysmally short and wide of their Memteth targets. The raiders jeered.

"It wonders me that Berta has left the Salvai's Damas alone to defend the west side."

"Berta must be short-handed," surmised Alba.

"Hnnh." Alaine shoved herself back. "It is time we move."

She and Alba edged back from the cliff edge and then jogged to the tree line where the others waited.

"Lotta, Eryn, Mieta, and Rhul," the Sirra designated each with a glance, "you are the best archers. I would have you remain here." She glanced sunward. It was riding low in the sky.

"They will not be expecting us," said Sirra Alaine to the rest of the troop. "Descend with all haste to the plateau, then spread yourselves out under cover of the forest.

"Rhul, allow us time to get in position, as you judge it,

and then send them a steady hail of arrows until we engage them. Then you must join us as soon as may be."

The senior archer nodded.

"Remember," the Sirra gathered all eyes, "if you fight hand to hand with a Memteth, they will use their teeth if disarmed."

All but the archers rapidly disappeared down the trail.

Sirra Alaine turned to solemnly regard Thera who determinedly followed her.

The Sirra sighed heavily.

"Lady, I would that you remain here. Let those of us trained to fight deal now with the Memteth," she forestalled Thera's protest with a raised hand, "you have done well, more than well." Her voice was low and her gaze somber, "The Salvai Keiris...does not thrive of late." The Sirra's brindled brows drew down and she looked toward the black smoke rising against the sky, "she is not tranquil of mind, and her body fails now also.

"I have seen how you put the heart in these," she gestured after the departed troop. "You commune with the Elanraigh and it treats you as its own. You have the gift of joining, and of reading hearts, I do believe." As Thera opened her mouth to protest, the Sirra raised her hand in an open-palmed plea, "You are too valuable to put at risk."

"Sirra! I will not sit aside and let all the others risk themselves."

"Lady Thera," The Sirra Alaine fixed a stern gaze upon her and it was as if a hand were laid firmly across her mouth. "You do yourself no discredit with any here. You know I am right in this."

Thera flashed a fulminating glance over the Sirra and read much. Impatience, yes, but also, disconcertingly, a very genuine concern for her.

The Sirra's impassive features would reveal nothing to most observers, yet Thera read that the Sirra burned to be with her troop. Here she was, detained by a headstrong young noblewoman who *might* choose to use common sense.

Thera felt her neck warming. *Why, I have fought Memteth, and destroyed their ship!* A thought came unbidden, *As Duke Leon's daughter, and Heir, I could take command of this troop and have my way.*

Sudden shame overcame her. Thera chewed her lip. *I take command? Oh? When I almost killed the sea hawk in my single-mindedness when attacking the Memteth leader? Look at the Sirra, an experienced fighter, who knows how to protect those in her charge.*

Thera folded her arms behind her back, at parade rest, a stance and gesture she unconsciously copied of her father.

"Then Sirra, at the One Tree we will meet, if not before."

The Sirra bowed slightly at receiving the ritual sending and bestowed her rare smile.

CHAPTER 20

*S*irra Alaine jogged down the path, sliding on loose scree. She leapt a rocky ledge, and disappeared into the trees far below.

Thera turned and walked back to the archers. Rhul nodded to her, then waved her group forward to the cliff edge. Thera hesitated, and then joined them. Hunkered down behind the lip of rock, the women quietly exchanged words as they checked their weapons.

A Memteth's triumphant cry suddenly echoed over the plateau. Thera scrambled to her knees in time to see a soldier fall back from position on Elankeep's east battlement, an arrow lodged in the breast.

Frowning, Rhul silently bent over the contents of the small leather bag she had detached from her belt; extra string, fletch, chamois.

Lotta, though, thumped her fist against the rock and cursed. Rhul's fingers locked on Lotta's wrist, restraining her. The look Lotta gave Rhul was strange and staring. Finally Lotta crumpled, sliding down the rock, the iron studs in her leathers grating against the stone. Giving Lotta a piercing look, Rhul released her and bent again to string her bow.

Lotta tugged off her helmet and jabbed her hands through the sweat-dampened tangle of her hair. Lying back against the rock face, she rolled her head to face Rhul. "That was Avra struck."

"Lotta. You cannot know that at this distance."

"I know it." Lotta raised herself to glare at the besieged keep again. "*When* do we strike?" She plucked her bowstring, "*I* will give that winding horn a new hole to blow through."

The raider whose arrow had struck Lotta's friend continued to yowl at the defenders. Then a many-voiced howling and banging of shields arose from the Memteth.

Thera and her companions scrambled again to the ledge. "There!" gasped Thera, pointing. On the west tower battlement, stood a tall woman, robed and veiled. She was flanked by a slender figure bearing a bow. The woman disregarded the Memteth below, and was facing the cliff where Rhul's small troop lay hidden.

"Blessings be!" moaned Rhul. "What can possess our Salvai to so expose herself?"

Thera was barely conscious of those beside her; she had fallen into deep rapport. She saw in close detail the face that was only a white blur to her physical eyes. To her inward vision, the Salvai stood before her; pale complexioned, her grey eyes glittering like steel shards. *There is not much resemblance to mother!* The sharp features of this face glowed with feverish interest as the Salvai similarly examined her. Thera read satisfaction, and underlying that, a wistful sadness. She felt the sensation of a cool, thin hand caressing her cheek.

"*I have long been expecting you, Thera ep Chadwyn...niece of mine.*"

"*Aunt Keiris?*" Thera's surprise at her aunt's gentle tones must have registered in her mental voice.

A rueful smile twitched the Salvai's thin lips, then her face sobered and her lips parted as if to use physical voice...

Jarringly, Thera was again fully present in her physical body; the Salvai only a distant blue-robed figure on the northwest parapet of Elankeep. Aware that it was the Elanraigh who had abruptly parted them, Thera's startled exclamation died unsent as she now saw the Memteth arrow arcing its trajectory toward the figure of her aunt.

Surely the Elanraigh has warned my aunt, why then does she remain unmoving?

With a thin scream, more like the keening of a hawk than human voice, Thera cried aloud.

Sound broke out all about her. Memteth heads swiveled, and from their mouths came hoarse cries of alarm. Rhul barked commands and the archers rose to their feet to send a sleet of arrows down upon the Memteth.

A wind shouldered past her, "*Therra, Therrra.*" Whether Sussara was scolding or encouraging, Thera was too stricken to consider. The small elemental flung itself toward the arrow, but its energy deflected it only slightly. Thera saw her aunt stagger from the blow. Gasping, hands clenched at her own breast, Thera wavered where she stood on the precipice as her aunt half-turned, and then fell.

Thera pressed the back of her hand against her lips. "*Elanraigh forgive! I have betrayed the presence of the troop, and still did not save the Salvai from injury.*"

"Rhul...?" she cried.

The archer, frowning furiously, spared a quick glance at Thera. "I do not know..." she muttered, then her expression cleared a little, "...Ah, look!"

Below, Thera saw the Memteth now clumped together,

their shields over their heads, forming a rough square as they tried to escape the deadly rain of arrows. The archers' rapid fire impressed her, for she knew what strength it took to use the longbow. Their movements were fluid and sure.

Thera saw the jeering raider fall sprawled on the grass, an arrow through his throat. Another nearby was struck through the eye and fell heavily, dead before he hit the earth. The Elankeep troop charged from the tree line.

"Hold!" commanded Rhul of her archers.

The Memteth were forced from their sheltering to engage the Elankeep swords. The clash of steel echoed off the cliff face. Thera heard a few faint cheers from the Elankeep battlements.

Young Edred, small and quick, was yipping fox-like cries as she swung her sword, dancing in and out of her opponent's reach.

Thera saw Sirra Alaine slam her small round shield inside a Memteth's larger one and she plunged her sword in his side. Pushing him away with her foot, Alaine freed her sword and turned immediately to assist Alba, who was hard pressed.

Alba's opponent hissed as he turned to face Sirra Alaine.

The raider the Sirra had just gutted began to crawl after her, almost tangling her feet before he lay still.

Rhul turned to Thera, her teeth bared in a grim smile. "Lady, odds are in *our* favor now."

The archer shoved back and bid the others, "Come now, soldiers of Elankeep, let us cleanse the forest of this horror." The small group plunged down the same game trail the Sirra Alaine had taken.

Thera, biting at the skin around her thumbnail, returned her attention to the fight.

A member of the Elankeep troop below had lost her

sword and now sought desperately to evade her opponent. She was armed only with dagger and shield against a Memteth swinging a broadsword. The swordswoman ducked a blow that whistled past her head. No. The blow must have glanced her helm, for the helmet clanged onto the rocks. The blonde-haired swordswoman, bleeding at her hairline, tucked and rolled. She was on her feet again, swiftly, swiping with her arm at the blood running into her eyes. The Memteth growled low and pressed on; the swordswoman giving ground steadily.

The Elankeep soldier must have been half-blind with the blood flow from her scalp wound, and Thera could see that she would soon be trapped against the cliff face. Jittering with the necessity of doing something, Thera desperately eyed the longbows Rhul and the archers had left with her. She stood only a head taller than the bow itself.

"Ne'er-do-naught," she muttered through clenched teeth, "just do it, you've drawn a bow before."

Thera clutched the nearest bow. Lotta's, she thought. She quickly slotted an arrow from Rhul's quiver, and drew. Her arm quivered, and sweat trickled down her sides. She could not sustain enough pull. Muttering Shamic's favorite curse, she gritted her teeth and drew again. Finally her breath gusted out. She had no hope of hitting her target.

The two combatants were closer. Thera could no longer see the Elankeep soldier, who was under the overhang of the cliff, but the Memteth was right below her. He roared as his sword sliced the air.

Thera heard a scuffle of loose rock, and small boulders bounced past the Memteth's legs. A human cry of pain echoed off the cliff rock.

The Memteth raider paused in his attack. An almost

reverent expression transfigured his features. He crooned words as he slowly raised the broadsword over his head.

Desperate, Thera grasped the largest rock she could lift with two hands and with a gabbled prayer to all powers of good, she shuffled as near the edge as she dared, and heaved it. Her pulse drummed in her ears as she watched the seemingly slow passage of her rock through the air. After a pause she measured in heartbeats, it plunged. She dropped to her knees at the cliff edge, her fingers gripping the rim. Her rock was on a true course for the Memteth's head.

His muscles were bunched for the killing blow, his gleaming sword at the apex of its arc, when Thera's missile impacted. The raider's head snapped back, his amazed gaze meeting hers even as his eyes glazed and he toppled.

Dizzy with relief, Thera dropped her head onto her arms. The only sound she heard was the pounding of her heart.

CHAPTER 21

A fading echo — Thera became aware that someone called her name. She stilled her breathing, listening past the pounding of her blood.

What?

She crawled toward the cliff edge. *It must be the injured Elankeep soldier who called.* She leaned forward just as a Memteth swung up over the cusp.

Fear screamed along Thera's nerves, contracting her muscles. *Run!*

The forest's energies rose like shimmering heat, only a few horse strides away, behind where the Memteth now stood.

She felt her vision darkening around the edges. Yet some other, wiser, part of her knew that fear would make her careless, and suppressed the overwhelming rush of panic. She was aware of her hand moving, drawing the Sha'Lace, of her feet shifting slightly, finding the right balance. Captain Lydia's endless drills ,blessings on her patience, schooled her muscles beyond the fear.

She forced herself to read the Memteth. He had moved,

swift as a lizard, to place himself between her and the forest. That escape was cut off. Yet, Thera now realized, he did not understand the true nature of the protection it offered her. To the Memteth it was merely a place she could hide from him. He loathed the strange, dark forest — but he did not understand that it was an intelligence, and that it roused against him.

Thera understood from this reading that he felt only that the forest was unwholesome. He believed the death of his companions in the ancient grove was caused by the *witch* in the keep.

Thera pulled free of the reading. This Memteth did not have even a portion of the intelligence that she had read in the captain of the Memteth ship, the one whose face she had scarred. This was the crudest of soldiers.

The Memteth was relaxing somewhat from his crouch. He ran his yellow eyes over Thera, then stared at her face. He straightened, looming tall over her.

He sheathed his sword.

Incredulous, Thera watched. *Does he mean to let me go?*

She shifted her weight, holding herself light, ready to run.

The Memteth also shifted. Keeping directly in front of her, he lifted his arms wide.

As if he was herding geese! Was Thera's absurd thought. Her hand sweated on the jeweled hilt of her dagger. She breathed deeply, loosening her grip, then readjusting.

May the Elanraigh accept my spirit if it should be freed this hour. Thera felt calmer as she sent her prayer.

The Memteth did not move closer.

Thera twitched in surprise as he began to sway — a slow, side-to-side movement. His yellow-eyed gaze remained fixed upon her. His lips parted and he growled, low and sonorous.

Thera felt her neck hairs lift.

The Memteth's throat was flushing bright scarlet.

Thera studied him, looking for some clue to this strange behavior. Her confusion mounted when she realized she could no longer read him.

The Memteth's spoke a word, "*Sinzet...*" he laughed to himself and resumed the strange humming. From under hooded lids, his eyes gleamed at her.

Thera flinched, body and soul. The heat of outrage and horror pulsed at her temples.

He swayed, his eyes drooped shut, and Thera sprinted for safety.

Quick as a toad's tongue he snatched at her, grabbing the neck of her tunic. Twisting his hand in the soft kidskin, he swung her against him.

Thera slashed with her dagger, but he eluded her effortlessly and her blade slid against the iron bands that fastened his cuirass. Deftly he shifted his hold on her, gripping her weapon hand.

He will snap my wrist like a dry twig!

His thumb pressed down, numbing her fingers.

He slid his yellow gaze into her vision. "*Ne-sinzet,*" he said, matter-of-factly.

Thera's *Sha'Lace* dropped to the ground and trampled under their feet as she struggled.

He snorted, a light flaring in his eyes, as she tore at his restraining fingers with her teeth. He grunted more words at her, sounding not particularly angry, then swept his foot behind her legs.

She fell to the ground, knocking the breath from her lungs. Her nostrils filled with his musky scent as he dropped to his knees astride her. Shoving his finger in her mouth, he laughed as if he encouraged her to bite him again, then he slid his hand heavily down her body.

Thera did scream then. She screamed when she realized that no act of will would make this horror stop. She sent a desperate, powerful call to the Elanraigh and thrashed wildly.

He slapped her. Once. Twice. "*Ne!*" he growled.

Her mind began to retreat — there was the Memteth kneeling above her, blocking the sun, then, abruptly, he was gone.

HER EARS RANG. It did not stop, not as she rolled away, realized what had happened, or crawled to retrieve her Sha'Lace.

The impact of the huge grey wolf's hurtling body striking the Memteth carried both combatants to the cliff's edge. They fought savagely, noisily, Farnash snarling as their bodies tumbled and twisted, scattering rocks and debris. The Memteth roared, struggling to rise. He heaved his body upward unable to shake off the wolf.

The Memteth flailed at Farnash, beating him about the head, but the grey wolf continued to grind the raider's arm in his jaws. His eyes glared into the Memteth's contorted face. The wolf's hind feet sent small rocks bouncing over the cliff as he dug his claws into the grainy dirt.

Thera crawled toward them, horrified at Farnash's peril so near the cliff edge. She heard herself whimper in fear. Farnash strained, gathering his haunches, as he resisted the Memteth's strength. The Memteth suddenly yelled and rolled, in a massive effort to loft the wolf over the cliff.

There was a snap as Farnash's jaws bit through bone and

the raider's arm fell useless to his side. Hissing, the Memteth lifted his legs, attempting to wrap them around the wolf's ribcage. Farnash leaped and twisted sinuously, snapping his jaws a finger's breadth from the Memteth's throat.

Thera felt her own lips curl in a feral snarl as the Memteth rolled to his knees, his uninjured arm and hand reaching for his blade. Farnash leaped again, this time slashing the Memteth's throat. The raider's blood sprayed in swift rhythmic pulses.

Farnash stood panting, legs braced and head lowered, his eyes never leaving the Memteth. The wolf's sides heaved and his raised ruff twitched across his shoulders. Stiff-legged, he circled the Memteth, growling low in his throat as the body shuddered in its death throes. Finally the wolf backed away, his pelt still flinching.

In the new stillness, the voices of the Elanraigh and Teacher burst in upon Thera's awareness. She shut them out. She felt vile and sick. She had been crawling, Sha'Lace in hand, toward the Memteth, determined to kill him before he killed Farnash. She was covered in the Memteth's blood.

Thera slumped. Her arms, suddenly heavy, went limp. As if from a distance, she watched her fingers slowly unclench to drop the knife. Folding her arms around her knees, she hugged herself, trying to stop the shaking. *His foul taste is scum in my mouth.* Great dry, heaves of retching convulsed her body.

Farnash sniffed the dead Memteth. After shaking himself, he padded, ears flat, over to Thera. Gently as he would caress a sleeping cub, he lapped her blood-spattered cheek.

Thera felt something release in her, and through gritted teeth, she began to moan — a strange keening sound she had never heard herself make before.

Farnash butted her with his huge head. She flung her arms about him, burying her face in his thick fur. His coat smelled of forest and clean air. Slowly he eased himself down.

Thera watched the sky darken. A small wind ruffled the wolf's silvery guard hairs.

The dead Memteth lay silhouetted, a jagged darkness against the evening sky. Thera shuddered.

"*You are Clan*," sent the grey wolf, licking blood from his muzzle. "*We protect our own.*"

CHAPTER 22

"*L*ady Thera!" A hand shook Thera's shoulder.

Thera slowly released the grey wolf's scruff. His eyes gleamed in the light of many torches. It was Alba bending over her, her forehead knotted. Her eyes widened as Thera winced.

"I'm...unharmed, First Sword." Thera tried to twist her mouth into some sort of reassuring smile; she could not. Alba continued to stare. Her hand tilted Thera's face to the light.

"Demon's heart, Lady!"

"The blood isn't mine..." said Thera, "...not mine."

There was a scuffling at the cliff edge as two Elankeep soldiers stripped weapons and gear off the dead Memteth. They rolled the corpse over the edge.

"We're burning 'em." Alba explained, glancing aside at the huge wolf. "It's over, Lady Thera."

Thera hugged the Elanraigh wolf and then raised herself stiffly. She could see the moon was high with a few tattered clouds tangling the stars. A friendly wind was blowing from shore to sea, dissipating the dark smoke from the pyre of Memteth dead.

Women's voices called from the plateau below, "*He's* a big 'un. Who got him?"

"The Lady Thera!" was the reply shouted down by Alba's two guards.

"No," Thera rasped. She cleared her throat. "No. It was Farnash. I owe my life to Farnash." Thera's hand searched for him. The grey wolf flagged his ears and nosed her hand. He too had risen to his feet, alert and proud.

Thera felt a mental nudge. "First Sword Alba, I present Farnash, grey wolf of the Elanraigh."

Alba's eyes glinted whitely, but she nodded her head, "I believe we met once before."

The grey wolf gaped his jaws in a good-humored fashion. His head butted Thera's hand once more and he turned, moving swiftly to the trees. He turned at the tree line. "*Sky Sister.*"

"*Blessings,*" sent Thera, trusting that her heart would color the inadequate sending.

"I MUST SEE MY AUNT — I feel it is most urgent."

"Impossible," replied Dama Ainise, the Salvai's First Lady.

The healing mistress, Rozalda, drew her thick, straight brows together. "Lady Thera, our Salvai sleeps deeply. I have given her a draught to ease her pain."

"Her wound...?"

Mistress Rozalda looked back toward the Salvai's chamber door, and her voice was low and troubled. "It is not a severe wound. It is not *that* which takes her strength, though she is no longer young."

Dama Ainise removed a filmy cloth from her sash, fluttered it open and touched it to her eyes. A sweet perfume wafted. "Rozalda! The wound is terrible! So much blood," She pressed the cloth against her lips, her blue-veined eyelids fluttering.

Rozalda frowned, but said nothing.

Thera laid her hand on the healer's arm. "I must see her myself; she might have words for me beyond your hearing."

As the healing mistress stared forthrightly at her, Thera flushed. Her words sounded presumptuous, even to her own ears. Who was she to claim powers here, at the Salvai's seat?

"I am sure if she had words for anyone, she would have spoken to me," quavered Dama Ainise in her courtly accent, "for I have been her First Lady all these years."

The healing mistress' warm hand suddenly covered Thera's. "As the Elanraigh wills, you *shall* see her." With a swirl of green robe, she turned.

Blessings be! Thera sighed with some relief and followed in Mistress Rozalda's wake. Dama Ainise's light footsteps hurried behind them.

Ever since Alba had escorted Thera into the keep, voices, barely audible, had been swirling around Thera's head — their whispers urging her make haste to this meeting.

They walked a long corridor slotted with latticed openings through which moonlight shone like paving stones at their feet. Mistress Rozalda indicated the Salvai's door to Thera, and then stepped aside. Dama Ainise making as if to follow Thera, was halted by Rozalda plucking and holding her sleeve. With one heartrending glance at the Salvai's closed door, Ainise allowed herself to be gathered into the crook of the healer's arm.

The torch nearby shivered, sending shadows dancing up the wall. Rozalda murmured, as if to herself, "The wind rises." She patted the shoulder of Dama Ainise, who wept into her gauze linen.

Thera's hand rested on the door's surface. Red cedar. Alive, and thrumming welcome. *The wind rises?* Something in the healing mistress's tone held her—though the planes of Rozalda's face were carved in shadow, Thera saw a silvery sheen on her cheek.

Mistress Rozalda pulled the hood of her cloak forward. "Lady, there are many wounded to be seen and tended. We will leave you here, if that be your will."

Pressured by a sense of urgency from within the chamber, Thera nodded, and then pushed on the door, which opened easily to her touch. "I thank you, both," she murmured. "I will stay with my aunt awhile."

Rozalda bowed.

Dama Ainise's slender fingers clenched her cloak into a tight gather of material at her neck. "Tell her we love her..." The First Lady's lips moved as if she shaped words she could not speak. Rozalda placed a firm hand under her elbow and turned her away.

Thera entered the tower chamber. The lattices were thrown back from the windows — one overlooking the sea, and the other facing the darkness of the Elanraigh. A restless fire gusted in the fireplace. The chamber was spare and neat. Salvai Keiris lay unmoving in the tall, canopied bed.

Thera's temples throbbed. She read the impression of a soul almost beating itself against the walls in its eagerness to be gone. The air was heavy with the scent of herbs and fragrant ointment. Her aunt's left arm and shoulder were neatly bandaged and bound. Her other arm lay alongside her body on top of the immaculate cover.

Quietly Thera pulled a small, woven-twig chair beside the bed. She gathered the Salvai's free hand into her own, and waited.

Settling her mind, she imagined herself sinking into a deep, quiet pond.

In that stillness they met.

"*I always thought you disliked me,*" blurted Thera, surprised again at the impression of a gentle caress. The Salvai's ghostly image sighed, a thin breath of sound. "*No!*" Then, "*Yes. It was envy I suffered from, child — Elanraigh forgive me my mortal blindness. Envy since I first saw you, my young, half-sister's only child. You were such a pretty child, chasing the salamanders that basked on the sunny walls of your mother's garden. I envied that child. You see, I knew the Elanraigh already loved you in a way it had never expressed with me. Forest-mind told me that you would be my successor — and more — a Salvai blessed with the old gifts.*

"*It was difficult for me to accept. The Elanraigh freely gave you its love.* Keiris continued, *All I ever wanted was for the Elanraigh to love me, and I thought that by dedication, duty, and will alone I could accomplish that.*"

The pale figure in Thera's vision looked yearningly toward the Elanraigh, then turned her face toward Thera. She continued, "*I think the Elanraigh took pity on me when first I escaped here, to Elankeep. I was a woman long past receiving the Sha'Lace. Your mother, Fideiya, was only fifteen when promised to ArNarone's heir. I had rejected suitor after suitor, 'till my father was long past patience and swore that he would arrange for my settlement — will I, nil I.*

"*It was a different bonding I craved. I always envied my older half-sister's relationship with the Elanraigh. It is your other aunt I speak of, Dysanna. Have you heard of her? She was dead long before you were ever born and when I was just sixteen. I dreamed* of being so loved by the Elanraigh. Everyone wondered that the Elanraigh would accept no new Salvai after Dysanna died. The Elanraigh mourned. As I grew I sensed the Elanraigh's need. I persisted in my prayers and finally the Elanraigh accepted. Blessings be. It was a good arrangement, I felt useful and at peace here. Though I knew the Elanraigh grieved as the hostility between the Ttamarini and Allenholme continued.

"Then one day, years after Dysanna's death, some Ttamarini came to Elankeep. Dysanna's son, Teckcharin, proposed a ritual union between us.

"By the One Tree! A half-bred savage! He must have sensed how I despised him, and how I cursed his father for ruining Dysanna.

"He stood silent, while their witch-woman spoke at length about a union between his folk and mine, as if such a thing could be. My sister suffered because such an alliance would not be tolerated by our people. She and the Ttamarini offers of peace were rejected out of hand. Your great-grandfather, Leif ArNarone and the Allenholme Council declared Dysanna as dead.

"As we stood there facing one another, that surly boy and I, I asked the winds of the Elanraigh to come and destroy them for their presumption!

"When my anger had stilled enough for me to once again sense my beloved Elanraigh, I felt only that it was both wounded and displeased by my outburst.

"So strong was my wish to please the Elanraigh that almost, for a moment I could bow to what it envisioned. Then I imagined that manling touching me — my mind went to darkness. I could not.

"I felt as if I smothered, and I flung the Elanraigh my refusal. The Elanraigh could have demanded my life of me, and I would have given it, but I could not do this. I do not remember what my rage and fear drove me to say to the Ttamarini's young chief.

"*My women came and I was led away in their care. When I awoke the next day, the Ttamarini were gone.*"

The ghostly Salvai trembled, and the thin hands came up to cover her face.

"*That was almost twenty winters ago. I have tried my best. Though the Elanraigh and I were loyal to each other, I was never its beloved. Not like Dysanna was, not like you are. I am the withered seed,*" whispered the frail voice. "*Yours is the life force it waits for.*"

Thera's brow puckered slightly as she stroked the cool hand she held. She knew there were women like her aunt Keiris who would never be life sworn, or joined with another. However, instinctively, she knew this withholding of self was disastrous in a Salvai. She considered the way she had responded to Chamakin, and felt heat rising to her skin. Yet, what if the first time she had faced another's desire had been the bestial Memteth on the ridge. How then? She shivered.

The Elanraigh gently nudged her attention;it forest-mind's will lay like a mentor's hand on her shoulder. She knew what the dying Salvai needed to know, and was too proud to ask. "*The Elanraigh welcomes you, aunt,*" Thera sent, "*as beloved sister. Be at peace. We shall all meet again at the One Tree.*"

Wind gusted through the latticed window and shadows crowded along the wall.

Surprised, Thera heard the voice she knew as Teacher's call softly, "*Keiris.*"

The vision of Keiris turned with her pale arms reaching and thin face transfigured.

"*Dysanna!*" Keiris cried in joyful recognition.

CHAPTER 23

*A*t last her aunt had the union she craved. The Elanraigh winds blew joyously in the chamber, tossing Thera's hair and dancing the flames. Thera released her aunt's cold hand. "Peace to you Salvai Keiris. May the One Tree guide and bless you."

Wearily, Thera rose to her feet, stretched, and moved to close the shutters against the wind. *Enough*, she admonished, as the shutter pulled from her grasp. The winds wrapped her in a caress and then careened toward the darkness of the Elanraigh. The sudden silence pressed itself against her as she gently drew the coverlet over her aunt's body.

THE SALVAI'S women were waiting outside the chamber door, some wept softly.

"We heard the wind," Mistress Rozalda explained.

Thera leaned against the wooden door frame, too tired

to wonder. "She went to the Elanraigh. She's with Teach–
the Lady Dysanna now."

"Blessings be," was the women's ragged response. Dama
Ainise sobbed and with trembling fingers, pressed her gauze
scarf to her lips.

The women clustered, as if irresolute, in front of Thera
for a moment. One turned a raised brow inquiringly to the
Healing Mistress. Rozalda shook her head, and with a brief
gesture of her hand waved them on.

The ladies filed into her aunt's chamber. Thera swayed,
her bones felt liquid with weariness. The Healing Mistress
placed a firm arm about her. "I will show you to a room
where you can rest, Lady. We will take care of Lady Keiris
now."

WHEN THERA WOKE, she lay a moment, taking in the details
of the room where she rested. The wood furniture was of
simple design, gleaming with the hand-rubbed glow of a
bride's treasured heirloom. There was a bedstead, wash-
stand, copper mirror, trunk, and desk. An intricately carved
spinning-wheel chair stood in one corner. Thick, woolly
sheepskin rugs lay scattered on the smooth planking of the
floor. Someone must just have been in to replenish the fire
against the morning chill, for though the flames snapped
cheerfully, the air in the chamber was cool.

Thera inhaled deeply of the moist air, rich with forest
scents, wafting through the one window. The chamber was
homely and pleasing. All she remembered of it from last
night was the bed's welcoming softness.

Flinging back the cover, she rose briskly. A kettle of water was simmering by the fire. Thera ladled some of the warm, herb-scented water into a ceramic washbasin. Stripping off her outer garments, she lathered herself with the fragrant soap. "Ssst," Thera hissed at the pain. She lifted her hands from the stinging water and eyed the numerous cuts and abrasions.

A Lady is known by her hands, Nan would say. Thera paused, then plunged her hands back into the warm water. *I will be their Salvai, and something more. Like Teacher, and like the Ttamarini's Maiya. A lady, yes, but also a warrior and a wise woman.* She sighed. *Someday, with the blessings and help of the Elanraigh.* The corners of Thera's mouth lifted a little. She could almost feel Nan's presence, like a warmth at her back. It was a good feeling. Abruptly she sluiced away the soap and dried with the fire-warmed towel.

A green gown, trimmed with amber at neck and cuff, had been laid out.

"Amber!" she murmured, reverently touching the beads, "Sacred gift of ancient trees." Biting her lip, Thera smoothed her fingers over the gown's material; a very fine wool, sliding like silk between her fingers. She held the gown against her, and then slipped it over her head. Raising her arms to lift her hair free, she twirled in front of the polished copper mirror. The gown clung to her breast and hips, its silky length brushing her ankles delicately. Her hair was wild, not braided or groomed as Nan would have had it.

Thera suddenly paused in her twirling; *I'm someone else, someone exotic and beautiful.* The woman in the mirror smiled seductively. *What if Chamakin could see me now?* Running her hands over her hips, she coyly turned, looking back over her shoulder at her hair hanging long and thick to the small of her back.

In the shining copper mirror, she saw her red tunic reflected, neatly folded, on top of the cedar chest. Someone must have retrieved the Elankeep troop's packs from where they had dropped them. She walked over and touched the garment. She felt her eyes well, an intense rush of love and homesickness. Someone had also cleaned her kidskin shirt and pants. In addition, her boots were supple and shining again.

Thera stared. Through most of her life she had thoughtlessly accepted, just such kind of services, today she felt warmed by the quiet thoughtfulness of these unbidden attentions.

With a small sigh, she pulled off the lovely gown, laying it aside. *That elegance is* for some other time and place. Instead, Thera slid the leather tunic over her head, and turned again to the mirror.

I am changed, she observed. Reflected in the polished copper sheet, her hair was still a dark, cloudy nimbus framing her face. *My face, this piercing, direct gaze, which is different.* Thera blinked. *I'm thinner.* She leaned forward, poking at her cheekbones. *My eyes seem bigger somehow and more green than before. Well, perhaps that is because my skin is darkened from the sun.* Thera touched her cheekbone again. Nan would have been scolding and applying goat milk to her skin in attempt to lighten it.

Her lips quirked ruefully. *So,* she thought, *I'm no Cythian Beauty, that is certain.* She fingered the upward sweep of her brows, like dark wings, rather than a fashionable arch. She watched her lips curve to a smile, a mouth too large to ever inspire Cythian songs of rosebud lips. "So. Well, it balances my chin."

She tilted that chin slightly. Chamakin admired her and wanted her. She knew that. She remembered the feel of his fingers on her skin, and the way his breath had quickened when he had touched her.

With a shaky "Huhh." of dismissal, she made vigorous use of a hairbrush. The pain of the tangles and knots soon diminished the disturbing sensations her thoughts of Chamakin had aroused.

She worked her hair into a single braid and then swung open the chamber door. An Elankeep guard was on duty outside her chamber.

"Blessings." Thera greeted her. She did not recall meeting this woman last night. "Where will I find the Sirra Alaine, or Mistress Rozalda?"

The guard limped as she turned; her face was swollen and blue with bruising. Her hairline was shaved back on the right side, exposing a sutured gash.

Thera's eyes widened as she recognized her. This was the same woman whose Memteth attacker Thera had killed with the stone.

The guard nodded stiffly, and she spoke from one side of her swollen mouth, "The Elanraigh's blessings on you, Lady. I will escort you to the dining hall. I believe the Sirra is still there with the Damas."

"I thank you." They turned to walk. "Swordswoman...?"

"I am Swordswoman Enid, Lady." The guard's gaze met Thera's firmly, "My sword is in your service." Thera nodded. The young swordswoman had uttered the ritual pledge with heartfelt warmth. The Swordswoman continued down the passageway. Thera followed Enid's limping progress, her brows creased in thought. *Father inspires just such looks from his soldiers, I have witnessed how his troops regard him.* Thera felt a heat burning her face. *These are my soldiers? If I am Salvai, it will be so.*

At the foot of a steep and narrow stair they turned toward a wider hall. Swordswoman Enid stood to the side of the arched entrance and drawing a deep breath, announced,

"Lady Thera ep Chadwyn Ned'ArNarone, Heir to Allenholme."

Thera's cheeks kept their glowing warmth as she entered the hall on the heels of such formality. She was further disconcerted to find the Sirra, Alba, and all but one of six Damas standing, to honor her rank.

Only one elder Dama remained seated. Her withered-apple cheeks puffed as her head swayed inquiringly to the women on either side of her.

"What be amiss *now*?" she demanded. She spoke with the loud, quavering voice of any deaf elder. The plump Dama standing beside her bent to whisper in the elder's ear.

"Eh? There's what? I have not finished my tea, Ella."

At that moment, the elder Dama caught sight of Thera in the doorway, and clasped her hands in a childish gesture of delight. "Ah, 'tis my Lady Dysanna come back. Blessings be!" The old Dama's hand scrabbled on the table for her linen. She dabbed at the tears that quickly filled her eyes. Then her gaze became worried and confused. "How can this be now?"

Thera moved forward with a nod to Sirra Alaine and the company in general, and crouched by the elder Dama's side.

"My name is Thera, Dama." Thera patted the hand which clasped and clung to hers. The old woman's bones felt thin under the loose skin.

"Lady Dysanna was my elder-aunt. I am the daughter of Lady Fideiya ep Chadwyn and Duke Leon ArNarone."

The Dama's pale blue eyes examined Thera's features. When she finally met Thera's smiling eyes, her own gaze seemed more lucid. She disengaged her hand from Thera's light hold, and moved it to touch Thera's face. Then the elder shot a look at Dama Ella, "I remember Fideiya," she stated, "a winsome, dutiful, girl *she* was. This be her child?"

"Yes, Dama Byrtha, yes." affirmed Ella. "Come now. Let me take you to your room for a nice rest."

Byrtha snatched her arm away from Ella's grasp. "I've yet to say to the girl."

Dama Byrtha turned her shoulder on Ella's long-suffering expression and leaned toward Thera, "I was Salvai Dysanna's First Lady, a long time ago." The old woman's eyes were soft with tears again, "Elanraigh bless her sweet soul." She grasped Thera's hand and tugged Thera toward her, "Will you come and talk with me?"

"Of course I will," replied Thera in the same conspiratorial tone.

The old woman sighed contentedly and patted Thera's cheek. "They be always taking me off to my chamber, you know," she said with a recriminating look around the table.

As Dama Ella assisted the elder woman from the dining hall, Thera turned to the others. "Please do be seated, all." Thera eyed the chair at the head of the table that sister Rozalda indicated for her.

"It is your right by birth," insisted Dama Ainise, "you are Lady Thera, daughter of Allenholme, and your lady mother is connected to the Royal House." As Thera sat, the others resumed their places. Ainise beckoned to a slender, brown-eyed girl, who placed a bowl of hot tea and a small loaf and cheese in front of Thera.

"Is that all there is for Lady Thera, Egrit?" demanded Dama Ainise of the girl.

It was Rozalda who answered in her calm voice. "The cookhouse is as yet in disorder, Ainise, and we wish to give the injured some days of rest, then we may present meals more suitable."

"The injured — of course. Very well, then." Ainise nodded and dismissed the brown-eyed girl with a wave of her gauze linen. Her fine brows arched inquiringly as she surveyed Thera. "I had laid out a gown for you, Lady. Suitable for a Salvai's own. I thought it would please you to change from your...riding clothes."

Thera had just bitten heartily into the nutty loaf. Chewing and swallowing, she considered her response. She had no wish to offend her aunt Keiris' former Lady companion.

Thera answered straightly, "I dress to be useful here." She wiped her fingers, and laid her hands flat upon the table. "I am not accustomed to being idle." Her glance crossed Sirra Alaine's, who regarded her with some inscrutable, half-smiling expression.

"I am good with the horses, even our old Sirra at home has found no fault with the care I give them, *and* I am a fair fisher." Thera did not miss the expression on Dama Ainise's face. Feeling some rising annoyance, which soon dissolved into amusement, Thera observed that elegant Dama dabbing at her lips as if in distaste. *By the One Tree! I'll have all understand I am not a useless ornament.*

She eyed these folk of Elankeep, her folk, should the Elanraigh proclaim her. Thera's gaze rested a moment on the brown-eyed girl, Egrit, who had brought her tea. The girl smiled shyly. Thera smiled back. "I cannot cook, however." She glanced to Sirra Alaine. "I hope that Sirra Alaine might allow me to study more of weaponry. I do not intend to be a soldier, but I would like to be stronger, and more skilled." She smiled to the gathering, "I hope that, except when necessary on High Days, we may dispense with formalities at table and hall. I intend to be a student here — yours and the Elanraigh's. I know I can learn so much, from all of you." An amazed expression still flexed Dama Ainise's delicate brows. Mistress Rozalda nodded attentively. Thera

hurried on. "When I was at Allenholme, it was my particular wish to learn many such things, you see. My father
could see no harm in my learning more of the daily tasks of
our folk. Indeed, he was proud of me for wanting to learn."
Thera's chin lifted slightly.

She saw the Sirra Alaine exchange a satisfied look with
the Healing Mistress.

Dama Ainise's shapely fingernails tapped the table,
"Really! *Dear* Lady Thera, you were a *child* then and it seems
your father indulged you. Believe me, in the south, in
Cythia, no gently reared young woman would ..."

Rozalda placed her large square hand on Ainise's arm,
who turned an annoyed frown on the Healing Mistress, but
subsided.

"Lady Thera," said Rozalda, blandly ignoring Ainise's
annoyance, "we, here at Elankeep, will honor your desire for
learning and appreciation of the life paths of others."

Mistress Rozalda's homely face glowed as she leaned
toward Thera. "The Sirra Alaine has related to us what she
knows of your gifts, Lady. It seems to me, the Elanraigh has
declared its intention. You are the Elanraigh's choice to be
Salvai."

"The Elanraigh knows what saplings grow in its shade,"
intoned a small rosy Dama to Rozalda's left.

"Blessings be," murmured the Damas.

"Indeed," replied Rozalda. She looked at Ainise, her
hand lightly patting that lady's arm, "and no one here will
interfere with your chosen life path. Or the way you choose
to serve, as Salvai of the forest.

Thera relaxed a little. She turned to Dama Ainise, with a
smile that had won even Shamic over to many favored
projects of hers. "It is also true, Dama, that I have never
been to the King's court in Bole, or to Cythia. It would be

good for me to learn what I must of courtly manners, so I may be a credit to my people of the northern holding."

Dama Ainise brightened immediately. Tipping her head, she observed, "You are a beautiful girl, my dear, and not in the ordinary way. And innately graceful, I have observed. It would be my pleasure to instruct you in courtly refinements becoming to a Lady." Dama Ainise's smile froze just a little as she glanced at Sirra Alaine, "When you are finished with your other pursuits, of course."

As they rose from the table, Thera turned toward the arched window. "Sirra Alaine. A moment, if you will." The Sirra came to her side. "Do you have carrier birds here?" Thera asked wistfully.

The Sirra shook her head slowly. "The birds' roosting pen was destroyed in the Memteth attack. Most all the birds escaped...," her glance crossed Rozalda's who nodded confirmation, "...and will return when the stench of smoke abates."

"I must tell my father of the death of our folk at Shawl Bay. My mother may have sensed the Salvai Keiris' passing. She will be distressed. They both need to know that I am safe here at Elankeep."

Thera's fingers were white as she clenched her hands together. "*Elanraigh bless*," she sent, "*I need to know how fares Allenholme, and the folk there.*"

Sirra Alaine grunted a laugh at the others' expressions when at that very moment a white carrier bird landed on the stone sill of the window, folded its wings, and stretched its iridescent neck toward Thera.

CHAPTER 24

" *L* ady Thera!"

Thera glanced over her shoulder. It was Rozalda who called. Thera rose and quickly swiped her hands clean. She had been inspecting the trampled vegetable garden with Eryn and Rhul, hoping to find Mulberry a carrot treat. Word had come from the stable that her mare had been found. "Aye, Lady," Eryn had confirmed, "found her, sweet as you please, sauntering by Bridal Veil Falls."

Rozalda, dressed for travel, waited at the keep's main gate to speak with her. Thera picked her way through the rows of tubers. Her smile of greeting wavered as she saw swordswomen Lotta and Mieta exiting the gate with her aunt's linen-wrapped body carried on the bough-woven bier between them. Lotta's eyes looked bruised and weary, her expression grim.

Last night, at the sea cliff's edge, the assembled women of Elankeep had gathered to sing the Lament. They sent their voices into the wind both for the Salvai, and for swordswoman Avra, Lotta's closest companion, who had that day died of her wound.

To Thera's mild surprise, it was shy Egrit who stepped forward to lead them in song. She called out the ritual greeting, "Elanraigh bless. Beneath its boughs may they rest. May their voices sing to us on the wind."

The assembled women answered, "Blessings be."

That done, they waited as the sun set, their lit torches roaring in the wind. The Lament would be sung when the evening star rose in the west.

Red clouds like wind-tossed plumes faded from the sky. In the deepening amethyst hue gleamed the first faint pulsing of the evening star. The winds lapsed and Thera felt a prickling of anticipation. Egrit lifted her voice. The girl sang the Lament in an ancient dialect, the notes rose like seabirds on the wind then descended, evoking the rich, dark depths of earth. The Elanraigh's hymn vibrated along Thera's bones. She felt forest-mind bending benevolent and close all that night.

"LADY THERA!" Rozalda called again, startling Thera from her thoughts. The Healing Mistress smiled.

Thera quickened her pace. She had already been told that the Salvai's body was to be carried into the forest. The Healing Mistress was in charge of the small funeral procession. Rozalda was cloaked and booted for her journey. Thera looked after the small, solemn group that had passed, carrying the bier northward.

"Where will you take her?" asked Thera.

"The Elanraigh will guide us to her resting place." Rozalda craned her neck, trying to adjust the harness of her travel pack. "I know only that Keiris' place of meditation was a tree cave somewhere above the little falls."

Thera paused in the process of assisting the Healing Mistress in the settling of her pack harness.

"A tree cave?" repeated Thera.

"Yes." Rozalda shot her a look from under her heavy brows, then turned her head to slip on the pack's shoulder straps. "Every Salvai is guided to some special retreat in the forest, usually a tree cave. It is a place she can always go to when she feels the need to be alone. When the Salvai dies, the tree will take her in, and then will seal itself."

Thera stared.

Rozalda studied her a moment, then lifted her gaze to the forest. "What greater comfort, *I* think, than to be laid to rest in the living forest's heart.

"Well. You are to be Salvai now. All here will serve you well."

Thera blushed, "Mistress, the Elanraigh has not yet proclaimed me Salvai."

Rozalda was still a moment, "Well. Even if it awaits the proclaiming, it has shown us clearly that you are its Anointed." She glanced behind her, her expression thoughtful. "I do not like to leave you with Elankeep in disorder and wounded still under care, but all seems well on the way to being mended and I should not be more than two days away. Sirra Alaine will best assist you in all things. I would have you feel confident to trust her judgment.

"Dama Ainise is the highest ranked of Keiris' ladies, but she is not practical. I say this though I am fond of her, mind you. She has had many disappointments in her life.

"Her brother, you know, managed to ruin the family estates. He survives by attaching himself to those in a more elevated a sphere of influence. He communicates gossip regularly to Ainise, some of which is useful, and we in turn relay it to your father.

"Ah, I've surprised you," she gave Thera a wry smile. "We do not spend all our days tending gardens and sheep. Our duty is to protect the Elanraigh, and knowledge of what goes on beyond the Elanraigh's southern border is of importance in this task."

Thera laughed and shook her head.

"Now," continued Rozalda, "I see Egrit, in her own quiet way, has established herself as your attendant. Are you content with this?"

Thera was still bemused at Rozalda's picture of the Elankeep attendants winnowing through Bole and Cythian court gossip. No wonder there was such a very *large* flock of carrier birds kept here.

"Oh yes." She nodded in answer to Rozalda's last question, her eyes dancing. Quiet and determined, Egrit had set about making herself indispensible. "Very much. Her ways suit me — she seems to anticipate all my wants as if that were her gift."

Rozalda pursed her lips in a small smile, and nodded her understanding. "She is a good girl," the Healing Mistress added, "I'd thought to apprentice her to healing, but she is like to be an excellent maid to you. She was always such a shy girl, but she is a wildcat where your needs are concerned.

"Hmm. Well." She eyed the bearers who waited for her at the forest edge. "I'll be on my way then."

Rozalda waved her walking staff over her head, "Blessings be," she called out. Answering cries and waves came from those on the tower and in the gardens.

Eryn and Rhul drifted up beside Thera, as did other

Elankeep folk. They stood together, watching in silence as the small cortege entered the forest.

THERA HAD JUST DROPPED her arm from its final wave, when Alba trotted over to her side.

"My Lady, Salvai Thera. Could you join us in the south field? There is a difficulty."

Thera turned and walked at Alba's quick pace past the keep's east wall. Rhul and Eryn had silently fallen in behind them. Thera glanced sideways at Alba's face. Her expression was stern and pensive, but not alarmed. As they crested the rolling ground of the south field, Thera could see a knot of guards from the keep standing at the forest edge. Past these trees would be Bridal Veil Falls. Thera looked in awe; the trees here were old giants.

As they neared the others, Alba spoke rapidly. "We knew from what the Elanraigh told you, that there be Memteth dead in there. We meant to cleanse the forest of them," she gestured to a pile of dead wood ringed with stone, "but I sense something amiss. I am not sure enough of my sensing, Lady, and we do not wish to offend by entering here if we be not wanted."

Thera knew immediately what it was Alba and the others had sensed. Old trees are slow to wrath, but the heaviness of the anger stirred against the Memteth still hung in the air. She directed her thoughts to the ancient trees.

"Old Ones, if you will, we come to remove the bodies of those who offended you and yours. We will send their dust home on the sea across which they came."

"Child. We know you, and all who are our own. Seek what you wish."

The forest-mind voices were somber, but not forbidding. Thera met Alba's enquiring gaze with a brief nod, and the small group fell in behind Thera and Alba as they passed into the darkness of the ancient grove. Once again Thera experienced a sensation as if a curtain had fallen behind her, shutting out all sound. The green-tinted gloom was unrelieved by sunlight; the ancient trees were so closely grown. Their coarse bark was hung with grey moss, resembling the beards of ancient patriarchs.

There was heaviness to the air that Thera knew was not natural to the Elanraigh. She saw Alba wince and mutter an appeasement when her foot snapped a limb from an old deadfall. There was no sound of the waterfalls, but Thera felt the vibration in her feet and knew Alba angled that way. Then they found their first Memteth body.

Or, what was left of it. It could be known only by the body armor. Of flesh there was nothing remaining but piles of chalk-like dust. Alba dropped to one knee, her hand hesitated, and then she pinched a small amount of the grey dust between her fingers. Alba's face was pale in the dim light of the forest as she looked up at Thera.

"No burning..." she whispered hoarsely, her brow furrowed, "...no matter how hot the fire, could reduce bone to this." The fine dust floated from her fingers, coating the top of a small bulbous fungus.

Thera held Alba's gaze, then turned to the others. "Quickly," she whispered, "gather together Memteth gear that's been left. The other bodies will be close by. We will not dally here or disturb the grove any further."

Nine Memteth dead were found the same as the first. The Elankeep women collected armor and weapons, all that the ancient grove had not taken into itself, and assembled the unwieldy gear into manageable loads.

Thera was troubled. "Where would the Memteth ships be anchored?" she asked Alba.

"They be smashed upon the rocks by now, like as not." replied Alba. "Why, Lady?"

"We could learn more about them." Thera gestured to the dust under the trees. "Or find out where they come from, if they have maps as we do. I feel it could be important, Alba."

Alba shifted her shoulders, glancing around her. "The only way to the falls, be through this grove, Lady."

"Yes. You and I can carry on to the falls. It's less intrusion on the grove that way. We will send the others back with this collection," she gestured to the pile of armor and weapons. "Alba, we can be back at Elankeep by noon meal." Thera smiled her brightest smile.

Alba frowned and shook her head. She bent to pick up a Memteth spear and hefted it appraisingly. "Well..." she drawled finally, baring her teeth in something not a smile, "let us be seeing, then."

CHAPTER 25

The walk to the falls took longer than Thera or Alba had judged. At times, as they travelled past the ancient trees, Thera felt as if she were wading through knee-deep water, so oppressive was the mood of the grove. When they came out upon a rocky ledge above the falls, the roar of the plunging river burst upon their ears.

Standing bathed in the sunlit spray from the falls, Thera was cheered and exhilarated. She smiled at Alba, who grinned in return and saluted lightly, spear tip to helm.

Bridal Veil Falls dropped from a sheer, ten pike lengths height, down to a foaming, turbulent bowl. From there the Spinfisher River ran swift, but navigable, to the ocean.

Alba leaned close and shouted, "The old caravan bridge is around the next two bends."

Thera nodded and shouted back, "Who built the bridge?"

Alba's dark brows drew downward and she rubbed a blunt finger across her chin. "I have heard the Salvai Keiris say it be the Cythian Works Masters who built it, by King Erod's order. That would be in your grandfather's time. All of the caravan trail was built at the King's command, in return for some service to do with the Ttamarini."

Alba turned and walked westward along the rocky verge. The faint path they followed declined steeply. As they rounded the first bend, Alba puffed, "They will likely be moored around the next bend, Lady. The river widens greatly there. The beach is broad and accessible. We will be cautious — in case they left a guard to watch the boats."

Thera compressed her lips, a slight crease between her brows. Surely this caution would not have been given to a member of the troop; it would not have been considered necessary. The knowledge caused her regret. Thera was surprised to find in herself a great desire to earn the respect of the Elankeep soldiers. Not the deference given due to bloodlines, or position. Something more like the respect her father had from *his* captains.

Ah, well. Respect must be earned.

They slowed their downhill pace. They were only two pike lengths above the water surface now. Concealed behind the rocks, they gazed down at the two Memteth ships. Thera felt a clenching in her gut as she observed the now familiar lines of a Memteth craft. These black sails were furled, and the decks appeared deserted. They were anchored bow and stern, but on one ship the stern line had broken and she had swung onto the rocks of the river's shore. The raider ship listed, aground. There was no sign of life.

"Lady, let us not go aboard. Let us burn them. Here and now." Alba spoke through clenched teeth.

Thera moistened her lips. There *was* something unsettling here, Thera could feel it too. She placed her hand on Alba's shoulder and spoke with more confidence than she felt. "We shall burn them, swordswoman, after we have examined their contents."

There was sweat sheen on Alba's forehead. Her brown eyes squinted as she studied the scene below.

However, she only said, "I will go down first, then. I do not smell wood smoke, but there may be guards camped near the river's edge."

Quietly, Alba slipped away. Thera waited impatiently, her mind probing at her own sense of unease, to no effect. *It is probably just a very natural repugnance at being close to anything Memteth,* Thera thought.

Thera was just about to descend to the river of her own accord when she saw Alba's helm appear below. The swordswoman moved further out on the boulder shore of the Spinfisher, and cupping her hands either side of her mouth, she whistled the unique call of a bush skree.

"Come forward," Thera recognized the signal. *"Blessings be."*

Alba waited for her in the shadow of a twisted tree growing out of the riverbank. They stood together a moment, observing. The river rush drowned out most sounds. Alba pointed to the rope ladders over the sides of both craft.

"Shallow here, no more than thigh deep," she said. "They must all have waded ashore. No sign of Memteth left aboard, or on the shore."

Thera and Alba waded toward the grounded Memteth boat. The water numbed Thera's legs and sunlight dancing off the water's surface dazzled her eyes. She lay her hand on the hull. Dead wood. Not like the ships of Allenholme folk — *that* wood sang with the strength and spirit of the Elanraigh.

Alba's brown hand reached past Thera to clench the rope ladder. She straddled the top rail as she drew sword, her head swinging fore and aft. Finally she leaned over, nodding to Thera.

Large numbers of barrels covered the deck, lashed together in the bow and around the pilothouse. Thera saw piles of oily coiled ropes and rusty grappling hooks along the sides.

Alba was approaching the dark opening that led to the pilothouse and, presumably, crew quarters and below deck. She took a step backward.

"Pagh! What a stench!"

Thera, gasping, clapped a hand over her nose. She turned to go back outside, when she saw chests with distinctive markings upon them, piled in the pilothouse.

"Alba! Look, these chests are from South Bole."

Alba ran her fingers over the markings. "Ahh. I fear they took the caravan, then, Lady. They were a merry crew, the caravaners from South Bole. There was a brown-skinned man with dark, laughing eyes that I took a shine to last Verdimas. I had hoped to see him again. Well...may his gods look upon him."

Alba turned. "So," she said brusquely, "what have we here, Lady?"

Alba's sorrow touched Thera, and she gazed one more moment at the First Sword. Alba's glance at her was bright and hard.

Understanding, Thera turned and lifted the top from a large barrel. "Oh look!"

Gleaming Bole pottery and plate lay nested in straw. They sifted through the top layers.

Beautiful workmanship! "Why would Memteth bother with such as this?"

Alba shrugged. "For trade, perhaps, Lady. Who knows?"

"Who do Memteth trade with? None in this land know

of them as anything but marauders." Thera gently replaced the jewel-toned pieces. Was it possible that Memteth admired and coveted beautiful things for their own sake? It did not match her understanding of them.

Stacked beside the barrel were four small chests which held a fortune in spices. Thera recognized the stenciling on the stoneware jars. These spices were so costly that Thera's mother kept them under lock and key, and they were used only on very special feast days. She sniffed experimentally. *Hmm.*

"Alba..." Alba was not beside her. "Alba?"

"Below." The swordswoman's voice was muffled and strange. "Do not venture down here, Lady. I'll come up."

Thera rose to her feet, staring at the stairwell where Alba had gone. Amber lamplight appeared on the wall and then a distorted darkness leapt within it. Thera reached for the spear Alba had left with her.

Alba emerged from the narrow door; her face pale and shining with sweat. With slow, deliberate care she placed the lantern on the chart bench by the pilot's wheel. With a small groan, she leaned, stiff-armed, over the top of the pottery barrel. She sagged a moment, then her somber gaze met Thera's concern.

"There be bodies down there, Lady. Two caravaners by their clothes."

"No!" Thera's face twisted. Her memory of Nan on the beach came again vividly to mind; her memory of ... "Are they womenfolk, Alba?" she whispered hoarsely.

Alba lifted off the barrel, and moved to the doorway. She hung there, inhaling deeply of the outside air. "I think not — but you see — something has been eating them."

Thera's hand shook on the jar she held. "No...! I have never heard that they..."

Alba's shoulders shifted, almost impatiently. "Nor have I." She continued, "It is likely they kept these poor folk to tell them where to find Elankeep. I had wondered how they knew of us. However, *some* beast has chewed on them. Perhaps the Memteth allowed it, to torment the poor souls into saying what they wanted to know." She turned and looked at Thera. "What else? I cannot think of any known scavenger beast which could swim water, and climb into a boat, and leave wounds as great as these."

Alba's voice grated in Thera's ears. "Let us give them to the fire, Lady. Burn the boats now."

Thera's brow puckered as she glanced about her. "There are great riches here, Alba. We should salvage what we can."

The swordswoman's features hardened — she regarded Thera steadily.

Thera did not notice. She continued, almost as if speaking to herself. "You see, a long time ago, or maybe it only seems long, I had an idea to establish a fund so that women could be free to practice a craft or trade of their choosing.

"I've heard tell of young folk who love each other but cannot marry because they have not the bride price demanded by father or brothers.

"Or of young women who must run away from their home, to a strange place, because they wish not to marry and have not the price to secure their freedom of choice.

"They are penniless, nameless women who suffer hardship because of it."

Thera's fingers clenched around the jar she held. "This fund can make a difference, Alba. These riches could be the start of such a fund." She gently placed the jar back with the others.

The hardness left Alba's face and a corner of her mouth

tugged downward. "Aye, Lady Thera," she said softly, "that *would* be a great thing."

"It is just the beginning of things I have thought to do," said Thera earnestly.

Alba folded her arms across her chest and smiled at her. "Aye. A beginning. Our Sirra Alaine said you would be a Salvai different than others."

The swordswoman rubbed her chin. "Well. If we lay some planks up to the rail, and then down to the beach on the listing side, we should be able to roll or rope most of these near enough to shore that we can pull them in."

They worked steadily, until the sun was past high. The raiders' ship was finally stripped of most valuables.

There was now only one box left on board — an elaborate black case. Alba discovered it in a cabinet under the chart bench. She was speechless upon opening it. Inside, wrapped in white silk, was a magnificent sword. The blade was the width of five fingers at the hilt, the handle of some white, smooth substance she had never seen before.

Thera watched Alba turn the blade over and over in her hands, her expression rapt and reverent.

It is as if she communes with the weapon, Thera thought, the way I do with the Elanraigh.

Thera looked to shore, feeling satisfied with the morning's work. They had secured the barrels and chests up off the beach, under a heavily bushed outcropping of rock. Maps and charts were wrapped in oilskin and tucked into chests and barrels.

She wiped her hands down her tunic. Her hands prickled with splinters; the rough planking of their improvised ramp had to be tediously moved and lifted each step of the way.

Finally released from her sword-spell, Alba exhaled gustily. She carefully replaced the weapon in its cloth.

"Such a prize, I never thought to see." Alba's voice became exuberant. "Ha! I can see the Sirra's face! I have no doubt she be thinking I was somewhere lying under a tree with a daisy stem in my mouth all this time."

Thera laughed then held her side, leaning back against the wall, she groaned. "Blessings! I ache all over."

"Aye. Well, I know all about aching. Perhaps you will be joining us in the hot springs after evening meal, Lady?" The invitation was almost shyly given.

The Salvai probably never went into the soldiers' quarters, Thera surmised.

Thera nodded assent with genuine pleasure. Then she looked about her; the emptied pilothouse looked battered and scarred. Thera's expression darkened.

"One last trip ashore with this chest and we're done. We can fire the ship and send the South Bole caravaners properly."

Alba reached for the lamp and cracked it briskly against the chart bench. She waved Thera out onto the deck as the oil spilled its dark stain against the wood. Thera leaned against the deck rail. There was no warmth left in the late afternoon sun.

Inside the pilothouse Alba moved rapidly, a darker form in its shadowy interior.

Thera felt drawn into the sounds around her, the water sucking at the void in the damaged hull, the restless creakings of the ship's timbers.

Her eyes flew open, fixed on the pilothouse roof. *Something huge!* Something slithered across the roof, and then quick as an indrawn breath, it disappeared through the hatch. Thera heard a thump on the pilothouse floor.

CHAPTER 26

*A*lba yelled.

There was a heavy thud against the wall of the pilothouse and a hiss, as of hot steel plunged into water.

Thera's hand clenched tighter on Alba's spear.

"Alba!" No response.

Calling on the Elanraigh for a blessing, Thera ran inside.

She had never seen such a creature before. Except for its great size, it resembled a sun-lizard, such as would bask on the castle walls come warm summer days.

She flinched back, heart tripping, as the lizard creature's huge tail swept past the door. The flat, reptilian head swung slowly toward her. Thera spared a quick, panicky glance over to where Alba lay sprawled.

"Alba...!"

Alba stirred, slowly, painfully. She shifted backward, propping her back in the corner. Her left arm dangled to her lap. Her right hand shook with tremors as she grasped her sword hilt. A dark stain spread across the material of her kilt. Blood seeped from under its hem and soaked into the deck floor.

"By the One Tree..." fear constricted Thera's throat. "...
Alba, how bad?"

The swordwoman's voice was flat. "Smacked me against
the wall with its tail. Took a bite of my leg...unnnn", Alba
groaned and panted, "...before my sword was even drawn. It
seems content to wait now."

Part of Thera's mind cringed and wailed its fear of the
foul creature, flashing images of death, the reptile tearing at
her entrails. Her pulse stumbled then raced.

So. Drawing a deep, shuddering breath, Thera weighed
what she must do. She touched briefly, horrified, at the creature's mind. *Uhh, it is truly beast, not sapient mind.* Gripping the
spear, she swung it before her in jabbing posture. She must
act now. Alba would bleed to death if she stood dithering.

"Hey-a!," she challenged, "You carrion-eating worm!"

The reptile fixed a yellow eye on Thera and its tongue
flickered. It shifted on its short, bowed legs.

Thera blinked. As the lizard-creature moved into the
dusky light by the portal, she saw flashes of color off its
neck. It wore a gold collar, studded with jewels.

*A Memteth's cherished pet beast? Does it sleep at its master's
feet as does father's deerhound?*

The setting sun poured through the portal, flooding the
pilothouse in dusty amber. The reptile's mouth gapped
open, slickly red. Fleshy gore clung to its rows of teeth.

It hissed, the pouches under its jaws pumping out the
sound like bellows. She was overwhelmed with the stench
from its mouth.

Again the debilitating fear constricted her chest. With a
deep breath, holding the spear before her, she edged warily
along the wall toward the wounded swordswoman.

She remembered the Elanraigh had told her a water

elemental held sway here at the Falls. She still sent a quick prayer to the Elanraigh. *"I must kill this Memteth's creature, so that Alba might live."*

It was Farnash's mind-voice that responded. *"You are Clan. Be one with us."*

"Farnash?" What does he mean? Oh.

Thera searched for the predator in herself. Almost wonderingly, she drew this aspect of herself forward. Her body remembered the sensations she had felt while in hawk form, and had felt emanating from the Elanraigh wolf as he battled the Memteth raider. She felt the clanship of hunting with the pack, running shoulder to shoulder. Her heart throbbed with a young hawk's feral joy, as it stooped to the kill.

Thera's body tautened. Her vision sharpened, focused on the creature before her. She observed how the light sparked the drops of moisture on its mauve-hued hide, and the hint of red color behind the dark pupil of its eye. One of the lizard's claws was torn and bled sluggishly. It favored the wounded foot as it turned toward her.

Drawing her lips back from her teeth, Thera snarled a challenge. Her spear tip jabbed out at the heavy dewlap of skin under the creature's jaw.

With a furious hiss the beast backed, its massive head swaying. It swung its tail at Thera's head. She lifted the spear, taking the worst of the blow on the shaft.

Even though the lizard's movements were hampered in the confines of the pilothouse, the force was enough to break the spear shaft between her hands and drop Thera to her knees.

With a scrabbling of claws, the beast charged her, swift and low.

Alba shouted hoarsely, some word, it was all a roaring in Thera's ears.

Now! Just as the boar hunters do.

Thera swung the broken, still deadly spear, before her and braced herself. The impact crushed her against the wall. Her head snapped back, and her vision sparkled.

Hissing, the reptile wrenched its body away. The spear shaft, embedded deep in its chest, tore painfully from Thera's grasp. She rolled as far away as she could get, pulling her dagger from her belt as the creature thrashed violently from one side of the pilothouse to the other.

Finally it lay on its side, skin twitching. Its jaws gaped as it labored to draw breath.

Thera moved immediately, a wary eye on its tail. With her dagger, she cut its throat.

"A mercy stroke," Thera murmured, "whatever you are."

She crawled over to Alba, her bloody fingers reaching for the pulse at Alba's throat.

The swordswoman's hand grasped her wrist. "I live."

Thera had felt the cold clamminess of Alba's flesh.

"The wound..." Thera gasped. "Let me see."

After a moment, Alba's hand dropped, and Thera moved the bloody cloth of her kilt away. She sucked in her breath. A vicious wound, flesh and muscle had gone with it, but Elanraigh bless, it seemed the tendons and bone were intact.

"I will splint this, Alba, but your shoulder is dislocated." She eased Alba down, and was about to rise, when the swordswoman's hand again grasped hers, restraining her.

"Bravely done. Oh bravely done." Her dark eyes, though glazed with shock, met Thera's squarely. "I would not like to have died in the jaws of that beast." Alba's eyelids drooped and her head sagged back across Thera's arm.

Biting her lip, Thera gently loosened Alba's hand and ran outside to obtain the materials she needed.

IT WAS full dark by the time Thera had bound Alba's wound and splinted her leg. The dislocated arm she bound to Alba's torso. Repairing that was a procedure best left to the healer. Alba had not regained consciousness. This was well, as the only way Thera had of moving the heavier woman was by dragging her on a blanket, over the same improvised ramps they had made in order to move the ship's cargo onto the beach.

Thera managed to drizzle some water down the swordswoman's throat, but though Alba mumbled, she did not waken. A small fire made from driftwood and bits of lumber from the Memteth ship was enough to keep them warm, but was not what she needed to summon assistance. The others from Elankeep would be searching for them by now, but they might confine their search to the ancient grove.

Thera tucked the blanket securely around Alba, then taking two brands from the fire, she waded into the river.

The ship anchored farthest out she fired first. She spilled lantern oil over its deck, and even as she waded on to the next anchored ship, flames were crackling and shooting sparks into the air.

Thera's body was so stiff and sore, she could barely haul herself over the side. Her jaws clenched as she again set foot on the deck.

The dead caravaners on this ship; it could have been us. It could have been Alba and I whose bodies now lay half devoured.

Thera stood a moment, eyes wide to the night, gripped by the horror of what might have been.

Again Farnash's voice rumbled in her mind, his tone matter-of-fact.

They died. We live. All is well.

CHAPTER 27

The burning ships lit the sky above the river. Thera was sure the Elankeep troop would find them quickly now, but she fretted as she constantly checked on Alba. The lizard creature's mouth had been so foul. Alba's wound might soon go bad without a healer's care. She sat, knees drawn up to her chest, rocking slightly, then reached over to lay her fingers on Alba's pulse just once more. Sighing, she lowered her head onto her bent knees.

A hand dropped on her shoulder. "Lady."

Her body flinched in reaction, though in the same instant she recognized the voice. She had not heard them come up behind her and here she was sleeping as soundly as a babe in its cradle. Her relief was tainted with chagrin. Yet, there was no reproof in Sirra Alaine's eyes.

Thera grasped the Sirra's hand. "Alba's hurt."

Sirra Alaine nodded slowly. She jerked her chin to where Mieta and Rhul worked at securing Alba's limp form onto a litter for portaging back up the steep trail.

The brackets at the corners of the Sirra's mouth deepened as she watched the swordswomen snugging Alba's form in blankets. Then she twitched her shoulders, looking down at Thera.

"It's a fine field dressing you made, Lady. Good as any a healer could have done." The Sirra squatted down and peered into Thera's face. "What happened here, Lady Thera?"

Thera saw that the Memteth ships had burned down to blackened framework. She collected her thoughts and began to tell Alaine what they had encountered here.

THERA SIGHED SHAKILY as the small rescue party re-entered the silence of the ancient grove. *We'll be home soon.*

She felt the forest greet her.

"*Thera.*"

"*Teacher?*" Thera felt strangely awkward. *How do I address this Elanraigh companion?* Thera now knew that in life, Teacher had been Lady Dysanna. If what Chamakin and Salvai Keiris had told her was true, and why should it not be, then Lady Dysanna had suffered much because of her...their...ancestors' bigotry.

"*Teacher.*" Thera projected the love and empathy she felt into her mind voice. "*You are...were...my elder-aunt, the Lady Dysanna?*"

"*Ah,*" the voice sighed. "*Thera. It is so and yet I have for so long been one with the Elanraigh, that my mortal lifetime seems to me as something seen from a mountaintop, distant and small. You are to be Salvai now, my dear, and a woman grown. I must no longer be 'Teacher'.*"

"*Do you leave me?*" Thera was struck with dismay — not another loss!

"We are always here for you. You are Salvai and we are the Elanraigh."

Dysanna's voice altered even as she spoke, deepening into the familiar rumble of the Elanraigh. *It is as if a soloist stepped back to join the chorus,* Thera mused.

THERE WAS a confusion of welcoming voices as they returned through the gates of Elankeep. Their torches had been spotted by the watch as they emerged from the ancient grove. Willing hands reached to relieve Alba's stretcher bearers. Questions were called out, which Alaine deflected.

"The wounded need attention and the Salvai needs rest. Leave be. You'll hear enough of rumor tonight. The story will be told when our Salvai is ready to offer it."

Egrit clawed her way to Thera's side.

"Lady!" Egrit's eyes widened at the blood stains on Thera's tunic.

Thera spoke quickly, to forestall her alarm. "I am well, Egrit. It is First Sword Alba who has paid the price of our adventure."

"Oh! Not Alba! Lady, did she fall?"

Dama Ainise barely glanced at the form on the stretcher as she too, pushed forward. "Alba is a strong, sturdy soldier, my Lady. The Sirra will see to her care. Do come with us, I pray you," her anxious eyes ran over Thera, "Egrit will draw you a bath and see to your meal."

Thera's brows drew down and she brushed from Ainise's light grasp. Too angry to trust her words, she turned to follow Alba's stretcher. Ainise lifted her gown hem and trotted after her. "Oh, my Lady, you should not go to the soldier's quarters."

Hissing a small sound, Thera spun on her heel, and was suddenly restrained by something in the elder Dama's face.

Calling on all her mother's teaching, Thera kept her voice kindly. "I will stay with swordswoman Alba a while, Dama Ainise. I am hungry, though. A bowl of soup would be good, if you would arrange for it to be sent to me in the infirmary. Enough soup for all, if you can manage that. Then you go to your rest, there are hands enough here for now."

Ainise reddened, curtsied, and turned to hurry about her errand. Thera watched after her a moment. "So."

"Pardon, Lady?"

Thera realized Egrit waited at her side.

"Egrit." Thera dragged the girl along with her. "Healing Mistress said she would be perhaps two days away, so she might return by tomorrow's eve. I pray so, for Alba's sake."

Egrit's eyes never left her face. "Lady," she spoke shyly, "I know something of healer's arts. Mistress Rozalda found me helpful when I was small, and could fetch and carry for her. She said I was quiet and did not get in her way.

"I learned much and she was patient with my questions. She said I had a healer's touch."

The girl flushed brightly, as Thera turned a warm gaze upon her. "Blessings be," murmured Thera, and further flustered the girl by grabbing her into a quick hug. "Come quickly."

They caught up with the stretcher bearers as they turned into the large chamber used as an infirmary. A fire crackled in the open-oven fireplace. A large iron kettle simmered on a hook. Herbs hung in fragrant clusters from the rafters. The walls of shelves were loaded with clay jars sealed with wax, other shelves held scrolls and leather bound tomes. In a corner by the window was a worktable and stool.

Clean white linens were folded neatly in a cedar wardrobe. At the far end of the room were four cots, one occupied, and the rest freshly made. Two women in woolen bed robes were relaxed in chairs by the fire, sipping a steaming brew from tin mugs. They rose to their feet as the small group entered and murmured in concern as Alba's stretcher appeared.

Sirra Alaine waved them to their seats. "Let us get her settled," she warned them.

Swordswoman Mieta walked over to the two convalescents, and they spoke in low tones as the others carefully transferred Alba to a cot.

Sirra Alaine and Thera then found themselves standing awkward and somewhat astonished, as the usually diffident Egrit began to issue brisk orders.

Her small hands quickly felt over Alba's head, neck, and limbs. "Out of my light," she demanded of Sirra Alaine, who immediately shuffled back.

Egrit stood with hands on hips, and chewed her lip a moment.

"I can repair the dislocation of the shoulder, but I will need help. Sirra, hold here if you please."

Thera found herself pressed back as the two others reset the shoulder. If she had not been so anxious, she would have been amused at with what alacrity the Sirra wordlessly jumped to little Egrit's soft commands.

"That is good." Egrit murmured, with a nod, as she rebound the shoulder and arm.

"Who did this splint?" she asked then, pointing to Alba's leg.

"I did." Thera replied, anxious.

"It was well done," Egrit commented. Her small fingers moved with a firm competency as she removed the splint to examine the wound.

Even the Sirra paled. The odor and color were unmistakable.

They both turned and looked at Thera.

"Lady, what did this?" Egrit's small face was bitter.

"A foul creature to be sure."

Egrit continued to stare bleakly at Thera.

"What?" Thera demanded. She glared, alarmed, at the two of them. "We have poultices for healing, do we not? You can draw out the poison."

Egrit spoke then, quiet and slow. Thera recognized the tone. Her father used it with his witless, high-bred racing horse.

"Lady, I will do all I can. But if the poison does not draw out by tomorrow, we must take her leg."

THERA PACED THE SOUTH TOWER. The sharp night wind lathed the sweat sheen off her skin.

Alba to lose her leg. Unthinkable. It was my *doing. I insisted we go onboard the ship.*

Hearing the steady shuff, shuff, of footsteps approaching up the steep wooden stairs, she marched back and forth angrily. *Blessings be! Can I not have a moment's solitude?*

The guard on duty glanced at Thera briefly, then discreetly turned her back and kept her distance across the tower.

It was Sirra Alaine who emerged from the trap door. Alaine regarded Thera, who continued her pacing.

*The dullest bovine cud-chewer in father's fields would sense
that I do not wish company right now. How not the Sirra?*

The Sirra strolled over to the granite balustrade, and
leaned there, her attitude contemplative.

"We are from the same village." Alaine finally said.

Thera jerked her shoulder at the intrusion of Alaine's
voice, but halted her pacing. She stood hunched, hugging
herself against the wind's chill.

"Alba be younger than I, of course." Alaine continued in
her stolid voice.

Thera made an effort to quell the queer temper that kept
rising like acid bile.

Alaine half turned, leaning on one elbow. "She sought
me out here, at Elankeep, after she had wandered some on
her own. You see, when she told her elder brother she
wanted to soldier, he tried to...dissuade her."

Thera felt some of the tension leave her shoulders and
she turned to join the Sirra at the parapet. She clenched her
hands before her. Shamed by the tears that glazed her eyes,
she could not look at Alaine. Tears seemed a childish
response to the trouble she had caused.

"Hnnh." Alaine cleared her throat. "When beatings
didn't work, when she still said she would go, her brothers
scarred her, with a knife."

The Sirra met Thera's shocked gaze steadily. Alaine's
own scar, a thin white line over her upper lip, distorted her
bitter smile.

"A common enough practice, Lady. You see, in some
places they think that forcing a woman to stay home as an
unmarriageable drudge is more respectable than allowing
her to seek such unwholesome independence."

Alaine turned from Thera's gaze. She leaned forward
again, looking over the grassy field now seared silver by

moonlight. "Not all are fortunate enough to find a place like the Elanraigh," she said, her voice reverent.

"The people from my part of the country are not a very forward thinking folk. Not all are like your people of Allenholme, Lady."

Thera bowed her head, scrubbing her fingers through the mass of her hair. "*My* folk have their blindside as well, Sirra," she said, her lips barely moving.

Alaine turned a sapient look on Thera. "Hnnh. So." Though the Sirra did not move, Thera felt as if a comforting arm had been thrown about her shoulders.

After a moment, Alaine continued. "Alba ran off finally. I can guess what that year on her own must have been like — her a scarred woman, penniless, of no name."

Alaine's voice turned droll. "She had some considerable sword skill by the time she found me. That be *her* gift. She'd worked with the caravans, I think. She'll not talk about those times much."

The childish tears would insist on coming. Thera wiped at her cheeks and blurted, "It is *my* fault she's in trouble now. I made her go on the ships. She wanted to burn them right away. She knew something was wrong. I did as well, but I was determined to go."

Alaine was silent. Bitterly Thera realized how much she would regret it if the Sirra and the women of Elankeep should shun her for her headstrong ways. Thera scrubbed at her face, her voice blurred behind her hands. "Some Salvai I prove to be. I'll never be as wise as either you or Alba."

Alaine proffered a neatly folded cloth from her belt kit. She gestured to Thera's now streaming eyes and nose.

"Wisdom. Hnnh. Seems to me, the best lessons learned come hard. Think on it. We were young as you once. We carry our scars to prove it." The Sirra shook her head. "Alba is strong, in ways I cannot even begin to describe. She will survive this, with her spirit intact. Elanraigh willing."

"I will pray for that," said Thera in subdued voice, and turning, she strode to the trap door and down the steep spiraling stair.

~

THE GATE GUARD WAS ALARMED.

"Lady?" The swordswoman cleared her throat. "Do you have an escort?"

Thera firmed her voice. "I will not be far. Be at ease." She strolled casually around the wall, out of the guard's line of sight, then ran lightly down the south side, toward the ancient grove. She could feel forest-mind driving her .

To what, she wondered.

It was very dark. Clouds obscured the stars and the wind hissed as it rushed through the dry grasses of the field.

Thera groped with her senses, but knew only a feeling of the grove awaiting her.

I'm right, she thought. *Something calls me there.*

She jogged on.

~

THE ROUTE she took was the same they had followed early that day. It was not as dark inside the grove as Thera had expected, for the ancient trees' bark gleamed like polished pewter. She felt a prickling on her skin as she neared where they had found the first Memteth body. On approaching the tree she was driven to her knees by the strength of forest-mind.

Her breath came fast as she extended her hands, but there were no dusty Memteth remains, just a profusion of cool waxy-green vines. The vine's roundish leaves were starred with delicate white flowers. Thera's fingers tingled pleasantly as she pinched off several long strands of the vine. She sniffed the broken stem; a clean, astringent aroma. On impulse she ran to another site where Memteth remains had been found. The vines lushly thrived there as well.

"*Blessings be,*" sent Thera, clenching the vines to her. "*Oh, Blessings be.*"

IT WAS change of watch as Thera returned to the front gates. The two guards, who were conferring, saluted her with obvious relief.

Thera felt almost giddy as she ran to the infirmary room, the bright green vines held close to her chest.

Egrit looked up from Alba's bedside as Thera burst in the room.

Carefully placing Alba's hand back down, Egrit rose, and moved to meet Thera at the healing mistress' worktable.

"Egrit! Look!" Thera extended the vine and watched anxiously as Egrit pinched a bit of leaf and sniffed the bitter-sweet aroma. She looked at Thera wonderingly. "Lady, I do not know this vine, I have never seen it before."

Thera shifted from one foot to the other. The heady scent enveloped the two of them. "Neither have I, Egrit. However, the Elanraigh led me to it. It was in...a special place." She rushed on, "I *feel* it will heal Alba's wound."

"You are the Salvai. Elanraigh bless us." Egrit held out her arms for the vines and without further word, turned to work.

Thera breathed in the scent lingering on her fingers and crossing to Alba's bed, laid her hand on the swordswoman's forehead. "The Elanraigh cares for you, Alba, and so do I. You *will* be well."

She lay down on the vacant bed beside Alba's, and as she watched the swordswoman's sleeping profile, her own lids drooped.

She awakened once, to see Egrit applying a poultice made from the waxy green leaves to Alba's wound. She drifted asleep again with the sharp, clean scent filling her nostrils. A warm sense of well-being enveloped her.

CHAPTER 28

*I*t was late morning when Thera awoke to find Egrit, heavy-eyed, but smiling, as she supported Alba to drink from a water gourd.

Egrit's voice was triumphant. "The poison has been drawn, Lady. Swordswoman Alba will mend."

Thera kicked off her coverlet and stood behind Egrit as she continued to offer Alba sips of water. Thera's fingers bit into Egrit's shoulder. "She is truly well?"

"Weak and disoriented, but she will be herself before long."

Alba's eyes opened a slit and she mumbled around the lip of the water gourd.

"Alba," Thera squeezed Alba's hand and leaned closer, "how do you feel?"

"Jus' tired. Next watch 's mine."

The swordswoman's eyes drooped shut again. Thera straightened and exchanged a wry look with Egrit. Alba's disorientation would pass. Thera knew enough healer's lore to rejoice at the return of healthy color to Alba's flesh.

Sirra Alaine was summoned. The Sirra's worn look lightened as she stood by the bed and observed Alba's improved appearance. Thera saw the Sirra's rough hand twitch slightly, then move to gently lift the sweat-dampened hair at Alba's temples.

Alba's eyes opened; her gaze clearer than before. She saw Alaine and a lopsided grin crooked Alba's mouth. "Huh. Feels like an old lizard chewed me up 'n spat me out."

"Hnnh." Alaine snorted. Her autumn-leaf eyes shone.

All that morning there was a steady flow of visitors as Alba's companions came off-duty, until Thera observed the slump shouldered weariness in Egrit's posture.

"Enough!" She gathered all eyes with a stern look. "Time to be off, all of you. If you but look, you will see that both patient and healer are in need of their rest." Thera had to chew down a smile at their chagrined expressions. The small troop began to shuffle past her to the infirmary door.

"Elanraigh bless, Lady," whispered Rhul from the doorway. Alba had spent much of the afternoon telling an elaborate and flattering tale of Thera's battle with the lizard creature to all her visitors. It had made her sound like a hero of old. Thera snorted to herself, and yet she had been so afraid she could barely hold her spear. Rhul's blessing was charged with warmth. Thera flushed.

Rhul's gaze swung over toward Egrit. "Elanraigh bless, *Healer*," she said with a respectful nod.

A chorus of good-natured *blessing-be's* echoed in the hall as Rhul, loudly shushing for quiet, pulled the door too.

Egrit, Thera thought, observing her maid's glowing pleasure that matched her own, *truth be known, has earned her way into the swordswomen's hearts.*

"Rhul," called Thera after the closing door, "ask Dama Ella if she will come to take over Alba's care while Egrit rests."

Rhul's dark head briefly reappeared to nod assent, "Yes, Salvai."

As Egrit passed her, Thera pressed her shoulder. "This is true healer's work you've done here, Egrit."

"It was you that found the vine, Lady."

The corner of Thera's mouth drew down. "Well, I was prodded, driven, by the Elanraigh to pick the plant it placed before my eyes. By all means, praise me if you will." Thera shook the shoulder she grasped. "It was you, Egrit, who knew what to do, not I."

Two days later healing mistress Rozalda returned. She swept into the infirmary room, escorted by Rhul and Lotta.

"What is this I hear of you feigning illness in my absence, Alba?" She shared a quick smile with Thera, before turning her penetrating gaze onto the patient.

Alba barked a laugh, then sobered. "It seems the Elanraigh choose to teach me to value that which I took for granted, mistress."

"Indeed," murmured Rozalda, laying her hand against Alba's cheek.

Even Thera could judge by Alba's appearance that the swordswoman was no longer fevered. Thera suspected the Healer's gesture was more affection than assessment.

Now Rozalda held her hand, palm downward, a finger's breadth above Alba's leg where it lay propped on a rolled sheepskin, and closed her eyes. Her hand hovered over Alba's wound. Then Rozalda's eyelids quivered and Thera saw her meditative expression alter to a frown.

Her voice was abrupt. "When is this dressing to be changed?"

Egrit blanched. Her gaze flickered, and then steadied. "Mistress, I change the dressing and wash the wound every watch."

Rozalda turned to Egrit and her frown cleared. "Egrit. My dear child," she said, her voice softened, "I have heard from all of the very excellent care you give our swordswoman here. But this!" she gestured at the bandaged leg, "This has been a most foul wound, I wish to see how it heals for myself and..."

Alba interjected, "Mistress. *Surely* it be time I was up and about." Alba propped herself up on her elbows. "I be right tired of laying abed," she grumbled.

Rozalda pressed her lips together thoughtfully. "It is early days yet, Alba."

Alba looked aggrieved.

Rozalda's heavy brows lifted. "Now then," she said, "I will first see for myself how the wound heals," she paused. "Perhaps next watch you may move to the chair by the fire for part of the day. We will find you some quiet, useful task."

She nodded at the brightening of Alba's expression, and gestured for Thera and Egrit to walk to her worktable with her.

Egrit looked disturbed.

Rozalda crooked a brow at the maid as she moved behind her worktable. "What troubles you, child?"

"Mistress," Egrit hesitated, then continued in a firmer voice, "is it not early yet for the swordswoman to be up?"

"My dear, I have found through long experience that when they start clamoring for their tasks or activities, I am best to give it them — be it shelling peas for cook, winding wool for Dama Brytha, or whetting a blade for their own use." She laughed a little, "Many's the time I've seen hands drop to laps and heads roll back on the chair as sleep overtakes them in the midst of what they are doing." She twinkled at Egrit from under her heavy brows, "Whereas, if I had confined them to bed, they'd have rolled and fretted and not had the healing sleep they needed.

"Now," she said briskly, "where *is* this vine that our Salvai found? Ah." She gently plucked the leaf Egrit offered from her apron pocket, and held it against the light.

"Blessings be!" she exclaimed. She rubbed the dry leaf between her fingers.

Carefully laying the leaf down, she used both hands to lift a heavy volume down from her shelves. Rozalda lightly ran her fingers down the tissue thin pages.

As Thera, Egrit, and Rozalda became engrossed in the old book of healers' lore, Rhul and Lotta moved across the room to sit on the edge of Alba's bed. The swordswomen shared some story with Alba. Thera warmed to hear Alba laugh.

Finally Mistress Rozalda closed the volume. Her fingers rested on the tooled leather cover. "Well," she mused, then looked up at Thera and Egrit, "it *is* lichenstrife."

A silence fell on the entire group.

"Lichen...what, mistress?" called Alba from her bed.

"A very rare plant. It has not been seen in *this* generation. ... it is written here," she smoothed the book's cover, "that there is nothing known to match its healing properties. The Elanraigh seems to grow it only when it is most needed.

"The last lichenstrife ever found in the Elanraigh was when lady Dysanna was Salvai at Elankeep, more than forty-five years ago.

"Indeed, there was much need of it in those times. It was when your great-grandfather was Duke at Allenholme, Lady Thera. There were constant territorial disputes between Allenholme and Ttamarini in those days."

The healing mistress held Thera's gaze. "It is said that the Ttamarini chieftain, Chemotin, mortally wounded, was

brought by his men to Elankeep. The tale is that the
Ttamarini were cut-off from their own healers. They
claimed they were guided by a spirit animal to bring their
wounded chief here, to the heart of the Elanraigh.

"Lady Dysanna hunted for and found lichenstrife
growing near her tree cave."

All the swordswomen present were familiar with the
story, but Thera heard Rhul mutter, "Bless me if I can understand how a Salvai can wish to meditate near a place she
knows will someday be her tomb.

"Ow. Sorry," Rhul amended as Lotta kicked her shin. "I
didn't mean to interrupt the story, mistress. Good story."

Thera searched her own feelings. No. She felt that the
hemlock tree cave would always be a sanctuary to her, now,
and whenever her last day should come. The Elanraigh
thrummed comfortingly at the base of her skull.

Even as she gazed unseeingly at her toes, Thera thought
she felt the healing mistress' glance.

"Well," Rozalda continued softly, "a Salvai must know
the darkness where grows a tree's roots, as well as the
sunlight where grow branch and leaf."

Lotta prompted. "Um. So, after Salvai Dysanna found
the lichenstrife, mistress?"

"Ah. Well. The lichenstrife healed the Ttamarini chieftain's wound. While he was convalescing here at Elankeep,
Lady Dysanna journeyed to Allenholme. She appealed to
her Duke, Leif ArNarone, Thera's great-grandfather, to hear
Chief Chemotin's peace proposal."

"But my great grandfather would not listen," said Thera
grimly.

Rozalda leveled a steady look at Thera. She spoke
slowly, "The Salvai was never said to condemn Allenholme's
royal house — her story ends with Allenholme's refusal to

treat with the Ttamarini. Soon after, Lady Dysanna herself, was dead. Perhaps elder Dama Brytha could tell you more."

"Ha," snorted Lotta. "*That* old soul cannot remember what happened yesterday!"

"True," replied Rozalda glancing up at Lotta. She returned her attention to Thera, "but she remembers forty-five years ago, very well indeed."

CHAPTER 29

*T*he elder Dama's chamber was pleasantly warm. It was located behind cook's work room, and just now, was fragrant with the scent of fresh baked bread. Thera, seated in the window niche, heard her stomach growl.

She lightly pushed open the window shutters. Bushes of anise grew below the window and as the morning sun warmed the yellow flowers, its sweet tang rose to delight her senses.

The elder Dama's voice broke into the comfortable silence that had fallen between them.

"That you, Ella?" she called out to the door.

Thera smiled in response to the conspiratorial twinkle in the old woman's eye.

Dama Ella appeared in the chamber doorway. "Oh." Ella twisted her apron in her hands, her cheeks slightly flushed. "I see you have a guest today, Dama Brytha." She made a courtesy in Thera's direction.

"Aye," The old woman drawled the word, and returned

her gaze to her knitting. "You needn't be bothering to listen at my door, Ella. I'll know if you do."

Affront stiffened Dama Ella's features. Thera bit her lip and turned her face to the garden view. For a moment the only sound in the room was the small tick of Brytha's needles.

"Well!" Ella puffed indignantly. "I only wished to be sure you fared well. And...and to see if there be aught you wanted. Well...," she said again, "I'll be about my work then."

Ella pointedly drew the door closed and soon pans were heard clattering. Brytha continued to rock in her chair, her knotted fingers manipulating wool and needles.

Then, as if there had been no lull or interruption in their conversation, the old Dama continued.

"Aye, child. Of course I remember my Dysanna." The old woman's voice became fierce. "So full of life and vitality she was." Her hands rested a moment and she smiled. "And a beauty she was too."

Her mouth pushed outward in a wrinkled pout. "Not at all like that poor thing that was Salvai here these last few years." After a moment Dama Brytha dutifully added, "May Elanraigh bless her and keep her soul in peace.

"Ah, but how fiercely the Elanraigh loved Dysanna. Often, often she would disappear into the forest for, oh, long periods of time. Bless me, how I fretted those times. When she came back she would be a-tangle with leaf and twigs in her hair. If I chide her, she would look at me, amazed.

"'Bry,' she would say so gently, 'how could I ever come to harm in the Elanraigh's care.'

"Many's the night I'd find her gone from her bed. She would be on the north tower, her hair all blowing about her, leaning into the wind as if she caressed it with her body."

"'Feel how soft the wind is, Bry!' she would say to me."

Dama Brytha chortled a little, "And me, bitten to the bone with the chill of it."

The knitting collapsed into a colorful mound. "She was like a wild thing of the forest herself, come to think."

Her voice quavered with anger. "I heard what Lady Keiris said when she came, years ago, to be Salvai here. I heard what she said of my Dysanna — Ainise couldn't wait to tell me." Dama Brytha's swollen fingers twisted, "She said that my Dysanna was as close to wanton as a high born lady can be."

Brytha's cheeks were flushed as she regarded Thera fixedly. Her tiny knotted hands bounced on her lap. "Wanton! My beautiful Dysanna! There were others, too who saw her as abandoned, something too strange and wild. But I never did. Dysanna was such as Keiris could never hope to be, and Keiris knew it."

The elder Dama sniffed and resumed her knitting. "The Elanraigh never loved Keiris, not as it did Dysanna — not as it does *you*, dear." The look she bent on Thera was warm and approving.

"You see, I was not especially well-born myself, as most First Ladies are. However, Lady Dysanna took a shine to me when she was still at her maiden home, and I was sent as a housekeeper's assistant there. So maybe I don't see things quite the way the others do. There were those here at Elankeep who thought they were better suited to be the Salvai's First Lady than me," she rolled her eyes toward the cook room. "That Ella was one."

The old Dama folded her lips and shook her head. "The things Ella said during those early years, mocking my ordinary speech or plain ways. This for instance," she lifted the knitting in a small gesture. "'Fishwives knit,' Ella said to me, '*Ladies* do needlework.'"

Thera offered, "I hate needlework."

Dama Brytha smiled. "Well, there are those here now who are glad enough of the leggings and vests I knit."

"There were some here who said I should never have let her be so wild. But she was ever in the Elanraigh's care more than mine. Then my lady went away with the Ttamarini Chief." Again tears welled in the elder Dama's eyes, "Oh, if you could have seen them together you would not have doubted it was right. I have no gift, but any could see, who chose, that the Elanraigh loved them both and wished for their union. The winds blew sweet those spring days they were here together. How happy she was, until word came from Allenholme.

"They would not countenance such an alliance. Dysanna was declared dead — severed — root and branch." The old lady paused in her rocking, "She bid us farewell that very day. I wished to go into exile with her. Indeed I begged to go. She would have none of it.

"In the days, months, then years that followed, I climbed to the north tower each night, even though my legs were no longer young." She shivered slightly. "I don't know what I hoped, I have told you I have no gift, perhaps just to hear or sense her upon the wind.

"One night, as I neared the trap door, I could feel the wind colder than ever before whistling through its planks. The door was snatched from my hand just as the very breath seemed dragged from my chest by its fierceness. Why I did not return immediately the way I had come, I do not know. I believe now that some part of me knew Dysanna was near. It was a struggle even to reach the wall, and when I looked out at the black trees it was to see their branches tossing wildly with a sound like a stormy sea. It was then the Elanraigh spoke to me for the first and only time — to tell me Dysanna had died."

Tear-blinded, Dama Brytha reached a frail hand to Thera. They touched a moment, then Dama Brytha reached up her cuff for a plain, immaculate linen, and dabbed at her eyes. "Did you know any of this, dear?"

"Salvai Keiris had told me some of it, in her own way." Thera chewed her lip, considering, then added, "And some of the story was told me by a Ttamarini who says he is Lady Dysanna's grandson." Thera patted the old lady's hand. "She lives in him, and she lives in the Elanraigh."

Dama Brytha sighed. It was not an unhappy sound. "Aye. I've felt her there. I'll join her soon." The elder Dama's gaze was a clear and bright blue as it travelled over Thera's features. "Do you know how like her you are, daughter?"

Thera nodded, too full of emotions to speak.

At that moment, there was a brisk tap at the door and Dama Ella entered with a tray of tea and scones. She bustled about the little room, arranging a linen cloth on a small table.

Brytha puckered her mouth and withdrawing her hand from Thera, resumed her knitting.

Thera repressed a smile. Dama Ella could not help but be aware that the ancient lady very deliberately ignored her.

"Here," Thera offered, "let me take the tray, I will serve Dama Brytha and myself."

Ella cast a reproachful look at Dama Brytha's averted face, "To be sure, my lady, I did not mean to interrupt. Healing mistress said she should eat small and regular, I was but thinking of her needs."

Dama Brytha finally looked up, "You were snooping, as always. I know."

Ella gasped. "Oh! How could you think...!"

Thera soothed Ella out the door, and returned to pour tea for the eldest Dama. The old lady seemed weary now and her thoughts wandered. She did not speak any more of Dysanna. Finally she nodded, asleep in her chair.

Thera called Ella in to help her to bed. She closed the chamber door on their voices.

"Ella, where have you been keeping! You know I nap after noon meal."

"Blessings, and me likely to get my head bitten off if I so much as look in the door."

CHAPTER 30

*T*hera walked to the window, flexing her arms forward and back, until she felt a deep satisfying pull on her shoulders.

By the One Tree! I ache!

A few days ago Swordswoman Enid had offered to help Thera improve her weapons skills.

"Lady Thera!" The soldier jogged to where Thera stood by the herb garden, and saluted.

Swordswoman Enid's forehead still glistened with salve.

"Enid. Blessings. How is your healing?"

"Well enough, Lady, when I recall I was preparing to offer my soul to the Elanraigh as that Memteth swung his blade, about to cleave my skull."

Thera nodded somberly, remembering.

Enid shifted to a slung-hip stance and jerked her chin toward the courtyard where some of the troop practiced weaponry. "Lady, you too were overpowered by a Memteth raider and most certainly he would have killed you had not the Elanraigh sent the grey wolf."

"I..." Thera flushed deeply.

Enid quickly interjected, "Lady, I do not say this to pain you," her color deepened also. "It is we who should be ashamed, who are sworn to protect the Salvai. I wish to offer my service to teach you any fighting skills you might wish to learn."

Thera stared at Enid, intent on her own thoughts.

"Salvai Thera. I do not mean to offend — I know weapons craft is not a Lady's task."

"Enid," Thera lightly touched Enid's tense forearm, "I am grateful for your offer, I was just...thinking within myself. You see, I was once told that the sword would not be my weapon. The shade of my great-grandfather told me this, but I would like to be stronger of body. Could you help me train as you do?"

Enid's features, still swollen from her injuries in the Memteth battle, cracked into what must have been a painful smile. "Elanraigh bless you, Lady! It will be my honor."

THERA RUBBED at her shoulders again. Enid kept her promise all too well. She had worked Thera hard the last few days.

Yet this physical exhaustion did not relieve the restlessness Thera now felt.

No word from Allenholme in eight days now. What does it mean?

Her mouth drew down ruefully, her father's missives had always been brief, but Thera needed those few scrawled words of home.

She lifted her head, sniffing the air and sending her thoughts out. Even the Elanraigh forest mind seemed distant from her right now, as if it were preoccupied.

Well. It seems I'm forgotten.

Outside her window, a dreary grey mist darkened the keep's walls and moisture dripped from the trees. Thera bounced a light, determined fist on the stone sill.

"I swear I will trek back to Allenholme. By the One Tree, I *will* go if I have not word of them by tomorrow."

A gust of wind swayed the hemlock trees with a sound like waves, and homesickness washed over her.

Mieta and Enid, dressed in light kilts and linen shirts, appeared in the courtyard below. Thera called to them.

"Enid...Mieta, Blessings!"

The swordswomen paused in their stretching routine. "Lady Thera, blessings of the new day! You are early to rise."

"No earlier than you, it seems."

Mieta grimaced. "We're a little ahead of the others this morning. We go on our run soon."

"I would like to join you!" Thera called.

Mieta looked so startled that Enid barked a laugh.

"Aye, Lady, do." Mieta called, recovering. "We'll be glad of your company to be sure, and perhaps the Sirra will choose an easier path than she threatened us with today."

Thera dressed quickly, in the same kilt, shirt, and leggings she had been wearing for her training sessions with Enid. She smiled. Enid couldn't wink with her eyes as swollen as they were, but she had flashed a conspiratorial smile as Thera spoke to Mieta.

She had asked Enid to keep their training sessions a secret, "No need to upset the elder Damas, Enid."

So, she continued to improve her penmanship and knowledge of courtly protocols with Dama Ainise, and, with more enthusiasm, studied healing lore with Mistress Rozalda.

In addition, there were welcome summons from the Elanraigh. On the latest of these quiet retreats forest-mind had taught her the Bear's Sleep Trance. Thera learned how to slow her body's functions; how to draw needed minerals from her bones, and how to break down her own body's wastes and reuse them, thus rebuilding what she had drawn from. This way, the Elanraigh explained, when she projected out of her physical body, even if for many days, she would not be so weakened and ill when she returned.

Thera ran down the main stairs, feeling the stretch and pull of the muscles in her legs. At the main hall she turned left and pushed through a small postern exiting into the north courtyard.

Mieta smiled an upside-down greeting from her spine-flexing bend. Thera followed Enid's warm-up moves until she no longer felt the morning's chill on her bare arms. As others straggled out, they gave her friendly nods and salutes.

When Sirra Alaine strode into the courtyard, she stopped by Thera's side. "Salvai?"

Now why did the Sirra choose to use her title? Did she mean to side with the Damas and point out that it was undignified of her to be here? Thera studied the Sirra's dark-oak features.

"I feel the need to — to be doing something, Sirra. The troops don't mind me joining them." Thera knew she jibbed like a restless colt, but she couldn't help it. She felt that she needed to fill her lungs with air and fling her body against the wind.

Sirra Alaine nodded.

Mieta grinned broadly, as did others.

Alaine, observing this, spoke dryly, "We plan to run hard today, Lady. There has been much lolling about close quarters, what with convalescents to tend and the Elankeep itself needing repair."

Mieta groaned dramatically, "My shins hurt already, Sirra. Bruised and sore, that's what they are. The way Alba flails those walking-sticks of hers."

Thera laughed with the others. Alba's rapid recovery had lightened many hearts around the keep.

"Sirra, I ran with you before, if you remember the day I first came to Elankeep." Thera's gaze swung around the group. She drawled, teasing, "I won't prevent the troop from being exercised to your liking."

THE SUN HAD ALMOST BURNED off the morning mist, when the small group returned toward Elankeep. Rhul panted, "It's going to be a steaming mug of Ella's blackberry tea, warm barley bannock, and creamy cheese for me!"

Thera felt no need of food. Her body felt light as the sea hawk's adrift on the wind — her blood ran hot under her wind-chilled skin. *I could run forever!*

"Alba!" Somebody behind her shouted.

Thera narrowed her gaze toward the keep. There was Alba, tottering on her walking-sticks and waving enthusiastically.

Alba is waving something — a letter! It has to be a letter from home!

Thera lengthened her stride. Edred laughingly matched her pace. They drew ahead of the others, who cheered them on. Thera reached for more speed as they passed the amazed guard at the gate, skidded past Alba, and collapsed against the keep wall. Their laughter echoed under the great stone arch.

"Cythian Hell!" Alba spun on her crutches as four hands reached to steady her.

"There is no one else here..." panted Edred, "...who can beat me at a foot race, Lady." Edred, a lean sliver of a woman, cast an amazed look at Thera.

Thera paced the small paved area by the door, one hand holding the stitch in her side. "I would be...hard put...to say whose foot first reached the entrance, Edred."

Edred smiled, and patted Alba's shoulder. "Which was first foot, Alba?"

"Do not be asking me to judge! All I saw was a whirling storm of arms and legs coming straight at me!"

Thera wheezed a laugh. "What have you...there, Alba?" she eagerly eyed the small scroll Alba held.

"Something important enough that I stood in such unexpected danger to get it to you, Lady." She handed the paper to Thera, "A carrier bird from Allenholme came in just now."

CHAPTER 31

*D*aughter,

Be assured that your lady mother and I are well.

The Memteth invaders increase the frequency of their harrying attacks on our shores. At Kenna Beach, a band of Ttamarini scouts fought to repel a landing of three Memteth ships. This battle was bloody, as the Ttamarini scouts who first encountered the Memteth were greatly outnumbered. Word came to me by way of a wounded Ttamarini sent to alert Allenholme and the Ttamarini encampment. We rode out after the Ttamarini warriors with such dispatch as our heavier horse and armor would allow. By the time we of Allenholme arrived at Kenna Beach, the scouts had been joined by the Ttamarini, and together we forced the raiders back.

We fought with the tide lapping at our feet. A line of Memteth took a stand at the water's edge and fought so fiercely that we were withheld while many of their number escaped to their ships. Our archers, lead by Sirra Maxin, did set afire one ship and men cheered to see its black sail catch

and burn. Another of the Memteth ships did cut sail to take
on crew from the burning ship. I do not believe this was
compassion for endangered comrades as much as a practical wish to preserve numbers. Teckcharin, however,
believes it bespeaks some code of honor.

Teckcharin did slay many invaders — as many, almost,
as I. Our Ttamarini is grim and silent in battle, unlike my
Heart's Own whose war cries fire the blood. I did only hear
Teckcharin call out once — when his son fell. After the
battle, Teckcharin was as a man possessed until the boy was
found and the old *Maiya* pronounced the wound not likely
to be mortal. The lad fought well. Indeed, he rode to defend
Dougall, who was trapped under his slain horse. Two
Memteth were about to finish him as he lay pinned. What
honor there, I ask you? Chamakin took his blow after killing
the one Memteth and mortally wounding the other. I am
grateful to this young warrior for saving the life of one so
dear to me, though the incoming tide almost accomplished
what the Memteth failed to do. Dougall was half-drowned
when we did get to him and the fallen Ttamarini youth. I
will tell you plainly, that I wish we had pursued peace with
these brave Ttamarini before now. The lad, Chamakin,
seemed feverish from his wound but after I spoke to him of
your being safe at Elankeep, he fared better. Perhaps, it was
Cook's possets that did the deed.

Your mother bids me tell you how it eases her heart to
know you are safe in the Elanraigh's care, but she is sorely
grieved to learn of Nan's death. The names of your escort
have been inscribed, into the scroll, with honor. Sadly, the
Lament has been sung for all too many.

We grimly prepare for attack on Allenholme itself. The
raiders grow ever bolder. Teckcharin feels these raids have
been but to take our measure. I have instructed Mika ep

Narin, Fishing Guild Master, to organize the fishing fleet — they cargo rocks to the harbor entrance and there off-load them. Some Memteth ships are rigged to sling fiery projectiles. These fearsome spheres hurl flaming fragments in all directions when they strike. We lost Arnott's father, Goodnath, as fine a fellow as I've met. Young Branson also — struck by one of these cursed flaming rocks before his sword was even blooded. Some others have since died of their wounds. We lost too many a fine horse as well.

These ships must not be allowed to approach Allen-holme. Mika ep Narin has vowed he will sink the fishing fleet itself, if he must, to form a barrier against the Memteth. I stared to hear him utter such words, for all know what each mariner's ship is to him. Yet I saw Mika's eyes as he pledged the vow. Elanriagh forbid. Yet, the old man's spirit did make my heart swell.

Be well, my own,

Your loving father,

Leon

~

HOT TEARS BURNED her eyes and her hand clenched, damaging the thin parchment of her father's letter.

Chamak wounded! She stopped, and smoothing the letter on her dresser, read it again.

"No, no, and no. I will not hide away here when my people are fighting and dying. Elanraigh Bless! What does all this mean if I do not fight for my home, my people, the ones I love." Her throat tightened.

Chamak. Chamak had been hurt and the Elanraigh had not told her!

Her hands gripped the window ledge, her arms aching with tension, *"How could you not tell me?"* She sent.

No response. Thera felt a frisson of foreboding. The Elanraigh *felt* elsewhere.

Sussara, however, swirled outside her window, the small wind elemental sounded worried. *"Therrra?"*

"Sussara. Blessings, it isn't you I'm angry at."

Sussara curled about her. *"Fly soon?"*

Thera's fingers relaxed their tension. *"Yes, Sussara. Now. We fly now. Meet me at the top of the tallest tower."*

She tried to ignore the clenching of her gut, as an increasing sense of urgency threatened to cloud her thinking. "Yes, I must see how things fare at home. I will call the sea hawk," she affirmed aloud, "I will enter the Bear's Sleep Trance. When they find me ..." her brow puckered, and she felt a pang, "...well, they will worry."

Thera paused, her hand gripping a thick woolen cloak, "Well I can't help that — I *must* go. I'll be back before anyone really misses me, and if I'm found, the healing mistress will know I am in trance, surely." She moved swiftly about the chamber. *I just want to see home.*

Thera shrugged into a warm jersey and threw on the cloak. Opening the chamber door, she listened for sound. She heard voices; however, they were far below. She was left in privacy to read her missive from home.

She ran along the hall and up the steep stairs that spiraled to the north tower roof.

Brisk winds had come and blown the morning's grey clouds away. Feeling the need of some kind of ritual to steady her, Thera turned to face the Elanraigh. She raised her arms and asked for Blessing.

Sussara was so excited by this time it was shouting in her

mind, "*Therraa! Want to go with you. Go now?*" The small wind elemental swirled in tight circles.

"*Hush now!*" Thera bid the elemental as she tried to confine her hair into the hood of her cape.

The wind dropped to a small cajoling breeze that buffed affectionately against her skin. Facing north, the Elanraigh and home, she sent her call.

"*Why not just Thera fly?*" whispered the wind elemental.

"*It is not safe for me to be formless for long. I get tired.*"

"*Wings.*" Thera imaged. "*To fly home.*" An image of Chamakin lying wounded flashed painfully behind her eyes. Her eyes snapped open. Thera rubbed the skin at her temples. "*Something's different!*"

Visions, not her own, began to fill her mind; Farnash on a rocky hillside, turning his pale, smoky eyes to her. Slowly, his head tilted and from his mouth the long "OOO," of the wolf's song.

She envisioned enormous wings beating golden against a cobalt sky. The raptor's shrill cry pierced her to the bone and filled her skull with its sound.

"*...an almost human aura!*" The response Thera felt was full of emotional nuance, unlike her hawk's simple sendings.

"*Recognition...love...welcome.*"

Thera yearned, body and spirit, toward what came closer with each beat of huge golden wings.

"*Oh!*"

"*Therra!*" whispered Sussara, its voice awed and small. "*Eiryana comes.*"

CHAPTER 32

*P*ulling the sheepskin cloak about her, Thera slumped back on the rough planking of the watch tower deck. Her eyes fixed on the bright swatch of azure sky above, her body already slipping into the Bear's Sleep rhythm. A winged shape drifted in to the patch of blue sky framed by the battlements.

"*Thera.*" The voice in her mind was feminine in tone and touch.

Not Teacher. Not the Elanraigh. Thera wondered, "*Who...?*"

"*Come, Thera. I am Eiryana Sky Weaver.*"

Thera's consciousness spiraled upward. Sussara trailed, for once subdued, behind her.

The eagle tilted her head, seeming to watch their progress toward her.

Eiryana. The name rolled like thunder through her soul. Thera remembered the Ttamarini Dream-speaker's words to her, 'When you fly as an eagle, child, then will you be fully fledged.'

Thera swirled below the span of Eiryana's great wings, wings that spread a full pike length, wingtip to wingtip.

"Such beauty and power!"

"Know that you are beautiful to me as well." The eagle's eye gleamed like sunlit amber. *"The Elanraigh has promised this joining since I was a nestling — I am in my first year of power, and you now enter yours. Let us be together."*

The warmth of Eiryana's welcome drew her.

"Oh the difference in this joining!"

Thera felt Eiryana's chest muscles momentarily tense in a reflex of surprise, and then her wings stroked powerfully. Thera understood.

The small wind elemental puffed out from under her wings like a bouncing ball. Sussara sent Thera and Eiryana the equivalent of giggling, joyful laughter.

"Eiryana. Are there many like you who can speak with a human?" Thera wondered.

"Very few, now. In the time of your ancestors, though, there were others of the Sky Weaver clan, and of the Grey Wolves, who soul-shared with human-folk. Most now have forgotten those bonds."

"Not one of my kin has ever spoken to me of those gifts," Thera mused. *"I do not think my people remember."*

"The Ttamarini remember those times," Eiryana replied.

"Ah. Well, the Ttamarini are very different."

"In the time of your ancient-ancestors, all were the same."

Thera mulled over this statement in silence as they skimmed the tall trees by Bridal Veil Falls. When Eiryana spoke again her tone of thought was wondering. *" I feel as if we are two nestlings long parted. With every wing beat that brings us closer, we share more of our feelings and experiences — do you feel so?"*

"*Yes! It is more like reunion than first meeting. Perhaps our ancient-ancestors knew each other this way.*"

Eiryana folded her wings and dove toward the waterfall's spray, through the mist and rainbow colors she did a tumbling roll. The roar of the falls thundered in her bones.

"*Thera of Allenholme, you are now woven into my song, with the Elanraigh, the wind, the sun, and sea, forever.*"

As EIRYANA ROSE, turning north toward Allenholme, Thera sent an expression of her joy toward the Elanraigh. "*Blessings be! Eiryana and I are myia!*" The Ttamarini term, *of one soul,* seemed so right.

The Elanraigh responded, its thrum was warm, yet distracted. The forest-mind's attention was on the north.

"*Eiryana?*"

"*I do not know, Thera. All seemed well when I passed your home at dawn.*"

They said no more and the young eagle swept her wings strongly, gaining height and following the shoreline northward. With a pang, Thera recognized the black rocks of Shawl Bay. Below them the waves crested, translucent green at their peaks, trailing white foam in the wane.

"*Poor fishing there today,*" observed Eiryana.

"*What? Oh.*" Indeed, Thera had sensed no hunger.

"*Good fishing at the Spinfisher River,*" added Eiryana in explanation.

"*Ah,*" Thera commented. Her thoughts were troubled. "*Eiryana, I would like to see Nan's cairn.*"

The eagle veered to fly low over the foaming water's edge. She settled on a spruce above the site where Thera had found Nan's body. Below them was the rough stone cairn the Elankeep troop had erected over the bodies of Nan, Innic, and Jon. Thera's grief thudded heavily through her veins. "*Oh, Nan.*"

Eiryana shifted on the sitka branch. "*Pain, Thera?*"

"*I miss her so, Eiryana. She died an ugly death.*"

Eiryana bent her head to preen under one wing, and withdrew her thoughts as if to give Thera privacy for her own.

"*Blessings, Nan,*" Thera sent, just as she had always greeted Nan.

"*Blessings is it now, and everyone looking high and low for Herself this day!*"

The voice Thera heard in her thoughts was Nan's, scolding just as she had when she'd found Thera asleep in mother's garden.

"*Nan!*" Thera wondered if this were a dream, something her mind produced out of its longing. She could barely articulate her thoughts. "*Are you with the Elanraigh? Are you with Innic — are you happy?*"

"*Oh, aye, Button. I've gone where I can have peace from children's questions.*"

Thera felt the sensation of Nan's arms warm about her, and leaned into it.

"*Go on with you now. Do not be lingering here — there be naught here but a grave.*"

A final caress of her cheek, and Thera was aware of no presence but the wind, and a small itching under Eiryana's wing.

"*Eiryana, we can go now.*"

The eagle lifted and sweeping through the spindrift thrown by the wild sea, she rose into the bright sky.

Thera's heart was too full for sharing thoughts until Eiryana asked in subdued tone, "*Thera, you have pain still?*"

"*Oh. Always I will miss her but she is happy. I feel a great weight is lifted from me.*" Realizing this was indeed true, Thera reflected on her good memories of Nan.

Some wing beats later, curiosity framed Eiryana's tone as she asked, "*Button?*"

CHAPTER 33

"*We're almost home, Eiryana!*" Thera's heart lifted as she saw the familiar landmark of Lorn a'Lea Point.

No smoke palled the sky, no clash of battle could be heard. With a rush of relief Thera realized how much she had feared she would find Allenholme under attack.

Eiryana whistled, startled, as they swept around the high rocky bluff above Lorn a'Lea Beach.

A huge ship, a ship unlike any Thera had ever seen, was making stately progress toward Allenholme. In the far distance, two of Allenholme's fishing fleet were underway as if to meet it.

"*This can only be the warship from Cythia!*" Thera surmised.

Incredulous, she eyed the ship's mainsail blazing molten-yellow in the bright sun, elaborate red-griffin banners undulated on the wind as the Cythian vessel slowly maneuvered toward Allenholme. Her numerous crews swarmed the deck as a hand of brilliantly dressed nobles lounged near the helm on the high-turreted stern. One noble had long blonde hair, neither braided nor tied, that blew in the wind. Others, soldiers Thera judged by their gear, kept watch or were at ease on the forward deck.

"*See!*" Eiryana's tone was dire. "*There!*"

Bent under the wind and the speed of their approach, sped at least five hands of Memteth ships.

"*They must be mad to attack the warship!*"

Eiryana's reply was a mental snort. "*Why? This vessel wallows like a fat duck.*"

Thera was forced to agree. Though a sight to see with her high turrets, bright sails and shining brass, she was turgid and slow. The Memteth ships approached swiftly, swooping like dark swallows low over the water.

Alarm rang out aboard the Cythian ship. She heard shouted orders and the thud of feet on the deck as the cross-bowmen scrambled into position. Behind the archers, the soldiers readied their pikes, preparing to repel boarders.

Thera watched the Memteth ships flare apart, to encircle the bigger warship.

"*Eiryana! Those that come from Allenholme — we must warn them if we can.*"

Eiryana swept toward the ships flying the Allenholme banner. Shouts carried faintly on the wind.

"*They've seen the Memteth!*" Thera was glad of Eiryana's eagle vision, many times better than her own.

"*That will be my father — see the crimson cloak near the prow of Bride O'Wind.*"

Oak Heart was turned to the crew, watching as Mika ep Narin directed them. At midships she recognized the Ttamarini Chief and Captain Dougall. Sun glinted off the helmets of a handful of archers; the rest on board the *Bride* were simple mariners.

On the second Allenholme ship Thera recognized

Captain Lydia and the Guild Master's assistant. This ship also carried archers as well as crew.

"*Elanraigh guard them! They hurry to help the Cythians.*"

Eiryana whistled her hunting challenge and swooped low over the heads of those on board the *Bride*. The Ttamarini chief pointed, gesturing animatedly to Duke Leon.

"The beauty!" cried Dougall, "An omen the Elanraigh is with us, lads!"

"An omen!" The men cried to each other. Mariners on the second Allenholme ship also cheered, their voices faint on the wind.

Teckcharin stared upward, one hand shading his eyes, the other gripping the rail. Thera saw the Ttamarini's gaze fixed upon her.

"*If only father would look again.*" Thera found herself willing her father to sense her presence.

Duke Leon turned to the men and pumped his fist into the air as he cheered them on. "A noble sign from the Elanraigh, *Araghna-hei! ArNarone!*"

"*ArNarone!*" The crews roared in response.

"So. Well." Thera sighed.

"*Thera. How could he know? Who among your people even dreams the dreams anymore? The Lord of Allenholme's gift is given of the sword and yours of the Elanraigh.*"

She broke off her circling of the *Bride O'Wind*.

Chief Teckcharin, though, raised hand to forehead. Eiryana whistled a single, soft note in courteous response, eliciting more cheers and war cries from the Allenholme men.

"*No, Thera. He does not know. It is just that the Ttamarini Chief has always honored our kind.*"

Memteth surrounded the Cythian warship — arrows

were fired by both sides. Cythian foot soldiers threw lances when any Memteth ventured within range, though the Memteth merely darted in and out with no attempts to grapple and board.

"*Eiryana, does it seem to you that the Memteth deliberately distract the Cythians from that larger, wider ship?*"

They watched this particular Memteth ship maneuver — it was armed with a shielded catapult device that now flung a black, pitch-like substance toward the Cythian vessel. Blotches of this substance adhered to the warship's sides, dark tendrils of slime oozing toward the waterline.

Eiryana hung in the airstream above the warship's mast. The Cythians seemed unable to effectively injure the swiftly moving Memteth. As it was, neither side was significantly damaging the other.

Thera remembered the *Grace O'Gull* as she'd been found after the Memteth attack on it — all the crew killed, their bodies carved and cut. "*They toy with the Cythians,*" she shared with Eiryana.

Just below them, a Cythian soldier yelled, then swore profusely. Alarmed, they looked to see only that he had been pelted with some of the Memteth's black substance. Other than his disgust he seemed unhurt.

"Blast ya Krist!" cried the man next to the besmirched Cythian soldier. "I thought at the least you'd been skewered! Blood of a Devil! You smell like bilge bottom." He shoved at the unfortunate Krist, then wiped his hands on his jerkin. "Ach. Now look. Pfah! You'd think they'd do better than fling their chamber pots at us."

"*Thera. See!*" Eiryana meant the rocks of the Lorn a'Lea point. The broad beam of the harried warship was close to running aground. They glanced at the helmsman. "*He knows.*"

The helmsman yelled desperately...something...to a sailor near him, who ran to the stern hauling aside a young mariner crouched below the turret wall. The sailor's face blanched and he skidded forward to hail the deck crew.

The blonde-haired nobleman near the stern grabbed the shrinking young mariner by his shirtfront, shouted into his face, and then flung him toward the stair. The youth stumbled, scrambled to his feet with a white-eyed glance over his shoulder and ran to join those mariners attempting to climb the mast. A moment later he fell to the deck with an arrow in his neck.

"*Fire! They are lighting fire!*" Horror rang in Eiryana's mind-shout.

"*Fire arrows!*" Closing in now, the Memteth fired volleys of flaming arrows at the warship, aiming for the thick black globs that clung like huge leeches all over the ship. Memteth raider ships now slewed off to intercept the Allenholme vessels that were almost upon them.

Frantic, they spared a glance, using Eryana's sharp sight, toward the Allenholme ships — they were preparing to engage the Memteth.

The cries of men angry and afraid were muffled by the roaring of the strange blue flames. Flames now leapt high over the Cythian vessel's sides. Like a dry wick, the mainsail caught and flames went shooting up the mast. The rush of rising heat under Eiryana's wings tossed her out of the fire's reach. The roar of it dinned in her head.

"*By the One Tree!*" cried Thera, as Eiryana panted in the dry, scorching air. "*What is it that makes this fire so fierce and strange?*"

Cythians were jumping overboard now. They saw the soldier, Krist, backing from the flames that consumed the ship's sides. He gathered himself as if to jump, when the eerie blue fire seemed suddenly to lean inward, snapping like wild dogs at prey. The flames howled as, afire, he ran through the wall of blue flames and tumbled, voiceless, toward the water. His companion whose hands and forearms were afire, writhed in agony, his screams shrill as a seabird's until he, too, struck the water.

Eiryana screamed, as Thera struggled with tearless horror and pity.

Many of the Cythian soldiers now leaping from the doomed ship, weighted by their gear or unable to swim, quickly sank beneath the water. Mariners who clung to floating debris were picked off by Memteth archers. The Memteths' shouts rang triumphant.

Thera could not tell Eiryana's anger from her own. The Cythian deaths were terrible — Memteth archers continuing to execute the exhausted burned survivors at will. The flaming ship drifted ever closer to Lorn a'Lea point, and the Elanraigh.

Eiryana whistled in alarm.

The Elanraigh!

CHAPTER 34

"*W*ithdraw!*" Thera's mental shout was full of the panic she felt. *Leave the endangered area!* Her mind flinched from visions of the Elanraigh tree elementals tormented and dying in the Memteth's fire.

The Elanraigh rumbled, "*With common fires we would, as you say, retreat from the stricken ones and group to form a barrier of our will, united we would smother the flames. This fire, though, also has will — we sense it. It hungers after us. We cannot chance it gaining foothold. We will not withdraw, child. Do not mourn — any of us would willingly die, to save The All that is Elanraigh.*"

They keened in frustration. The loss of even one tree elemental was grievous. Thera remembered the forest's rage when the Memteth had cut down the sitka.

"*Eiryana, you hear the Elanraigh — how many elementals will be lost in a battle of this kind?*"

"*Forest-mind is strong,*" Eiryana's mind-voice expressed hope.

"*I know. Remember, I told you of the bodies of the Memteth raiders in the ancient grove — like husks ground between the miller's stones. They are right, this blue fire has consciousness. I feel awareness of it like the aftermath of nightmare."*

Eiryana whistled mournfully.

"Don't despair. This thing must not overwhelm us, or distract from our belief in the Powers of Good. Elanraigh bless, I must think of something!"

They circled silently, and then Thera gasped. *"Wind!"* she sent to the Elanraigh, *"You can call the wind. It will come for you."*

"We touch minds, child, with those cousins of the air, but we do not command."

"Oh? What of Sussara? Just a few like Sussara and we can accomplish this!" Thera flung out a calling to the wind elemental.

"Thera", warned the Elanraigh, *"They are unpredictable!"*

"They will come. I feel it."

"They must come." Thera kept that thought between she and Eiryana.

Eiryana whistled softly. She swept toward the Allenholme ships. The *Bride* was grappled to a Memteth raider ship, their crews a heaving mass, fighting hand to hand. *Father!*

"Eiryana, where is my father? Where is he? The red cloak — do you see it?"

Eiryana whistled, her wings sweeping back. Below them a red-cloaked warrior struggled, clenched in a spine-cracking embrace by the largest Memteth Thera had yet seen.

Leon's neck arched back — tendons straining, teeth bared. His upturned face was a taut mask as he blindly met her gaze. With a throat-tearing roar, he broke free.

Eiryana's keen sense of smell warned Thera that the deck surface was beslimed with blood. Oak Heart slipped, falling hard on his hip. The Memteth howled and charged. Leon rolled, grabbed his sword, deflecting the Memteth's powerful down stroke. Thera's scream was an eagle's shrill-pitched call as they watched her father struggle to his feet.

He limps! He cannot keep this up! Oh where are the others?

A wounded mariner lay propped against the mast. His eyes on his Duke, he inched the fingers of his uninjured arm toward a bloodied iron gaff. Thera smelled his sweat, and fear. *Do it, good boy! A distraction, anything!*

They saw Dougall, hard-pressed, casting frantic looks aft, striving to hack his way to the Oak Heart's side. Teckcharin fought with strength and skill but there was something about his footing...

The Ttamarini may never have been at sea before, and look how the deck is tossing!

A throbbing cry burst from the throat of another Memteth on the raider ship. This one grabbed a pike and vaulted the gap between the two ships to join his companion.

Eiryana shrilled her hunting cry, and before Thera could even form the thought, folded her wings and attacked.

Both Memteth wore helmets, but the pike-wielder's was made only of leather. The eagle's vision was focused on her chosen prey, though the speed of their plunge would have dizzied Thera's human perceptions. She attacked from high and behind the pikeman. Oak Heart's eyes widened in surprise as he saw what came towards him. Eiryana, talons extended, struck hard. Thera felt terrific impact as her hurtling weight snapped the Memteth pikeman's neck and propelled his body against his companion's sword.

She heard the cracking of bone and smelled the scent of rising blood.

Thera refused to submit to the lightning-like flash of

exaltation that now blinded Eiryana to all other senses. "*I will not allow you to be hurt as the young sea hawk was. Eiryana. Arrows! Get out of range of their arrows. Quickly!*"

"*Eiryana!*" Thera's mind-voice almost sobbed with anxious care.

"*I will kill this other one! Leave be!*"

"*Do you think the Memteth will stand still to watch? Eiryana Sky Weaver is not foolish. Now!*" Understanding too well how Eiryana felt, Thera exerted the steady pressure of her will even as Eiryana opened herself like a floodgate to share with her the rapture of this victory.

"*No!*"

Finally Eiryana obeyed. Snapping her wings, she lifted away. Memteth, crying out in consternation, sent arrows to harass their flight. Eiryana screamed defiance.

Oak Heart, recovered from the surprise of the giant raptor's attack, swung his sword striking the Memteth's shoulder. The raider roared. Planting his foot against his dead companion's chest, he shoved the corpse off his sword. Shifting his weapon to his uninjured arm, seeming oblivious to his massive wound, he charged forward. Leon ducked beneath the wild sweeps of the giant's sword.

Leon's injured leg betrayed him. It gave out, crumpling beneath him. The Memteth raised his weapon high.

Eiryana screamed.

With a hoarsely yelled curse the wounded mariner at the mast lunged for the barbed gaff, grabbed and threw it, striking the Memteth's groin.

Wild-eyed, the Memteth stared at the protruding hook. Leon levered to his feet with a yell, and swung his sword at the giant Memteth's neck.

The raider fell to his knees; his head wobbled

grotesquely and fell to the deck an instant before the corpse dropped.

Cries went up. Thera saw Dougall thrust his sword into his attacker and break free, sprinting to Oak Heart's side. Teckcharin growled something to the Memteth before him and grinned wolfishly. The raider retreated toward his ship. Allenholme mariners cheered.

"*Thera.*" Eiryana warned. Distracted, Thera heard the sound before she saw. Groaning like a suffering beast the Cythian warship grated across the farthest rocks of Lorn a'Lea islets.

Thera's heart pounded. "*Perhaps she'll catch and hold.*"

Eiryana shrilled, sharing the hope, her voice carrying even over the roar of flames. Thera prayed to the Powers of Good that the flaming ship would indeed be held off from the forested beach, but the ship lifted clear to drift slowly shoreward again. Two men, one, the blonde-haired noble, the other all in black, vaulted from the warship's stern, past the fire and into the water. They bobbed to the surface, swimming for the rocks of Lorn a'Lea.

"*Therrra! Therraaa! I've come with family! All want to help the tree cousins. Are we going to make a wave?*"

Thera almost wept with relief.

She felt Eiryana's surprised grunt as the covey of wind elementals tossed her exuberantly.

"*Sussara, Blessings on you. However, do stop now and listen. No. This time we need to make a big wind. A wind big enough to blow that burning ship away from the beach.*"

Sussara swirled. "*Nasty fire folk,*" it commented. "*Push and shove at me when I went to get help. Huh. Brought* all *my family. Now we'll see.*"

"*Sussara! Can you do it? Can you save the Elanraigh?*"

Sussara gusted. *"Family say that ship will be hard to move until the tide turns."*

"When does the tide turn?" asked Thera, trying to keep anxious haste from her mind-voice.

"Soon, family say."

"Sussara, we must try now. For the Elanraigh. The terrible flames are so close to the trees."

Sussara swirled, apparently communing with the family of wind elementals. Thera could get no sense of the "family's" mind-voice.

"Family say they will try. Therrra, they say it would be good to move the little ships that still have the wind catchers on them."

Thera checked with Eiryana, who was as baffled as she. *"But they're not on fire, little one."*

"Yesss. We know. But Therra, Eiryana Sky Weaver, and Elanraigh tree-cousins would like to see them go away. Yesss?"

Eiryana grunted in surprise again, loosing height, as the riotous covey of wind elementals departed.

"Eiryana, where are they? Can you tell?"

"They have gone to the top of Lorn a'Lea cliff. Perhaps they commune with the Elanraigh."

"Ah." Thera could sense them now. They spun above the cliff, faster and faster in tight circles, then plunged in an ever increasing gust down the cliff face and out over the water.

The wind elementals couldn't affect the burning warship directly, but they could affect the water around her. The ship slowly righted. Spinning slightly, she tipped back, away from the shore. The flames howled eerily, flattening, snapping like werehounds at the wind.

"It's working! Elanraigh Bless! If they can just hold her there until she burns completely away. She's almost down to blackened beams now — surely the flames must die when the ship is gone?"

Eiryana whistled.

Memteths' voices carried in snatches over the wild winds as the crews of the raider ships adjusted their "wind catchers," as Sussara called them.

"Yes," commented Thera, bitter satisfaction laced her mind-voice as she and Eiryana skirted the edge of the maelstrom. *"Imagine how mystified they are by this "freak" wind!"*

Horrified cries rose from the raider ships closest to the Cythian vessel as the perverse wind forced them against the burning hulk. Flames eagerly leapt to their new havens. Once alight, the raider ships were blown toward their companions' ships as they made haste to be underway.

"So, the fire is equally merciless to its own creators," Thera murmured, subduing an unwelcome welling of pity for even the Memteth as they leapt wrapped in whirling flames into the waters of the bay.

Eiryana veered toward the point.

"What?"

"A Memteth lizard beast. Below us."

The huge reptile, shifting nervously, stood at the stern of a Memteth ship. Ship's crew must already have jumped overboard. It swayed, forked tongue questing the air. As the flames hurried toward it, it too slid into the water. The flat, reptilian head soon reappeared at the water surface. The beast swam, arrowing for the rocks where the two Cythian nobles had pulled themselves to safety.

Thera could see the blonde man and his dark companion casting about for, anything, presumably, they could use to defend themselves.

Thera felt all the horror she had on her first encounter with a Memteth lizard. Eiryana appraised the creature, *"Reptiles are good. I frequently take them if there is no fish."*

"*Ptah!*" Thera commented, "*Can we help these Cythians, Eiryana? Is it too dangerous for you?*"

"*It is much bigger than a bluefish or even a bristlefang. It will be difficult to kill. I will not be able to carry it,*" she added.

"*Blessings no! If we can just keep it from the Cythians, it will be well.*"

Eiryana winged for height. Thera held herself quiet as Eiryana prepared. She experienced the sharpening of vision as Eiryana became completely focused on the giant lizard. Then, once again that sudden drop as Eiryana folded her wings, diving through the driving winds toward the snake-like head.

Thera heard the blonde Cythian's shout, peripherally saw his gesture of pointing. His black-robed companion with one hand on the younger man's shoulder, shaded his eyes with the other, watching. Wind elementals lashed at the dark man's long black hair and sweeping moustaches. He moved his hand, absently, as if swatting flies, and the elementals recoiled in disorder. Thera had no time to wonder.

Eiryana struck. Just behind the reptile's head. Her talons pierced the tough skin and clenched on muscle. The beast thrashed and Eiryana held, half lifting, then tearing loose just as it rolled and submerged itself into the eddies of its own blood.

The blunt head re-appeared several pike lengths away, the beast deflected from its earlier course and now swimming for the beach.

"*Eiryana, are you all right?*" Thera felt the young eagle's pain.

"*Well enough. Hind talon. It's a heavy beast.*"

"*Its wound is bad, Eiryana. You may have killed it!*"

On the shore of Lorn a'Lea Beach were a double-hand of

Ttamarini and Duke's soldiers equipped with ropes, buckets, and shovels. A continuous string of riders were edging down the steep trail.

"*They must have come to defend the Elanraigh against the fire. Blessings on them.*" Thera shared.

"*We will drive the Memteth's beast to them.*" Diving and swooping, Eiryana harried the lizard. Snapping at them, it rolled, its limbs convulsed then loosened. The body washed ashore. The men on shore who were shouting and cheering the eagle on, fell silent as they observed the creature.

"Spawn of a Sea Fiend!" exclaimed one as they circled it.

"What be it?" asked Kirten, his youthful voice cracking.

"What matter?" replied Ent. "Some form of filthy Memteth creature." He shaded his good eye in a long look at the eagle drifting above him. "It be an omen. Yon fine, brave creature of the Elanraigh has destroyed this vile beast. Tore its throat."

"Worse teeth than a bristlefang!" whispered Kirten. He crouched at its head and reached to finger the gaping jaw.

"Ware!" yelled Ent. He laughed uproariously as Kirten flinched back a full body length, scrambling for his spear.

Wiping his eye with the back of his hand, Ent subsided, only to start up again as he observed the youth's wrathful face.

"You one-eyed old sedgemole! If you weren't older than my granda I'd make you pay for that!"

"Oh-huu-huu-huu!" Ent hooted, pointing. "Oh, aye. Aye." He finally turned, hefting his own spear. "Damned young fool. Your old granda would have known better. It's not dead yet. This beast could still take your arm off." He prodded it with the spear tip, and the jaws snapped. "Be done with you," Ent snarled and plunged his spear into the lizard's chest. The lizard's massive tail lashed, sweeping sand into Kirten's startled face, before it lay still.

Her heart thudding light and swift, Thera vividly recalled her own battle with a Memteth lizard beast. Eiryana, swept along with Thera's feelings, screamed her hunting cry. Below them, faces upturned and voices hailed Eiryana with their war cries.

Sirra Maxin, whose face Thera recognized among the rest, now turned and barked at soldiers, Allenholme and Ttamarini alike. "Away with you now from gawking at the beasties." Some he sent to the grisly task of collecting the bodies of Cythian and Memteth dead; some to scouting southward along the forest edge for survivors.

The two Memteth ships that had survived the battle were already mere specks on the horizon. The *Bride* was under way to rescue the Cythian noblemen from their perch on the rocks of Lorn a'Lea Beach. Already the noblemen were up to their knees in the incoming tide. Winging closer, they saw Oak Heart standing with Dougall and Teckcharin. Duke Leon limped heavily when he moved, but his voice rang out with vigor enough.

The two Cythian noblemen watched as the *Bride O'Wind* approached. The younger man reached behind his head, tying his hair that had loosened in the wind. He seemed a handsome man of fair complexion. His nose was small, but well shaped. Now he frowned and leaned toward his companion, speaking swiftly. His teeth were very white and even. His neck flared smoothly to broad shoulders. She heard his voice rise on the wind, a clear tenor.

The wind elementals were again tearing at the blonde man's taller companion. The man stood, arms folded across his chest, seemingly unperturbed by the frenzied wind elementals.

"*They really seem to dislike this black-robed man,*" Thera observed with surprise.

Eiryana whistled softly.

"Yes," replied Thera. She, too, felt a queer uneasiness as she examined him. He was older than her father. His long black hair was graying. He was tall and wide shouldered and as the wild winds molded his wet robe to him, Thera could see he was of a gaunt leanness. His eyes were deep-set. Even with Eiryana's excellent vision, she could not determine their color, only that they were dark. His mouth was a red slash of color below his long black moustaches — his skin very white.

The *Bride* launched a skiff to pick up the Cythians, the rowers pulling hard toward the awash survivors.

"*Eiryana.*" Thera felt weary to her soul. "*I must return to Elankeep.*"

"*What will you do now?*"

"*Sleep. Then I will gather the Elankeep troop and return to Allenholme.*"

"*Rest, then.*" Eiryana banked and with several strong beats of her wings, the battle scene was far behind them. "*We will be at Elankeep by sunset.*"

CHAPTER 35

Thera slitted open her eyes to the glow of blurred, amber light. *What?*

"*Thera! Are you well?*"

"*Eiryana — where?*" Thera felt the weight and contours of her own human form. "*I'm in my body — how?*"

"*I sent you back. The bond between you and your physical body drew you safely.*" She added in wry voice, "*you did not even wake.*"

Thera's tongue felt thick in her mouth. "Hunn." Thera snorted a small laugh. "*I didn't know we could do that.*"

"*Nor I.*"

"*I am curiously light-headed. And you? Where are you?*

"*Near. A fine roosting tree on the promontory.*"

"Thera!" A different voice, a human voice, dinned in her ear while a hand shook her shoulder. "Thera."

Thera opened her eyes fully — *I'm on a bed, not the planks of the north tower.* The amber glow resolved itself into the lamp at the corner of the infirmary, a dark shadow into the Healing Mistress' face. "Rozalda. Blessings," Thera swallowed, "so thirsty."

Healing Mistress Rozalda looked weary, though the crease in her brow smoothed somewhat as Thera spoke. She disappeared from Thera's view to reappear with a water dipper.

"Here." As Rozalda raised her shoulders and helped her to drink, Thera heard a murmuring of voices. "Yes," Rozalda tossed over her shoulder, "she's awake."

Egrit and Sirra Alaine loomed into Thera's line of sight. Their faces were worried and grim respectively.

"I've been home," Thera said, "I have such things to tell you!"

Rozalda motioned to Egrit and the girl plumped the pillows behind Thera's back, propping her up in the bed. Thera bore Egrit's fussing behind her with pricklings of impatience. To her surprise, she read disapproval in those about her.

"Eiryana, they are angry with me — after all we've done!"

Eiryana's response in her mind was sympathetic.

Rozalda, sitting very straight, hands clasped tightly in her lap, spoke first. "You have been in the deepest trance I have ever witnessed! Hardly breathing and impossible to arouse. It was Enid who found you at noontide when she went on watch. She thought you were dead. You've lain here, almost lifeless, a full day. It is near midnight now."

"I *had* to see home," Thera said. "I thought I would be back before anyone even knew I was gone. You shouldn't worry about me." Thera eyed them. "Blessings be! I am no longer a child to be coddled so. I know what I am doing."

Egrit looked unhappy. Alaine drew a quick breath — then gusted it out after a quick look and shake of the head from Rozalda. "Now," Rozalda grasped Thera's wrist and shook it. "Thera, all here are pledged to defend you; you are the Salvai. You have won their hearts as well as their loyalty

— you should not abuse them so. How could any of us be sure this was a self-induced trance, when trance it has finally proved to be? How could we know what was happening to you, wherever you had gone or been taken? You did not see Enid's face when she carried you down here after finding you on the north tower. Or Alba and the others, who have been in and out here all day, helpless to know what to do."

Thera stared.

"*Read past their anger*," came Eiryana's voice.

Thera folded her arms across her chest and frowned. "*No*," she sent back. "*They are so wise and sure. They will be sorry when they realize how they've wronged us.*"

"*Thera. Do.*"

Clenching her jaw on her own anger, she slipped into her unique way of *reading*, and studied her friends' energies. She sent Eiryana a terse acknowledgement. "*Yes. I see.*"

"*And* your *anger?*"

"*Eiryana!*"

"*Do.*"

Goaded, Thera read her own emotions, quick as if dipping her finger into simmering water.

"*All right*," she acknowledged. "*Much of my temper stems from shame at worrying them so. Blessings be. I may now be 'flying with eagles,' as the Maiya said I would, but all this love tethers me.*"

Eiryana's warm chuckle in her mind soothed the last of her ill mood. "*All life is interwoven, Thera. They are learning too.*"

Thera reached her hand, touching Sirra Alaine's sleeve. "I'm sorry to have grieved you."

Alaine's rough hand gripped Thera's painfully. "Next

time, trust us. We will ward you. Promise me, as Salvai." Her throat moved as if swallowing unspoken words.

Thera nodded solemnly.

Egrit swiped at her eyes with a corner of her apron. "I'll get us tea," she said, walking briskly to the fire.

The Healing Mistress leaned forward and tapped Thera on the leg. "Do not think the only enemies your father has are the Memteth, Thera. Among the royal houses there are those who fear and loathe Duke Leon."

"Who? Why would...?"

"Any one of many powerful men and women who influence the court." Rozalda interjected. "Men and women, who live and die for favors and influence, equate honesty with stupidity. Until now, they have allowed that the stalwart ArNarone clan is well enough placed in its remote northern holding. It is fortunate, too, that the king, though generally a fickle man, always speaks warmly of the ArNarone, and especially of your father who is his cousin's son."

Rozalda leaned back in her chair. "We are never complacent, however. Ours is a king surrounded with many clever and corrupt courtiers." She paused, staring at the lantern, her gaze unfocused. "His idea, I think, is to retain those most dangerous near him, at court, where he can keep his eye on them. Though the king keeps his powerful houses on tight leash, ArNarone has enjoyed a kind of negligent indulgence. But now," Rozalda returned her gaze to Thera, "with this new alliance of ArNarone with the Ttamarini — your father has disturbed the balance of power."

"Rozalda," Thera whispered, "how do you know all this?"

"As I told you before, Ainise and her brother belong to one of the minor houses that happen to be in the king's favor. Her brother, however, with his unfortunate love of gaming has managed to impoverish the estates. Ainise made a place for herself here, serving Salvai Keiris."

"Did he gamble away even Ainise's bride price then?" asked Thera. "It is surprising she is not more bitter than she is."

"Actually she bears great affection for her brother, and he for her. He manages to maintain a position, of sorts, at court. He has his privileges of rank still, and earns his keep ferreting out secrets to sell. He regularly sends court gossip to Ainise. As a result we are amazingly well informed."

"This is all so — disgusting," Thera raked her hair back. Her scalp felt twitchy with irritation. *Like Farnash's pelt when he is disturbed*, Thera thought. "Well I have no wish to ever go to court. We don't need Bole, or Cythia, or any of them." She tilted her chin. "Hah! We defeated the Memteth without help from either the King of Bole, or Cythia." Thera smiled, "And we have alliance with the Ttamarini now."

Rozalda's brow knit and she sighed, shaking her head. "The King of Bole, Thera, is a jealous and acquisitive man who handles his snarling pack of hounds with a firm hand and a tight leash. Do not assume he is unconcerned with what happens even in the small and remote parts of his kingdom.

"We have learned that Duke Perrod of Cythia is sending his son and Heir, Ambrauld, by ship to Allenholme. This is possibly at the king's bidding. The Cythian Heir's official position is that of emissary, but of course we know his purpose is to assess this alliance with the Ttamarini. What is more disturbing is that a Besteri accompanies the Heir."

"What is a *Besteri*?" asked Thera.

"Pagh!" Sirra Alaine spat the word. "I know of them. They be vicious as were-weasels and just as sly."

Rozalda nodded. "They are an obscure cult from the far

south. They are magicians of sorts — seemingly their gift is for *knowing* a thing. Their craft is for hire. Some few Besteri have settled in Cythia. One called Willestar has found favor with the Cythian Duke." Rozalda frowned, "It is said that a Besteri, like most mage, use the *knowing* only in order to compel."

"Aye," muttered Alaine. "Perverse."

Thera rubbed her arms as a chill riffed over her skin.

The gleaming white's of Egrit's eyes showed as she glanced from the Healing Mistress, to Alain, to Thera. "Please," she said, her soft voice seeming to break the chill spell, "I would like to hear now what happened to Lady Thera."

CHAPTER 36

Thera's audience were as enthralled with her tale as she could have wished. The Memteths' strange blue fire and the threat it had posed to the Elanraigh struck them speechless with horror. Thera's account of the sighting of the Cythian Heir and the man she now knew, thanks to Dama Ainise's brother's gleanings of court gossip, to be the Besteri mage, was swept away in their exclamations.

"Wind elementals," mused Rozalda. "I always felt that there must be something like elementals of the air. Well — and why, when you think of it, would they *not* fight to save the Elanraigh? Trees commune between earth and sky." She sighed and nodded. "It is harmonious. It feels right that they would help each other."

"Aye," Sirra Alaine eyed Thera with a satisfied expression, "and you bonded with an eagle."

"Eiryana."

"Eiryana. You fought off the Memteth, saving your father when he fell — and destroyed the Memteth reptile. It is a hero's tale, Lady." Alaine cocked an eyebrow. "Soon you will not need our meager help."

"Sirra," Thera felt both pleased and embarrassed by the praise, "it was Eiryana's self that fought the brave fight — I was just there as moral support, if you will."

"Oh, aye. But it was your will that saved the noble Eiryana's hide from the Memteth arrows, and your combined wills that saved the Elanraigh." She rubbed her hands together. "Enough to spin a fireside tale worthy of many ales!"

Thera sipped tea from her mug, and then said, "Sirra, I feel my gift of joining with the raptor birds of Elanraigh, with Eiryana, should be kept between us. Whether sent by the Elanraigh or my own intuition, I've learned to trust these feelings."

Rozalda and Alaine shared a look.

The corner of Thera's mouth quirked, "Especially, I do not wish to tell my parents about the extent of my gift — at this time, anyway."

Alaine's shoulders jerked as she swallowed a laugh with her tea. Rozalda chided, "No parents could love a child more, Thera, than do ..."

"I know, that's it exactly," Thera interrupted. "In their fervor to protect me they will attempt to do as *they* judge best."

Thera decided now was a good time to elaborate on her feelings. "It is time now for me to follow my own inner guidance." She smiled, "Haven't I been trained by the best for this — by those at Allenholme; by the Elanraigh forest-mind; by all of you here at Elankeep, and now Eiryana."

Thera placed the tea mug on the table. "You must trust me, too."

Alaine's autumn-leaf eyes danced and placing hands on knees she rocked forward. "You are right, Lady Thera," she said, rising to feet. "Do just tell us what it is you want and where you want to go. We will get you there."

Thera smiled brightly. "Then, Sirra, I want to go home."

CHAPTER 37

*J*t was still dark outside the infirmary window, yet footsteps pounded back and forth outside the door and voices echoed in the courtyard. Awake immediately, Thera quickly dressed.

"*Eiryana?*"

A very faint response, "*Hunting.*"

"*Good.*" *Blessings be, Eiryana is very hungry.* Thera grimaced and rubbed at her own midriff to subdue the rumbling there. A kettle of tea sat on the hearth beside a cloth-covered pot of oatmeal. Thera crouched, spooning some porridge into a bowl and dipping a spoon of honey over the grains. She ate ravenously.

The infirmary door cracked open, then swung wide. Sirra Alaine and First Sword Alba clattered in.

"Alba, you're not using your sticks today!" Thera exclaimed. Alba smiled broadly. *Though yet limping, she walks well,* Thera observed. *No dragging. Blessings be.*

Alba lowered herself into a chair beside Thera.

"Pardon, Lady," she carefully stretched the injured leg

before her, "wish I could reach the tea," she said to the room at large.

Alaine slanted a knowing look at Alba, but moved to pour two cups of tea, and fill two bowls of porridge. Handing Alba hers, she leaned back, one foot propped behind her against the fireplace stones.

"Sirra, won't you sit?" invited Thera.

"I thank you, Lady. But there is an old soldiers' saying that, 'a standing belly fills the fullest.'"

"Honey," mused Alba loudly and mournfully as she stared at her bowl. "No honey."

Thera laughed, shaking her head, as Alaine moved to open the honey crock. "Never mind, Lady," drawled Alaine, slopping a spoonful into Alba's tea and more into her bowl. "Once that injury of hers is healed, that muscle in our First Sword's leg will need hard work to stretch it again. Then will I come into my own."

Alba spluttered.

"Hot?" inquired Alaine. "Well, Lady," she turned to Thera. "We make ready to travel."

"Today!" Thera's heart thudded. *Home. Chamak.*

"No." Alaine's brows twitched. "No, but by the time the sun blesses the Elanraigh tomorrow we will be ready to depart.

"I wonder, Lady, if you know if we must take the coastal route or if the Elanraigh will permit us the forest track home? It is a difference of four days."

Thera communed with forest-mind.

She roused when Alaine touched her arm. "You are smiling, Lady, the news is good?"

"Oh, blessings be, Sirra," Thera wiped her eyes, "the Elanraigh is singing again and I was bound in its spell." Thera continued, "Yes, it tells me it senses no Memteth pres-

ence anywhere near. It will gladly open a forest track."
Thera's happiness at the shortened journey time brought an
affectionate rumble from the Elanraigh.

Alba slapped her leg jubilantly, then winced. "Ahh!
Demons of Hell."

THE FOLLOWING dawn was thick with fog. The travelers
assembled in the front courtyard. Horses snorted at the
chill air; their breath gusting into the fog that crept along
the ground and clung to the stone walls. Harness creaked
and jingled. The Elankeep soldiers' voices were muffled by
the fog as they spoke among each other and to their
mounts.

"I wish you could come with us," Thera said to the
Healing Mistress. She was checking Mulberry's hooves
when Rozalda joined her in the courtyard. Rising, Thera
stoked the mare's nose. "Though, of course, I understand."

Rozalda reached her hand to the mare's shoulder,
smoothing the glossy hide. "Yes. I would have liked to see
Allenholme again, and your lady mother, Thera. It has been
many years since I've seen Fideiya. But, there are the elderly
Damas to think of as well as the recovering wounded.
Alaine has assigned the light duty wounded to guard and
maintain the keep. The Elanraigh's assurance to you that the
Memteth have left this area does much to lighten heart and
mind."

Thera glanced over to First Sword Alba. Although Sirra
Alaine had adjured, then entreated her to remain behind
with the wounded, Alba would not hear of it. Even now, her
head swung belligerently at any voice, as if expecting a
rescinding of the grudging consent. She hobbled about her

horse and gear, muttering, "...think I was infirm, to hear them. Huh..."

Alaine, coming to join Thera and Rozalda, said, "Better to have her along than trying to follow on her own. Hnnh. Stubborn."

"She'll be fine, Sirra," said Thera watching Alba hop-hobbling around her placid horse.

"Aye." Alaine slowly nodded. "So I think. Stubborn — always was." Alaine swung onto her mount.

Thera caught the glimmer of Alaine's headband, the silver Sirra's emblem glinting in the light of the wall torch as she moved. As a matter of fact, the entire troop wore their dress greens, kilts, and cloaks. The garments looked freshly fulled, and every piece of metal harness and gear gleamed.

Sirra Alaine twisted back, observing the party; four hands of soldiers and Egrit to serve Thera, ten horses, and a string of five mules. Those that marched afoot were already underway.

Thera embraced the Healing Mistress and quickly mounted. Mulberry danced sideways, snorting and blowing. Rozalda laughed. "Whatever possessed Duke Leon to give you such a flighty mount, Thera?"

"Oh, but her blood lines are good. She is always restive at first; she'll test me a little, and then settle in very well. She's of good heart."

"Aye." Rozalda looked at Thera a long moment. "Aye," she repeated. "Elanraigh guard you, Salvai."

"I'll send word as soon as we're home, Rozalda." Thera impulsively reached to grasp the Healing Mistress's arm. "I will remember all your words to me."

Rozalda nodded, lips compressed. She stepped back, tucking her hands into her sleeves.

Thera turned, waving energetically to the Damas clustered at the entrance to Elankeep's hall.

Hands rose in formal blessing, their voices small in the heavy fog, the Damas chorused their various farewells. Dama Brytha, though, her bent form supported by Dama Ella, blew Thera a kiss.

How like her, Thera thought, feeling a tightness in her throat. *Blessings on them.* She dropped her arm to her side, and turned Mulberry to the gate.

"Tcht-tcht," heeling the mare to a trot, Thera rode forward to join Sirra Alaine.

CHAPTER 38

They rode single file from Elankeep, rising into weak sunlight past Bridal Veil Falls and eastward along the Spinfisher River. Looking back, Thera saw dark treetops spiking through the gauzy veils of fog.

Thera heard a sudden arpeggio of clear notes. "*Elanraigh*." She reined to a halt. Rising in her saddle she saw a trail through the heavy forest, wide enough for two abreast to ride. "*Blessings be*," she sent warm thanks.

"Sirra. There," Thera pointed. Alaine hand signaled the troop and reined in beside Thera. The two of them waited as the entire troop, wide-eyed and silent, entered the tunnel-like opening through the giant trees. Thera continued to hear the Elanraigh's singing until after she and Alaine had entered. Looking back, the saw the path obscuring behind them

Their party made better time then, the horses' legs brushing easily through moist fern and shining salal. Riding near Alaine and Alba, Thera told them about the people of Allenholme. "I hope you will come to regard them as I do," she said finally, "and feel at home when there. Though

Allenholme is not in the midst of the Elanraigh, it is on its very borders."

"Our place is at your side now, Lady. You have pledged to the Elanraigh, and we have pledged to you. It is one and the same."

Thera fell silent. Alaine observed Thera's expression and lifted her brow inquiringly.

Thera sighed. "All my life I have felt this bond with the Elanraigh, accepted the Elanraigh's love which seems to be given me unconditionally — never yet has the Elanraigh demanded any pledge or vow from me. I wonder about it. I do not know how the choosing happens with other Salvai. What do tales tell of how it was when Lady Dysanna pledged to be Salvai?"

Alaine's chin dropped to her chest as she considered. "Hnnh. It would be better to ask the Healing Mistress such history. Or even Elder Dama Brytha." Her eyes met Thera's, "But it is my understanding that there is *always* a vow taken."

"Blessings be!" cried Alba suddenly.

Thera and Alaine pulled up their horses — the troop fanning out behind them.

"If the One Tree is to be found anywhere on this earth," said Alba in hushed voice, as she gazed upward toward the distant tree canopy, "Surely this is where it will be."

Mulberry danced her feet nervously as Thera slid to the ground. "Hush now," she murmured to the mare. Standing at Mulberry's head, she gazed around her. *It is a sight to set the soul singing*, she thought.

Here, far from the pearly mists of Bridal Veil Falls, the sunlight slanted through the evergreens like sheets of molten copper, illuminating the mossy trunks of the largest trees Thera had ever seen. Handing her reins to Alba, who took them silently, Thera walked forward. An eagle whistled high above her, but no mind-voice intruded. Even the singing of the small birds of the Elanraigh suddenly hushed.

She approached the nearest forest giant. Its base was so wide that all of the troop, finger-tip to finger-tip, could not have spanned its width. The sitka's huge base spread to grip the earth like the paw of some mythical beast.

Thera's breath quickened as she came close, reaching her hand to touch the ancient tree's bark. Energy, like a shower of sparks leapt into her body. Thera gasped, caught in the tree's powerful grip. Her breath came quick and shallow as visions began to flow; dappled sunlight, flowing swift as years passed in the single beat of her mighty heart; her roots delving the dark loam to grip the rocky bones of earth itself. Thera was dizzied by the spinning vision of eons of stars wheeling overhead. *How many hundreds of years!*

"Ancient One, Blessings be," Thera whispered her greeting. Never had she felt so small and insignificant. The sitka elemental's mind-voice merged with the wind that moved through the branches so high above her head.

"*Thera, daughter of Allenholme, your vow will soon be demanded. It must be the true choice of your heart.*"

Thera felt tears rising. "*Do you doubt my love?*"

Warmth and understanding enfolded her. "*Child, you are our hope, but the vow must be made with full understanding. You must know your heart before you pledge it.*"

"*I am ready now.*" Thera felt tears on her face. "*I will never choose other than to serve the Elanraigh.*"

"*No. Soon.*

Thera folded down, leaning against the tree giant. It comforted her — yet, though it surrounded her with its love, it would not yet take her vow.

Finally she felt a gentle nudge, "*Continue your journey, you will be at Allenholme by dark. We guard your way.*"

Drawing a deep breath, Thera bid the sitka farewell. "*I will prove my heart to you,*" she promised. "*I pray to do so.*"

As Thera walked back to the troop the forest sang — it was a paean of both joy and longing. She saw Alba freeze where she stood, one foot in the stirrup. The First Sword's head tipped upward, her eyes squinting against the dancing, brilliant light. "Lady," she murmured, "do you hear that?"

"Yes, Alba. You can?"

"Aye. Beautiful, yet..." Alba placed her hand over heart, her brow furrowing as she sought the words.

"*Piercing the heart like a spear of light,*" Thera responded, remembering the words of an old folk ballad.

"Aye," Alba breathed.

The troop crossed the grove; the forest closed like a curtain behind them.

CHAPTER 39

*E*ven Mulberry sensed that home was near. She tossed her head, continually trying to edge into a trot. Thera patted her neck. "Yes, you fractious child, we're almost there. Blessing be. Perhaps the climb up Lorn a'Lea will settle you down."

Alaine eyed the young pair and her lips pursed. "Aye, like mistress, like beast, I think. Eager to be home." She smiled at Thera who laughed appreciatively. "Hnnh. We are close to Allenholme then, if this be Lorn a'Lea point?"

"Yes. Almost home now." She breathed deeply. "Do you smell the air?"

"It is the same good, sweet air I have smelled all along, Salvai." Thera lifted her brows expectantly, so Alaine shrugged and rose in her stirrups, taking several deep breaths. She sat back, meeting Thera's look. "Perhaps a touch more of the salt water tang here, than at Elankeep. And something else—"

"Yes," Thera beamed, "cailia bloom and salt tang. Home." She heeled Mulberry up the rising trail.

Emerging into the clearing at the top of Lorn a'Lea, they were challenged, "Halt! Who travels in ArNarone domain?"

Thera nearly blurted a happy greeting on hearing the familiar voice, but Sirra Alaine was already responding. "Lady Thera, Heir of Allenholme and Salvai to the Elanraigh, and her escort."

"Captain Lydia!" Thera couldn't wait, she swung off Mulberry and tossing back the hood of her cloak ran forward. "I've come home."

"Blessing be," choked Lydia, grasping Thera by the upper arms. "The Elanraigh has just granted your father's dearest wish." She took in Thera's appearance, met Thera's eyes with a small nod. "I see, Lady," she said softly, "that you command your own now. These be the Elankeep soldiers by their gear."

Thera nodded, "Their service honors me. Captain Lydia, this is Sirra Alaine and First Sword Alba."

As Lydia returned the soldiers' salutes, her glance over them was lively and interested. She jerked her chin over her shoulder, "We have a small watch-fire in the hollow, and some hot tea. It will be full dark soon. Do come and warm yourselves and then I will escort you in."

She called to one of the two figures silhouetted against the fire's light, "Kirten! Come tend to these horses while our Lady Thera refreshes herself."

CAPTAIN LYDIA JOINED Thera where she stood, hands wrapped around the warm mug of tea, watching sky and sea lit with the sun's last fire. Lydia glanced at her, then spoke quietly, "It harrowed our souls to hear of the danger you'd passed through on the Coast Trail, Lady." Thera glanced up, blinking at Lydia's profile, mauve-shadowed against the dying light. "We sang the Lament for Innic, Jon, and your Nan." Lydia, sighed, "We've sung the Lament too often. A great deal has happened while you have been at Elankeep, Lady. But," she smiled at Thera, "that will be your father's tale to tell first."

"Some of it I know, Lydia — from father's letter."

Lydia laughed. "Aye. He doesn't like the writing of them — though he was ever eager to receive yours, be sure."

Thera spoke into her tea mug before taking a small sip. "The Ttamarini — are they still here?"

"Oh, aye." Lydia glanced at her, then away. "We've all come to honor them as allies and friends. They stay to celebrate the victory over the Memteth. Your father has invited the Ttamarini Heir to remain as a guest, if he wishes. The Memteth are gone ..."

"Pardon?" asked Thera, feeling distracted.

"The Memteth. Gone. No sign of them for days now. The Elanraigh speaks ...?

"The Elanraigh does not feel them anywhere near," Thera murmured. *Father invited Chamak to stay on?*

"Ah," Lydia nodded. "That is good news. Lady Fideiya thought the Elanraigh might be sending you home. She said that the last two days an eagle has circled the keep, calling. Lady Fideiya said it made her feel you were somehow near. Eagles are good omen to our folk these days."

Thera and Lydia fell silent a moment. Captain Lydia watched the Elankeep soldiers as they talked among themselves. "They look like fine companions," she remarked. Then she laughed, "I can't wait to see Harle's face!"

"Horsemaster Harle?"

"Aye. The only way he came finally to accept *me* was when he convinced himself I must be an exception, a freak of nature." She shook her head and gestured at the Elan-keep troop. "All these fine women soldiers will quite overset him.

"Well. If you are ready, Lady, I will have the great pleasure of escorting you home."

THERA SAW her father and mother standing with Captain Dougall and the Heart's Own at the South Gate. Kirten had indeed hurried ahead with word of her arrival. Torchlight and shadows alternately washed over the Allenholme party in the chill night wind—her father's red-gold hair, glitter of mail and jeweled badges, all swimming before her eyes.

A small sob broke from her and Thera was off her horse and in her mother's embrace — scent of sealily and calla. Her mother's small, chilled fingers touched her face, tilting her head to the light. "Oh, my dear one," she murmured.

"Thera!" growled Leon, and her father's arms surrounded them both.

MORNING SUN BURNISHED the copper bowls on Thera's cedar chest and freshly picked blue hyacinth released their scent. Slowly, lovingly, Thera drank in the familiar sight of her own room. Yet, it was all somehow different now.

Last night she had been bundled quickly toward her parents retiring room, her mother ordering refreshments brought. "My troop, father," Thera had protested against her father's propelling arm.

"You are weary. Maxim will see to them."

"I am not that weary, sir. I will order them settled."

Leon paused, dropping his arm from her shoulder. He regarded her with approval. "Well, daughter, that is well spoken."

Thera turned. "Sirra Maxim, kindly escort Sirra Alaine and the soldiers of Elankeep to the east wing." Thera glanced at her father. "I would have them quartered with the Heart's Own, sir." Leon nodded.

Sirra Maxim and Sirra Alaine saluted. After conferring briefly, Alaine signaled the troop, and they followed Maxim toward the east wing.

In her parents' retiring room, tucked into a large chair and sipping mulled wine, Thera listened to her father tell the tale of events since she had been gone from Allenholme. As he told of the Memteth assault on the Cythian warship and the battle at Lorn a'Lea, Thera felt the strangeness of hearing the story told from such a different perspective than her own. His account of the bitter fight with the Memteth giant was told in a bright-eyed, vigorous tone of reminiscence. When he spoke of the eagle coming to his aid, he said, "It was as if the very spirit of the Elanraigh formed itself into that shape and fought at our side. I cannot explain it, or adequately describe it."

Thera mused, *Well. That is close enough to the truth of it.*

Leon's face darkened. "The Memteth have ravaged up and down our coast. Many good people have died--villagers and townsfolk alike. When I was a half-day's ride to the north, engaged against a Memteth raid on Brachna village, a small party of raiders managed to set fire to our ships, right here at Allenholme. We lost half the fishing fleet before the flames were beaten." Leon sat with chin resting on fist, staring at the crackling fire. Thera eyed the pulse throbbing at her father's temple. She flinched as a blackened log tumbled to the hearthstones.

Leon stirred, and continued, "Mika ep Narin ordered the burning ships cut loose," Leon's breath came harsh as he spoke. "There was nothing else he could do. No one could get near the raging inferno those vessels were by then." Her father paused, breathing heavily, then continued. "Some youths — children, truth be said, sons and daughter of mariners — knowing what the ships meant to their fathers, defied their Guild Master and fought the flames. They perished, every one. Their fathers netted their charred remains from the sea."

Fideiya's hands clenched on the needlework she held, her eyes starkly fixed on Leon. Seeing her stricken gaze, Leon sighed. He reached over, placing his hand on hers, "Surely the Elanraigh took those brave young souls straight to its heart."

Thera felt stunned. She knew so many of the young fisher folk. Bright faces gathered in a dusty circle, playing spin crystal games. "Thera, I challenge you for the blue quartz!" And there was Thera, as begrimed as the rest, sitting in the dust, at least until Nan caught her. "Blues are worth two whites — let me see your bet, Adon." The echoes of their shouts and laughter rang in Thera's memory.

Again patting Fideiya's hand, Leon got up from his chair. He crouched before Thera, and reached his hand to touch her hair. "I am a soldier and I have seen death in many forms. It is a terrible thing for a parent to have to bury a child. Your mother and I give thanks that the Elanraigh has brought you safely home." Planting a quick kiss on both their heads, Leon left the room.

Blessings be, Thera agreed, *that the troubles are at last truly over.*

CHAPTER 40

*T*hera leaned at her window, drinking in familiar sounds and smells. *I have slept late — the sun is well above the tree line.*

High and distant, Eiryana whistled.

"Blessings, dear one!" Thera sent.

Eiryana's mind-touch caressed Thera. *"We have been waiting to greet you,"* she chided.

"We?"

A wind stormed past her, *"It is I, Therra!"* It swirled chaotically through her chamber, tossing petals from the overblown flowers and fluttering loose the ties of her nightgown in a teasing fashion before exiting the chamber.

"Sussara!" Thera laughed and retied her lacings, *"Blessings of the day, Little Mischief."*

"I'm going to help Eiryana Sky Weaver to fish this morning."

"Oh my," sent Thera to Eiryana with a rueful smile.

Eiryana's mind-voice was warm with affection, *"I have learned from my sky-sister to have a fondness for this little one."*

Thera laughed her agreement and stood enjoying their

rapport until Eiryana became focused on the waves below her.

A melodious trill captured Thera's attention from Eiryana's fading presence. Peering over the window's edge, Thera saw Tenatik, the Ttamarini horsemaster, seated cross-legged on the grass by the stable path. Placing a small reed flute to his lips he blew a low, murmurous sound, followed by a rapid glissando of notes.

Sussara twined affectionately around the musician. *"Therra, listen. It sounds like wind through grass and birds in the morning."*

"Yes, little one. Tenatik is gifted, for that is just how it sounds."

Booted footsteps crunched along the path and voices came into her hearing, "...five mares in foal. Blessings be." Oak Heart's rough voice drifted up. Dougall responded something, too softly for Thera to hear, and someone shouted a laugh in response.

"Ah," Thera leaned further outward, "Oak Heart, Dougall, Sirra Alaine, and — Chamak!" Sensations as ambiguous as frost burn, heat and cold, flashed over her. Chamak, for it was he she had heard laughing, called to Tenatik.

"Ten', did you tire of waiting for us that you torment the birds so?"

"His arm is bandaged still," Thera inventoried Chamak's appearance, *"Father didn't say exactly what his injuries were. He sounds well, even happy,"* she smiled — a smile that froze — *"has he forgotten about me?"*

Tenatik rose to his feet, a grin deepened the crevices bracketing his mouth. He wiped the flute, placed it in his belt, and saluted. "Anything, oh son-of-a-great-chieftain, to forestall you raising up the game-scaring croak you claim is a singing voice." Chamak and Sirra Alaine paused beside Tenatik, their voices lowered again, but Chamak's gestures suggested introductions being made. As Tenatik began speaking with Alaine, Chamakin turned, looking up toward Thera's window.

Thera flung herself back inside, her heart thudding a panicked rhythm. *What is the matter with me?* Thera wondered. *I want to see him, to look in his eyes and know if he still feels the same way about me. So why do I hide from him?*

She paced, halting in front of her polished bronze mirror — *because I want to be ready when I meet him again*, Thera acknowledged. She smoothed her nightdress to her, turning this way and that, trying to see herself as Chamak would see her. Thera smiled, the mirror reflecting the flash of whiteness. Humming Tenatik's lilting tune, she twirled, moving her body with rising joy.

THERA VIGOROUSLY WORKED her brush over Mulberry's hide. She muttered to the mare, "So. Where are they? I'm sure I heard Tenatik offer to show Alaine the stable, and Chamak followed them." Her lips quirked wryly as she straightened, flexing her back. "Here I rushed to the stable as quickly as may be, expecting to conquer my lover once and for all, and no one is here." The mare whufflled at her shoulder. "Except you, dear one, of course," Thera glanced over the mare's haunch, "and one small stable boy."

She dipped her hand into a sack of carrots and retrieved one for the mare. "Here, greedy child." Thera glanced up, heart tripping, at the sound of multiple footsteps approaching.

Is it — oh. Thera recognized the Cythians, accompanied by one of her father's guards as escort.

She quickly wiped her hand on her grooming cloth. The

Cythian Heir, Ambrauld, stopped, squinting slightly in the brightness outside the stable. His companion, the Besteri mage, swung his head in Thera's direction.

"Lady Thera," the guard saluted, "I was to escort Lord Ambrauld to join Duke Leon and his party. I thought they were at the stables."

So did I. "I believe they must have been here earlier, Guardsman Bran."

Before the guard could speak further, the Cythian Heir approached her, his handsome face lit with a delighted smile. "Finally! Well met Lady Thera." He stared at her face a long moment, brows lifting and eyes wide, then his gaze roamed over her in a manner Thera found utterly embarrassing. Her face grew hot. As he reached for her hand, Thera quickly dropped the grooming rag to the straw. Catching sight of the grimy stains on her fingers, she flushed again as he gently pressed his lips to her fingertips. After suffering a brief awkwardness, she suddenly laughed.

"I am sorry, my Lord," she apologized quickly seeing the look of surprise on his face. Shaking her head, she delicately withdrew her hand. "Somehow the stable does not seem the place for such courtly courtesies. I should have met you in my father's Great Hall with all appropriate ceremony." She smiled winningly and the Cythian Heir beamed down at her.

"Your ingenuousness disarms me, Lady."

His accent is definitely of the south — very refined. How he stares!

Thera, in turn, quickly appraised this young Lord. He is as tall as Chamakin, she thought, though heavier muscled. Then, Thera judged, he is some years older. His eyes are a paler blue than father's — almost colorless. Thera continued to read him, as his eyes glinted with amusement.

He is amused at the little female who sizes him up like a combatant on the battlefield. There is arrogance in the set of that jaw. Perhaps that is not surprising, Thera conceded, considering his noble rank and physical appearance. *Yes, his looks agree with what I read of him. He is not a man used to being thwarted, in anything. There is implacability in him.*

The guard cleared his throat and offered, "Perhaps my Duke took the Ttamarini Heir and his party to view the hunting birds — their pen is by the Northwest Gate, Lord Ambrauld. We might find them there."

"Be at ease, man," snapped Ambrauld, his eyes fixed on Thera. He gestured toward the dark shadow at his shoulder. "Lady Thera, allow me to introduce Willestar, a mage of the Besteri, who serves as Councilor to my father's house."

Thera was not prepared for the intensity of the dark regard that lingered insolently long on her face before the tall man bent gracefully.

"My Lady Thera, I am your servant."

Thera nodded stiffly as the mage rose to his full height again. The Besteri's full red lips pursed, his heavy-lidded eyes glinted as he again stared. "My pardon, Lady, but I must ask — I sense something of *gift* in you. Is it the Old Teachings? *Who would have taught you this?* he mused, *The Ttamarini's Maiya might have the skill, perhaps.*

The mage did not move closer, his hands were tucked within his sleeves, yet Thera felt as if chill, spectral fingers brushed her forehead. Instinctively her spirit flung itself to the *place within* that was hers alone. The Besteri's mind-touch never reached her, passing like a wind in the high trees of her mind-place. The Besteri looked surprised. His moist lips pressed together, his eyes darkling and arrested. Then he smiled, and withdrawing his hands from his robe, he gestured — a slow opening of his hands to her view.

Surrender or apology? I cannot read this man. Thera felt shaken.

Ambrauld's voice broke the tension between Thera and the mage. The Cythian's eyes were on Thera's horse. "Ahh, Willestar, look at this! She is yours, obviously, Lady Thera. A beauty."

Thera, distracted, stared as if she had not heard him. *When I read people through my gift, does it feel so to them? No. No one ever looks disturbed — perhaps only if one reads another who is also gifted?*

She could barely forebear rubbing at the spot on her forehead where the Besteri had reached with his magic to read her. *So invasive! He reached for it as casually as opening his wardrobe door.*

Mulberry bumped her from behind. "Oh." The strange chill departed at the mare's touch and she belatedly answered the Cythian Heir. "Yes," Thera stroked the mare's withers, "she was a gift from my father."

Ambrauld reached for the mare. Mulberry danced sideways, arching her neck and flattening her ears.

"Sir. She doesn't take to strangers," Thera warned, pressing her hand against Ambrauld's arm.

"Here," offered Willestar, and, muttering a quick string of words under his breath, he strode forward, grasping the mare's halter. He raised his hand.

Thera tensed, about to intervene, but Ambrauld had gripped her elbow. "Do not fear. He will not harm her, Lady. Watch, you will see. It is a marvel how he can handle animals."

"What —?" Thera flashed Ambrauld an angry look. *If the mage strikes Mulberry I will deal him back double the blow.* Ignoring the Cythian's grip, Thera snapped her attention back to the Besteri. Mulberry, to Thera's surprise, was standing perfectly still as Willestar placed his hands on her. His long, pale fingers smoothed down over her neck and withers. Thera was incredulous until she saw the mare's eyes roll toward the mage, her skin flinching under his touch.

He forces her! He forces her to stand for him against her will.

"Do not!" Thera swallowed against the repugnance she felt. Swinging around to Ambrauld, she lowered her voice in an attempt to disguise her shaking anger. *Honored guest in my father's house.*

"My Lord Ambrauld, she does not like it."

Ambrauld looked down at her with a gentle smile. "My dear Lady, surely you can see the benefit in a fractious young beast being so easily controlled with no harm done to it or its handlers?"

"Do not. I beg you," repeated Thera. "I do not wish to break her spirit so."

"You are a sensitive." Ambrauld patted the arm he had taken again in a familial grip during Thera's distraction. "Sensitivity is woman's special gift. You do not displease me.

"Willestar," Ambrauld flicked his eyes away from the mare.

"Yes, of course, my Lord. I would not wish to distress the Lady ArNarone." Willestar's voice was deep and smooth, rich as port wine. His hand lingered a last moment, caressingly, on the mare's flank. Then, staring at Thera, the mage traced a sign in the air and Mulberry reared, shook her head and sidled to the back of her stall. The Besteri folded his pale hands back into his sleeves and turned to Lord Ambrauld with a pleased smile. "She is beautiful, and she has excellent spirit."

CHAPTER 41

*A*mbrauld poured wine into his goblet "You frightened her, Willestar," he said, glancing over his shoulder at the mage. He strolled to the window, inhaling the fresh breeze that stirred the shadows within the chamber. "This is a wild, yet beautiful place," the Cythian mused.

"It is damp," muttered Willestar, "and the forest oppresses me."

Ambrauld turned his pale eyes on the mage.

Willestar shrugged and continued, "Frightened her?" He cast an amused look at the Cythian Heir. "I think not. Disturbed her, yes. That." Willestar rested his chin on his hand, his finger moved across his lips as he gazed at the fire. The light sharply defined the planes and shadows of his face. "She has talent, that one. My kind of talent."

Ambrauld snorted, surprised. "A woman's magic. So? What harm in that?"

Willestar said nothing as he regarded the younger man a long moment. He lowered his eyes and stared meditatively into the wine cup held in his hand. "You are much taken with this maiden."

Ambrauld savored the sweet wine in his mouth as stared out toward the sea. "Yes. I cannot stop thinking of her. She is like this place — her beautiful eyes that are the color of the forest, the freshness of her skin and the amber fire in her dark hair." He drank again, "How sweetly she blushed when I kissed her hand." Ambrauld grunted a laugh. "A noblewoman who grooms her own horse." He shook his head, "It is appalling that ArNarone allows her to run so wild." He turned the goblet in his hand, his thumb tracing the carved pattern. "Did you hear her laugh? A lovely laugh, like sparkling water. When you were not upsetting her that is." Ambrauld slid a glance at the Besteri who continued to stare at the fire, a small cynical smile on his lips. Ambrauld again looked out the window, absently watching the reconstruction activity at the West Harbor. The Memteths' attacks had greatly damaged Allenholme's wharf area. Teams of heavy horse rumbled past, dragging fresh-cut timbers down the winding hill to the harbor.

"Cythia has not fully appreciated the resources of this northern duchy," Ambrauld mused—*fine timber, skilled wood crafters. The fighting men are superbly trained. This young northern heiress would bring great wealth to Cythia. Such riches.* Ambrauld smiled.

"And her figure," he continued aloud to Willestar, "is goddess-like. I never guessed a gently reared maiden could inflame me so. What sons we would make, and how joyously!" He turned his head and looked at Willestar under his brows, "Not like Ethelwidde, poor soul." The wine goblet swung in a sloppy toast to his deceased wife.

Willestar pursed his lips. One brow lifted. "She was — frail."

"Oh, indeed, gods rest her. Her bloodlines were impeccable, and her face plain as a tinker's damn. She was always afraid of me— though, god's witness, I tried to be gentle with her." Ambrauld shrugged, and rose to fill his cup again. "But this one ..."

Willestar declined with a languid gesture as Ambrauld waggled the decanter. The Cythian shrugged and splashed more into his cup.

"...*she* would not be running to hide amongst her women every night."

Willestar leaned forward to lift the poker and prod the fire. "The ArNarone Heiress has quite the opposite temperament indeed, my Lord. She will require very different handling."

Ambrauld's smile flashed like white heat in the deepening dusk.

The Besteri carefully controlled his distaste. *The lusting dolt has no idea beyond the girl's beauty.* Calming his flash of irritation, he again focused his attention on the fire. He drew a deep breath, holding it long before releasing it. As he meditated on the young Lord's desire, he was only marginally aware of the arrival of a manservant and Ambrauld's good-humored preparations to dress for his requested meeting with Duke ArNarone.

Ambrauld has a rival. I have seen how the Ttamarini Heir watches us. Willestar shifted again. *Danger. Strong forces are working here, but to effect what destiny I cannot yet determine, except they do not lie with Cythian interests.*

The ArNarone heiress is, indeed, all the things Ambrauld rhapsodized about. A beautiful girl — soon to be a beautiful and formidable woman. Willestar's lips twitched into a smile. *When Ambrauld weds and beds the girl I must quickly take a hand with her, or she could very well manage to harness the Cythian Heir to her chariot.*

No. That would never do. She surprised me with her ability to resist my gentle probe of her talents. Yes, surprises and intrigues me. She must be controlled, but skillfully.

As with the girl's own concern for her horse, Willestar found he did not particularly wish to have to break her spirit.

A child from her will strengthen the dilute bloodlines of the noble Cythian house. The King of Bole has no issue — he has blood ties to ArNarone, as well, it is said, as a great fondness for that stalwart line. However, Cythia is next only to Bole itself in wealth and power. Yes. A male child it must be, born with the girl's gifts and raised under my tutelage. They will have a future King, shaped to Besteri design.

Willestar stroked his upper lip with one finger as he mused on. Duke Perrod of Cythia had been appalled at his sickly daughter-in-law presenting him with a deformed grandson.

Poor Ethelwidde, indeed. Willestar had reassured Duke Perrod that neither mother nor child was thriving after the difficult birth, but the Duke had not wished it left to chance.

Fortunately, Ambrauld had not asked to see his "stillborn" son. He had publicly, dutifully mourned the child and poor, plain Ethelwidde, who had never looked better than when she was a corpse.

"I WONDER if we should put all your hair up, Lady?" Egrit pondered aloud as she rubbed cailia-scented balm into her palms and massaged it into Thera's hair. She peered around into Thera's face, "The noble guest from Cythia is so handsome. He looks and speaks so fair. I cannot believe he is one of the wicked courtiers that Healing Mistress told us of."

"Hmm? The Cythian? He is handsome enough. But I find I do not like Cythian ways," Thera said. *It is a good thing Mulberry was unharmed.* Thera had stayed to soothe the mare, who, blessings be, recovered quickly enough from the Besteri's handling.

Egrit held thick swatches of Thera's hair between her fingers and wove them neatly together at the crown of her head. "Of course the Ttamarini Heir is more striking, but," Egrit shivered, "I cannot be comfortable around him. He is like a wolf, I think, fierce and solitary. His eyes look as if they see the very shadows of your soul. I would be afraid if he so much as spoke to me. But he did not. There." One hand firmly holding the hair in place, Egrit sorted through Thera's jewelry box with the other.

He is not solitary. He waits for his mate, Thera thought with a small frisson of excitement. She tilted her head, smiling in the mirror at Egrit. "You make me look beautiful, Egrit. I am in danger of becoming as vain as a Cythian bolari dancer."

Indeed, thought Thera, wondering at herself, *today I feel glorious and invincible.*

'I wish, she sent to the Elanraigh, *I knew if you are responsible for this feeling, or if it comes from somewhere in me?'* The Elanraigh hummed along her nerves — there was a decided air of satisfaction in the Elanraigh's mood.

A young maidservant entered Thera's chamber to light the oil lamps. Russet highlights flared to life in the dark mass of Thera's hair. "The red must be from your father's side, Lady," said Egrit. "Ah, this is the one for tonight." Egrit choose a topaz and gold clasp to fasten the twists of Thera's hair. She brushed energetically at the rest until it flowed down her back.

Thera stepped into the moss-green gown and savored the silky slipping of the fine clothes up her body. She watched in the mirror while Egrit fastened the back. Amber beads gleamed at the gown's neck, cascading over shoulders and bodice. The gown clung to breast and hip in undulating shadows of deeper green. Amber, sewn a hand-span deep at the hem, made a pleasing sound when she walked.

"Lady," Egrit's eyes shone, "always I knew you were lovely — never more so than now."

"Egrit," Thera clasped the maid's hands. "I thank you for your words, because tonight," a smile tipped the corners of her mouth, "tonight *he* is here for me and I will make him mine."

"Which one, Lady?" asked Egrit with a dimpled smile of her own.

"Which? Oh, tch." Thera mock-frowned over her shoulder.

Egrit was still smiling as she answered a tap on the chamber door. Swordswoman Enid, on guard duty outside Thera's chamber, announced a messenger from Duke Leon. Thera glanced up and nodded. Enid swung the door wider and an unfamiliar youth in recruit's colors entered. Glancing sideways at Enid as he passed, the young man's gaze arrested on the ugly scar that marred Enid's forehead and scalp. He reddened as Enid flatly returned his stare.

"A soldier's scars are common enough these days, I would've thought, recruit?" she drawled.

The recruit sweated in the heat of his chagrin as he turned to salute Thera. "L-Lady Thera. Recruit Sword Eagin at your ser-service. Lady, your father wishes to see you privately in his conference room. I am to escort you there."

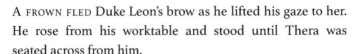

A FROWN FLED Duke Leon's brow as he lifted his gaze to her. He rose from his worktable and stood until Thera was seated across from him.

"You look lovely, my own." He shook his head. "Am I soon to be left in the dust of memories of my little girl heeling a fat pony to a jog in the exercise yard?"

Thera laughed, but examined her father with the gift. *"His words and manner are light, but he is heavily troubled."*

Leon sat, leaning back in the high-backed chair. His head tipped down and chin on chest, he stared rather bleakly at a closely written scroll. His thick fingers drummed the tabletop.

Thera clasped her hands in her lap. She eyed her father anxiously. It was unusual for her to be called to this room — as a child only after the worst misdemeanors. Her father's old wolfhound rose heavily to his feet and swayed over to her. She fondled his head then pushed the grey muzzle aside. "No, you old ruffian, I am dressed for the hall."

Her father roused and snapped his fingers, calling the old hound to him. As the wolfhound settled at his feet with a heavy sigh, Leon directed a keen and focused look at Thera.

"Thera," Leon flicked a finger against the scroll. "I have here a formal request for your hand in marriage."

Chamakin! Could it be? Mother said before I left for Elankeep that he had already asked and father had told him he must wait. Thera felt a heat rising under her skin and excitement tingled along her nerves. Her father's fair brow rose as he scrutinized her. The corners of his mouth drew down.

"This does not seem to have come entirely as a surprise then?" Leon's tone was heavy and Thera felt a squeeze of apprehension. A frown rumpled his brow as he toyed with the scroll, then shoving papers, scrolls, and maps aside, he rested his arms on the desktop. Thera abided in deepest anxiety while her father, cracking his knuckles, remained in thought.

"Well, my dear," he said at last, "it is a noble offer. But...," he glanced sternly at her, "you are very young yet and so I told him."

Thera found herself clenching her hands together painfully. She deliberately relaxed her fingers, spreading them against the softness of cloth that draped her thighs.

"Father..."

Leon lifted his hand. "Well. The young noble is as full of ardor and promises to cherish you as any father could wish to hear. Indeed, my dear, I am only too aware of all that recommends this union." Leon's mouth drew down even further, "He seems a man enough—cocksure and arrogant for one so untried," Leon muttered. He observed Thera's puzzled frown, "but — but he is yet a young man. He will grow into the wisdom he needs. I am aware that a house of such wealth and status as Duke Perrod's could choose a bride from any Duchy. To be sure, my dear," her father's lip curled slightly, "he touched on that most delicately. But — but I had hoped — Thera, what is it?"

"Perrod! You mean it is Lord Ambrauld of whom you speak?" Thera reared to her feet.

"Why, yes. Who did you — ah!" Leon too, levered from his chair. He paced a few steps and then spun on his heel, his expression bright. "Hah!" He strode toward Thera, taking her hands in his. "Then you are not taken with Perrod's Heir?"

"No, father! No. I had thought you were speaking of —" Thera flushed and she bit her lip.

Leon gazed down at her a moment, then backed, pulling her with him, to sit hip-slung on his worktable. His mouth quirked in a small smile as he looked at her. "I see. My dear, let me tell you that over these past months I have come to have a great regard for our Ttamarini allies. In truth, Teckcharin is a man I could proudly call brother — and the son is very like his father."

Thera felt she must be shining with joy. "Then you do not hold with great-grandfather's feelings?"

"What is this?" Leon's brow rumpled.

"Duke Leif ArNarone and the others refused to condone a marriage between Ttamarini and Allenholme — in Lady Dysanna's time," Thera reminded her father.

"Elanraigh bless you, lass — that old tale. Why would you think so? I have ever judged a man as *I* find him."

"Will this cause trouble for us with Cythia?" Thera asked.

Leon smiled even more broadly. "Well, I will send the young Cythian away, as soon as may be, right smarting from his thwarted love. Though I must credit him with good taste in his first choice, he strikes me as a young man who will soon be smitten again, come along another beauty of noble house. My own," Leon fingered one of Thera's curls, "I was troubled, feeling he was not worthy of you. We can well endure Cythia's pique — we have Ttamarini allies by our side and I will make sure to have the favor of the King." Leon slung his arm around Thera and walked her toward the map on the wall. He sighed. "It will be necessary to travel to court to formally present our new alliance and receive the King's sanction of it. Tch. It is a tedious journey, and I am ever loath to leave Allenholme. However, the King must know the northern part of his kingdom to be at peace and strongly held." Leon hugged her shoulders, "If he is the man I remember, the King will see reason, and be as satisfied with the Allenholme and Ttamarini alliance — and your betrothal, as are we."

"Father!" Thera hugged Leon tightly, then leaned back to look at him, "but I have not seen Chamakin since I've returned. What if he does not feel the same about me?"

"Hah!" laughed Leon. "His father and I have long noted his increasing edginess, his lean and hungry wolfishness. These days he chooses to ride alone—fast and hard— over widow-maker trails.

"I was just the same way, you know, when I first saw and loved your mother. Old Lord Chadwyn denied my courtship of your mother until my anointing by the King as Heir to Allenholme. This ceremony, as you know, does not happen until your nineteenth year. Young Chamakin is just the same as I was that year." Leon threw back his head in another laugh and hugged her against his side.

"My recruits dread arms drill these days, so fiercely does your Chamakin glare and bash at them in the practice yard. Hah! Just so did my Heart's Own bear many more bruises than usual from the ferocity of our arms practice during those months I was held off from your mother. Oh yes, he loves you, my dear."

Thera felt the welling of joyful tears. She swiped at her eyes with her fingertips. "He is a wonderful warrior, is he not, father? So brave in the battles with the Memteth, yet the *Maiya's* teachings have made him both thoughtful and wise beyond his years."

"Aye. Aye, lass, he is a good man. You never knew I extracted a promise from him, before you left for Elankeep, that he would not approach you until he had my consent for you to be courted. I told him you were too young, and so you are, but the Cythian's interest has now forced my hand.

"I knew how difficult it was for Chamakin to not be there when you left for Elankeep, but I thought it best, and so I told him to grant you a time of growth at Elankeep. I knew he was a young man of honor and would keep his word to me, though it cost him, Elanraigh knows what pain, to let you go.

"A betrothal now with the wedding next Verdemas — that would be acceptable to your mother and I." Leon cleared his throat, "Yes. Well, I have two young men to speak with this evening then — one I must disappoint and one I will gladly grant his heart's desire." Leon returned to the chair at his worktable, "Well then. I will see you again at evening meal. Your mother has arranged to have the tables laid in the garden. Send that recruit, Eagin, to me, if you will, my dear. I have messages."

Thera spun happily on her heel with a muted tinkling of amber beads, "Yes, father. Right away."

AFTER SENDING the recruit in to her father, Thera carried on toward the Great Hall. The huge outside doors had been pushed open and servants were busy carrying the long tables to the flagstone patio outside. Steward Valan came toward her and bowed. "Lady, is there anything I can help you with? Do you seek Lady Fideiya?"

"No, I thank you, Valan, I just came from my father. When do we dine?"

"At full eventide, Lady."

A while yet. "Thank you." Thera turned, and from the corner of her eye caught sight of a tall Ttamarini, just as her heart quickened she recognized him as Zujeck, Chamak's close companion. The young Ttamarini saw her and veered her way. His handsome face was solemn as he saluted her, but he visibly warmed as Thera greeted him.

"Zujeck, Goddess bless."

"Blessings, Lady ArNarone."

Thera turned to walk toward the main doors, the Ttamarini pacing at her side. "You fared well in the Memteth battles, Zujeck? No injuries?"

"Yes, Lady, thanks be. Nothing to mention."

They emerged into the soft air of late afternoon, the lowering sun already staining rocks and trees in dusky amber. "Not all, I hear, were so fortunate?" prodded Thera.

"No indeed, Lady, there were losses and injuries enough." Zujeck paused and Thera halted. Standing straight, hands behind his back, he tipped his head down to meet her gaze. "My own friend, Chamak, was seriously injured at the battle by Kenna Beach."

"Chamak is recovered now?"

Zujeck shook his head slowly, his long hair swaying at his shoulders, though his face remained serious, his eyes began to dance. "The wounds healed cleanly and well, yet something seems to ail him. A continuing infection perhaps remains. We hope he will begin to mend soon, now."

"I will offer prayer to the Elanraigh for his full recovery, Zujeck." She smiled up into the warrior companion's face.

Zujeck's lips curved into a slow smile and he bowed gracefully. "I can imagine nothing more efficacious, Lady, than your intervention."

"I will see you at the evening meal then," said Thera happily, "is — is Chamak now at your encampment?"

"Well," replied Zujeck, "our *Maiya* commanded him to go and meditate, she was concerned with him, 'scattering his energy', when he was soon likely to need his wits about him."

Thera felt a dimming of the joy within. "Oh." *Where could he be and for how long?*

Zujeck rocked on his heels, hands at his back. He eyed the top of the old sitka tree on Lorn a'Lea Point where an eagle now perched. "I believe he has found some special place near here where he prefers to go when in the mood to be alone with his thoughts. He told me he met his destiny there once." Zujeck regarded her keenly and Thera flushed to the tops of her ears. Zujeck returned his gaze to Lorn a'Lea with a satisfied nod while a smile tugged the corner of his mouth. "Yes. I believe Chamak told me that his spirit brother, the grey wolf, appeared to him there."

As Thera reached the old sitka, she paused as she always did to commune with the old tree. "*To think how close we came to losing you and so many others to that malevolent Memteth fire.*" The pounding of her heart stilled somewhat and she breathed deeply the tang of salt and pungent evergreen boughs. A mind-touch, light as a feather, told her that Eiryana was close by and withholding herself so Thera could have this time alone.

"*Blessings, dear one,*" Thera sent in return.

She steadied herself a moment, her hand resting on the old sitka, as the sky rapidly deepened it's color from lemon to orange, then red.

In the next few moments my life's path will be set.

Thera pushed away from the tree then, and began the climb, her eyes fixed on the granite spur of rock — "*and right below is the mossy ravine where Chamak and I sat only three moons ago.*" The Elanraigh's presence was strongly with her and it sang to her the rightness of her choice.

"*Blessings be!*" sent Thera, "*He is my only choice! Did you for one heart beat believe I could have chosen the other over him? Is this the choice of my soul that had to be made before you would take my vow?*"

A wind rose in the tree tops, as if the Elanraigh cavorted in its sharing of her joy.

"*Will you take my vow now? Will you believe that we, Chamak and I, will work to bring our people close to you again, as it was long ago?*"

Like a warm hand at her back the Elanraigh urged her on. *Thera, you are our own*, it thrummed. A shadow detached itself from the base of a huge tree and padded toward her. Thera felt the brush of the wolf's pelt below her fingers.

"*Farnash!*" She knelt and fondled the huge head. "*Oh, Farnash,*" tears flowed freely down her face. The wolf head-butted her gently and the bright tongue lolled, then he turned his muzzle, nostrils distended, toward the cliff. "*Yes. He is there. Do you come for him as well?*"

"*He is myia, brother of my soul.*"

They reached the top of the granite rock together. Below them sat Chamakin, his hands resting on his knees. Two kirshrews were curled in the starmoss beside him. Though the little creatures shuddered and twitched in their dream sleep, Chamakin sat perfectly still, bathed in the setting sun's red light. Thera felt herself reaching out to him, as if with physical hands, she touched his face. His eyes flashed open. He stared blankly a moment. Thera could imagine how they must look to him, woman and beast, dark silhouettes again the fading light. She saw his lips move. *Thera.* Then with a small sound, he passed his hand across his brow.

Thera could wait no more. "Chamak!" She ran down the

narrow trail that led to the ravine with Farnash leaping like a tame dog at her heels.

Chamakin sprang to his feet, "Thera!" He grunted as Thera flung herself against his chest. "Is it really you, Chaunika *myia*? Ahh —" and he crushed Thera to him with one arm and lifted the bandaged arm to trace the side of her face with the backs of gentle fingers. His eyes searched hers, then flickered to meet those of the grey wolf. "Chaunika *myia*, what company you keep. Blessings, *brother of my soul*," he murmured.

"Do you wonder," he said to Thera, "that I thought I was seeing visions."

"He is here to be your companion, Chamak, his name is..."

"Farnash. Yes," Chamak's face lit with his entranced wonder, "I hear his voice and he has given me his name."

Farnash loped forward toward Chamak, dropped to his haunches and lifted his head to Chamak's hand. Above them Eiryana whistled her high-pitched call.

"Sky Sister," Chamak said, looking up at the watching eagle, then at Thera, "Farnash calls you Sky Sister."

"Yes." Thera felt like both laughing and crying, her emotions were in such tumult. She saw Chamak look up and gaze around him. Wind tossed the high branches and evening shadows flew like dark birds across their small clearing.

"What is that sound I hear?" Chamak looked at Thera, his face reflecting her own wonder and joy, as the sound grew around them.

"It is the Elanraigh, my own," Thera sobbed with joy. "It is the Elanraigh singing. Oh, I have so much to tell you!"

"*Warrior and priestess, wolf and eagle are One — the forest rejoices*," declared Farnash.

EPILOGUE

*T*hera couldn't help but compare the differences between this feast and that one at which she'd first met Chamak, only three months ago. Chamak then had seemed so grave and stern, whereas now his hand sought hers as he was animatedly exchanging a battle story with Captain Dougall, Zujeck, and Sirra Alaine. Thera could hardly contain the joy she felt as she and Chamak were bathed in the love and well wishing of family and friends.

Of Allenholme's council, only Mika ep Narin, the Fishing Guild Master was absent. Oak Heart said the Cythian Heir had been determined to return to his own domain immediately. Mika volunteered to journey them home on the *Bride O'Wind*. Mika observed the peeved and thwarted expression on the Cythian Heir's face as he whispered to the Besteri Mage, and the old sailor clenched his pipe between his teeth to suppress a grin.

Mika would have been disturbed however, had he overheard the whispered exchange between Ambraud and Willestar.

"It is obscene, Willestar—he wastes her on the barbarian. What can he be thinking?"

Willestar responded mildly, "My Lord, he must yet win consent of the King. Much can happen in the meantime."

"I want her and none other," affirmed Ambraud.

THERA PRIVATELY REJOICED to know she'd have no further encounters with the Besteri mage. Indeed, on hearing the Cythian Heir and his mage had departed, Thera felt completely lifted in spirit — *nothing now to dim my happiness in this evening's celebration.*

"Friends, My Own," her father rose with his cup in hand, "I offer this toast to our victory, thanks to our honored allies and the Elanraigh..." The roar of response thundered from all tables. Leon waited until this had somewhat subsided, then raised his hand, "and with the greatest joy, her Lady mother and I, wish to announce the betrothal of my daughter and Heir," Leon gestured Thera and Chamak to their feet, "to Chamakin Dysan Chikei of the Ttamarini — Elanraigh bless them!"

This time the thunder of cheers and mugs beating the tables seemed likely never to end, until a sudden gust of warm wind snapped the torch flames, flared through the courtyard, creaking the branches of the old oak. As the people subsided their noise and looked about them, voices began to murmur, "What is that? That sound?"

Thera knew, and her heart swelled as she grasped Chamak's hand. Chamak raised her hand to his lips, and a shiver of sheer joy thrilled her. The Elanraigh was singing, and her people for the first time were hearing the unearthly beauty of its voices lifted in an upwelling peon of joy.

All present were enthralled by the Elanraigh's otherworldly chorus, until gradually, it receded and the sounds of night returned.

Some there remained on their feet, awestruck — some quietly wiped tears from their eyes as they slipped back into their chairs.

Thera's clear voice spoke into the reverent silence. "Dear friends, old and new," her gesture included those of Allenholme and the Ttamarini present, as well as those from Elankeep. "It has been given me as gift, to commune with the Elanraigh forest-mind. Forest-mind knowing our future need has groomed me to be your Salvai. I will be present amongst you, and there will be frequent and open commerce between Allenholme and Elankeep. The forest paths will be open. The Elanraigh blesses you."

This time there was no silencing of the cheers and joyful thunder of many hands pounding the tables.

DEAR READER

Thank you so much for reading *The Guardian Forest: Elanraigh: Book I*

I hope my love of these characters, who have absorbed so much of my life, reflects itself in the writing. I hope you too enjoyed it and will look for the upcoming sequel, *A Scourge of Shadows, Elanraigh: Book II.*

Kindly do me the honor of leaving an honest review, wherever you purchased this novel. Authors so appreciate hearing that readers enjoyed their books, and hopefully others will read your comments and choose to enter the world of the *Elanraigh* as well.

ABOUT THE AUTHOR

Sandra A Hunter has always lived at the edges of ocean and forest in the Pacific Northwest, so it came naturally to have a sentient forest as a major character in her Elanraigh series beginning with *The Guardian Forest* and its sequel *A Scourge of Shadows* (YA/Adult High Fantasy).

The Guardian Forest (first published by Caliburn Press as *Elanraigh: The Vow*) was awarded the Dante Rossetti Award (2014), First in Category, Young Adult High Fantasy, from Chanticleer Book Reviews.

Sandra's short story, *And the Coyotes Sang*, won Spinetingler's Dark Fiction Writing Competition; and she has been published in On Spec, and poetry in Gaslight, Lynx and Women & Recovery.

Sandra's a member of SF Canada, The Burnaby Writers Society, and W.I.P. (a Vancouver Island writers group).

She's a "fair weather" kayaker, and a lousy gardener—but tries hard.

She has a ready sense of humour and an optimistic outlook (a good thing, when you're a writer). She enjoys time spent either on her deck, or in her office, laptop at hand, a glass of wine and a view of either ocean or coastal mountains— and being spirited away by her characters.

~

Follow Sandra on...

Facebook: www.facebook.com/sandra.a.hunter
Twitter: www.twitter.com/furorescribindi
Pinterest: www.pinterest.ca/sandraahunterauthor

Made in the USA
Middletown, DE
20 June 2021

42786090R00179